DISCOVERING HOPE

Chautona Havig

Edited by: Katherine Britton and Susannah Cox

Fonts: Book Antiqua
Art font—"Jailbird Jenna" by KevinandAmanda.com (commercial license)

Cover photos: IKO/shutterstock.com

Cover art by: Chautona Havig

The events and people in this book are fictional, and (aside from a passing nod to a man I've only heard of but never met) any resemblance to actual people is purely coincidental and I'd love to meet them!

Visit me at **http://chautona.com** or follow me on Twitter **@chautona**

All Scripture references are from the NASB. NASB passages are taken from the NEW AMERICAN STANDARD BIBLE (registered), Copyright 1960, 1962, 1963, 1968, 1971, 1972, 1973, 1975, 1977, 1995 by The Lockman Foundation.

For Dell

You have walked me through and cheered me on through many books, but this one I could not have done without you. For all the questions that you emailed your friends, I thank you. Raj is dedicated to your friend, of course. The jokes, Jay's last name—none of it would have been "just right" without you sharing them with me.

In Memory of Becca

In the months before I started this book, many online friends and I, all around the world, prayed for baby Becca—first before she was born, and then as she went through one medical trial after another. She died just days before I typed the first words of what was then titled, "Hope 101." As I wrote, I shared each chapter with Becca's mother. Each time I think of Hope and Jay, I remember those hours of messenger conversations with Mama Adrienne and thank the Lord for that little girl's touch on all of our lives.

Tamil Words and Phrases

Azhagghee — beauty

Edhirparppu — hope

Kadhal — love

Kaalai vanakkam — The equivalent of "good morning"

Naan eppavume unnai kadhalippen — I will love you forever.

Naan unnai kadalikiren — I love you.

CHAPTER 1

"Hey, hey! Lookie who I found. Evangeline."

The words reached Jay as he sat beneath a nearby sycamore.

"Hello, Josh." The young woman sounded put out.

The guy knocked a backpack to the ground and grabbed a book from her hands. Jay's eyes shot to the girl—Evangeline. Interesting name. The strain on the girl's face prompted him to stand. He edged closer, watching for some sign that she needed help, physically and intellectually ready to crush "Josh" at the slightest encouragement.

Josh almost leered at the cover of the book. "*As You Like It*. Very interesting. How *do* you like it, Miss Evangeline?"

"I like it far away from you. Give me the book."

Jay inched closer at the sight of indignation in the girl's eyes. She was seriously ticked. A small smile hovered just inside his mouth, not quite making it to his lips. The idiot obviously didn't yet realize that he was in over his head.

All patience drained from the girl's face as she stood, snatched the book back from Josh's hands, and marched past Jay, unaware that he observed. Josh, either oblivious to the brush off or too certain of his desirability, followed her, cajoling and pleading with her about some paper.

"Give me a break. Just leave me alone. I'm not going to do your lit research paper for you. You don't have enough money to tempt me."

"What about a thou—"

"Have a check on my doorstep for any amount tomorrow and I'll just take it to the dean's office and report you for harassment." She stopped for just a moment and growled, "Do not ever talk to me again. I won't put up with this."

Shocked, Josh watched as the girl sauntered down the breezeway as though she hadn't just flattened with him. Jay grabbed his backpack and rushed after her. As he passed, he glared at Josh, hoping to reinforce her words.

As he neared the girl, just steps behind her, Jay asked, "Is your name really Evangeline?" He jumped back as she whirled to face him, his hands raised in defense as she.

"Oh! Sorry. I thought you were someone else."

Jay watched the effects of adrenaline slowly dissipate from her expression. "I overheard—wanted to make sure you were ok."

"I'm fine." She inched away from him. "Gonna be late for class if I don't start walking."

"Mind if I follow? Still curious about your name…"

"Sure. Name—" She shook her head. "No, that's not my real name. They tagged me with it the first week in anthropology."

"Why Evangeline?"

She shifted her backpack before she answered. "Because when Professor Terrell insisted that I defend my objection to Darwinism, he wasn't satisfied with my scientific answers."

"Faith?"

"Yep. He pushed until I had to add my faith into the mix or get docked for 'lack of participation.'" She grinned. "He wanted to humiliate me."

He knew the answer before he asked, but couldn't resist. "I take it you don't humiliate easily?"

"I think he was disappointed."

She turned to cross the grass that separated the humanities building from the fine arts complex. The breeze caught her hair, tossing it over her shoulder. The movement was instinctive—habitual. She tossed it behind her, letting it fall down her back, settling between her shoulder blades.

8

From her side, he saw his arm next to hers—an almost unbelievably different contrast. She looked Nordic—silky blond hair, blue eyes, pale but warm skin. *She should model ski gear.* What prompted that thought? He was taller—almost a foot. Something about that appealed to him. Definitely darker. His Indian skin was nearly as dark as that of his friend from Ethiopia.

Richly colored leaves crunched beneath their feet as they strolled under a canopy of fiery red and gold maple leaves, jerking him from his thoughts. The building loomed a hundred yards away. He didn't have much time.

"So, if your name isn't Evangeline, what is it?"

"Hope—Hope Senior."

"A senior? What's your major?"

Laughing, Hope shook her head. "No, my last name is Senior. I start my third semester in January."

"I'm Jay, by the way. Jay Brown—Business grad."

He waited for it—there was the hesitation—and she asked. "Okay, sorry, but I have to ask. How does a guy with an Indian accent end up with a name like Jay Brown?"

"Jay's just a nickname," he admitted. "Full name is Sanjay."

She stopped just a few feet from the door. "So, mother is Indian and father... British?"

"Nope. I was born in India—came to America when I was a child."

She reached for the door, but Jay pulled it open for her. Smiling, she stepped inside and waved. "I'll have to ask about Brown some other time. I'm late for my drama class."

Jay watched her as she disappeared around the corner before making up his mind. He followed her inside and to her class, relieved that she hadn't noticed. She'd put him in the "Josh the Stalker" category, and he wouldn't blame her. Through the open door to the theater, he heard a heavy Scottish brogue call for those with singing parts to gather near the piano.

"Come wi' ye neow," a woman, whom Jay assumed was the director, shouted above the din of the class.

A student mentioned the need for white floral spray paint for heather and the director flipped. "Where's yer brogue? I want to hear ye soundin' like Robert Burns hissel'!"

The director called for the class's attention and made an announcement. "This is Drama. Whether ye are a soloist, a main characther, a minor characther, a musician, costume arthist, prop technician, or gopher, ye are a member of the cast and wi' take part—completely. Brogues for all. I grade on participation as well as technical merit. I am not afraid to give piur grades. Do not think this class is an aisy A. Ye'll be siurely disappointed."

Half the class groaned.

A grin split Jay's face. The woman had obviously dragged out her speech as she looked for words to emphasize with a heavier brogue. As he turned, the director called for the first victim of the day. "Now, Fiona. Come hither and let us hear about how ye're waitin' these days."

Two steps from the door, he paused. A voice rang out through the theater to his ears. Hope. He inched back to the door and leaned against it, listening.

The director stopped the song several times, adjusting tempo or pronunciation until Jay wanted to kick something in frustration. She sounded great to him. How could she stand the constant criticism?

The alarm on his phone buzzed. Class in twenty. He strolled from the building with one thought in mind. *Opening night. Definitely going to be there.*

CHAPTER 2

Jay pushed his food around the plate. All around him, the students talked, joked, read, and studied as they ingested their tasteless meals. Why had it seemed like a good idea to stay on campus to eat? As he twirled his salad around on his fork, he watched the room as people came and went. The wilted salad repulsed him, and the rubbery fish on his plate looked equally unappetizing.

He recognized the futility of resistance and dragged himself from the chair, clearing his place. Lost in a mental jungle of restaurant options, Jay almost missed Hope as she reached for the door. "Hope?"

She dropped her hand and glanced up, recognition lighting her eyes. "Oh... names. Yeah, not so good with those. Um... don't tell me. You were born in India but the name doesn't sound Indian. Um..." She sighed. "I give up.

"Jay. Sanjay Brown. I tried to rescue you from a paper extortionist, but you didn't need me."

"I'm just going to get something to eat... you hungry?" Hope reached for the door again before adding, "I'm famished."

"Just leaving. The food is particularly unappetizing tonight. I was leaving to eat somewhere else." He hesitated before adding, "Would you like to come with me?"

Hope's lips pursed to one side as she considered the invitation. To Jay's consternation, he found it distractively charming. Her fingers closed over the door handle as if she had

11

decided against his invitation and then stepped back.

"Thanks. I'm not in the mood for icky food and I don't feel like going home for Mom's cooking." As she stepped out of the way to let in another unsuspecting victim of indigestion on a platter, she said, "So where are we going?"

They climbed aboard a bus and discussed their dinner options as it crawled across the campus. "I want something hot... and yummy." Her eyes sparkled under the lights of the bus. "Eloquent and decisive, aren't I?"

Jay studied her, as he thought about the places closest to the first stop. "There's that sandwich, salad, and soup place just a block from the bus stop. They make killer pies too."

"Sounds good to me."

They sat, facing one another, in the bench seats that lined the sides of the bus. Jay's arms lay crossed over his chest and Hope's hands fiddled with her purse strap. Awkwardness hung between them as they rolled farther and farther from the center of campus.

Hope sat up straighter and leaned forward, studying him. "So, you're business administration, right?"

"Yep." A chuckle escaped before he could stop himself.

"What?"

"What, what?"

"You laughed."

"Technically, I believe that would be called a snicker or chuckle, but yeah. I amuse easily, I suppose."

"Care to let me in on the joke?"

"The joke is on me. I've wondered about you since that day, but I was too chicken to look for you. Then you show up when I'm ready to flee."

There it was—a flash of embarrassment before she lowered her eyes. "I want to lie and say I'd forgotten all about it..."

Bus brakes squeaked as it pulled over to their stop. Could timing be worse? She stood and waited for him before hurrying off the bus. "Oooh! Nippy out here."

Again, her comments amused him. He attempted a little sarcasm. "It was so balmy ten minutes ago..."

"I think you owe me pie for that one."

12

The restaurant was almost half-empty, but Jay knew it wouldn't last. The moment the game was over, people would flood all restaurants near campus, looking for better food and a warm building. He didn't even open his menu when the server brought it.

"So you know what you want."

"Yep." He nudged her menu. "And you don't. So you should start looking."

Several more seconds passed before she frowned and dropped her menu atop his. "Fine. Then you choose for me. It all looks good. I'm too hungry."

"That's why I know what I want."

She started to ask and then shook her head. "You're smart."

"You are observant — probably intuitive as well."

"How do you know that I'm intuitive?"

Jay laughed and crossed his arms across his chest, leaning back in his chair. "Okay, you tell me. Why am I smart?"

"Because you figure out what you love most at any place you eat and keep it in your back pocket for times like this."

"And see, you are observant and intuitive to recognize that in me. Most people think that if I don't look at a menu, then I only order one thing every time."

Impatient fingers swept her bangs from her eyes. "So, you are business administration..."

"You said that."

"Yes, I did. And you never answered." Hope wrinkled her nose just the slightest before adding, "So spill it."

"There is not much to say. I'm working on my MBA — almost ready for graduation, actually — and I work part time for Finch Investments."

"Impressive."

He shrugged. "A lot less exciting than your drama class."

Those words threw up the curtain and flicked on the stage lights of the conversation. Hope came alive as she answered the questions he fired at her. She spoke with her eyes, hands — every facet of her person and personality eagerly taking part in the discussion.

"Y'know, I wasn't going to take drama until later — kind of

13

as a breather between harder classes, but when I heard they were doing *Brigadoon*, I just had to."

He'd never heard of it. "*Brigadoon*. What is it? How did you know the play before the class?"

"Oh, it's been my favorite since like the fifth grade. Mom rented the movie version for me one time when I was home sick." Her sigh couldn't have been more perfectly placed had she tried. "I was so in love with Gene Kelly. Broke my heart when Mom told me he was dead."

"So what's the story about?" Before she could answer he folded his hands, leaning his forearms against the table. "I should tell you that I followed you to your class that day. I've never taken a drama class. You made me curious."

"You followed me?"

"Yep. Hid in the hall and hoped you wouldn't see me." He snickered and then laughed as she rolled her eyes. "You must hate hearing that anyone hoped anything."

"Pretty much."

In an attempt to distract her, he continued, "So, tell me about the play. What is it about? The director said something about everyone sounding Scottish, so it must take place in Scotland..."

"Yep!" She leaned back to leave room for their server to set down her plate of salad. After shaking salad dressing over the pile of greens, she picked up her fork—and used it to gesticulate rather than eat as she described the legend of Brigadoon and her part in the play. "I still can't believe I got the part of Fiona."

"I heard you sing—it was great. Beautiful." He took a bite, hoping she'd follow suit, and smiled when she speared a small tomato. "That director though," he said as he speared another forkful of salad, "she was really critical that day. I don't know what her problem was."

"Ms. Gomez is amazing. She knows how to get the best performance out of you. I had no idea all the little things I did that would make a note go a little sharp or whatever."

As they ate their salads, Jay tossed question after question at her—just enough to keep her on a running dialogue about the play, her other classes, and occasionally, herself. By the time

14

their soup arrived, Hope refused to answer another question. "Nope. It's your turn."

"Okay..."

"I know your year and major now, so I can't ask those again—"

"Sure you can. You can make sure I am not making up stories."

An eyebrow rose, slowly followed by the other one. "Okay, fine. What year are you; what is your major; how long have you been in America; and where do your parents live?"

"Would you like to know anything else?

"Of course, but that's good for a start." Hope took a bite of her cream of broccoli soup and moaned, "This is so good."

"Well, as I said, I am a graduate student, working for my MBA, we moved to America when I was eight, and my parents live in Westbury."

"And now that we have the Twitter version of it, how about you tell me a little more? Tell me about India."

"Let's see..." He almost winked, caught himself, and then did it anyway. "My parents are from one of the southern Indian states. After they married, they decided that they wanted to move to America and began working hard, saving..."

"Do you have brothers and sisters?"

"No—just me. My parents wanted to be sure they could afford to come before I was old enough for high school, so they only had me." He leaned forward. "I would love to tell you exciting stories of fleeing tigers or riding royal elephants beneath the Indian stars, but I'm sorry to say I don't remember much of it—not really."

Hope chuckled. "I can just see a little you joy-riding on a maharajah's elephant." She started to ask another question and stopped. "Wait—really? You don't remember anything? I can tell you everything I did the summer I was eight... seven... five even!"

"Really." The question inevitably came when people asked about his homeland. "I played football in high school, got injured, have brain damage, and don't have an accurate memory bank anymore."

15

"What? No, wait. You can't just leave it at that. What happened?"

He should have known she'd want every detail. "I was stupid and played one night when I was really sick. Poor Coach didn't know I was sick until I collapsed holding the ball for a kickoff."

Eyes wide, she sucked in her breath. "Oh no... I see where this is going."

"Yes. They don't know if it was my illness or if I was just arrogant enough to be careless, but my helmet wasn't buckled right. It rolled off just as I fell over. The quarterback kicked my head instead of the ball—just couldn't stop himself."

"Ouch!" The wide-eyed horror in Hope's eyes—priceless.

"Yes. The doctors said I should have been paralyzed—or worse. I just ended up with a weird semi-amnesia thing."

"What's it called? What do you mean semi-amnesia?" As if she hadn't asked questions, her eyes roamed over him. "I can't see any scars. Of course, you've got the thickest, blackest hair I've ever seen on a guy. It's probably hidden, huh?"

"Yeah." He accepted his chicken and bacon hoagie and thanked the server before answering her questions. "It's hard to explain—the amnesia thing. I remember but I never know if what I remember happened, or if I saw or read it somewhere. They're kind of jumbled."

"So, did you have to learn stuff all over again or what?"

"Some, but not most things. I had some short-term memory loss at the time. Recent stuff in school—gone. I had to repeat that semester just to catch up again. My *amma* says I forgot more than the doctors think—little minor things that you don't usually think of unless someone says something."

"Oh, like when someone says, 'Hey, remember the time that guy dropped all the plates in the restaurant?'"

Jay nodded. "Exactly. Things that I wasn't really a part of. Most of the rest of it, though, most is still there—sort of."

"Sort of?" She stared at her sandwich as if confused as to when it had arrived. "Chicken bacon?"

"Yep."

"Yum. I love bacon." She moved his hand as he reached for

his sandwich. "Nuh, uh. You tell me about how it's 'sort of' and then you eat."

As his hand reached to pull the plate away from her, she snagged it and held it off to one side like a caricature of a waiter. Resigned, he threw up his hands. "Okay, okay. It's just that if I watched a movie as a kid or read a book or something, if I don't see it again to put it into the right box of fact or fiction, I can't tell if it happened or if I heard or read about it — or saw it."

"Wow." She passed him his plate, joking, "And you look so normal."

"I don't know if I'd say that..."

They finished their sandwiches in silence, exchanging curious glances when they expected the other not to notice. To Jay's chagrin, they seemed too in sync to avoid eye contact in their surreptitious efforts. As she shoved the last half of her sandwich aside, Hope's eyes grew wide. "Oh! Wait. You forgot to tell me the most important thing!"

Although he had anticipated the question, he put on an exaggerated air of ignorance and played along asking, "What question would that be?"

"Your name. How did Sanjay from India get the very American-sounding last name of Brown?"

"I think you will be disappointed; it's not very exciting." At her pointed look, he continued. "See, our province in India — there, people don't have surnames. When we came to America, the officials offered us a list of suggested last names — the ones most Indians in the U.S. use."

"And most Indian-Americans choose names like Brown?"

Jay shook his head. "No. More like Patel or Singh. My *appa* said that he wanted a real American last name. No one could make him understand that all names here come from other places. So, they suggested a name like Wilson, but when *Appa* found out it meant 'Will's son' he refused. 'I am not the son of Will; I will not be called that.'"

Curiosity filled her expression. "And so he chose Brown?"

"After a long debate over other names. He wasn't a smith, didn't think Jones sounded good with Raj, so when they got to the colors, it got really interesting."

17

"I think I hear it already..."

"Yep, he said, 'I am not black or white or green. Brown. I like Brown. It describe me!'"

"I think I like your father's sense of humor." She accepted a to-go box from their server and tucked her sandwich inside. As if lost in her own thoughts, she murmured, "I can just see him there wearing a tunic thing—"

"Kurta."

"Yeah, kurta and your mom in a sari—oh, tell me she was wearing a sari."

"She was. She still wears them often."

Hope beamed. "All standing there talking about names. You were probably adorable, watching everything with big brown eyes, totally confused as to what this name business was all about anyway. Your dad joking about which name to choose for life in a new country." She shook her head as the server asked if they wanted pie. "Too full." To Jay, she added, "Oh yeah, he has got to have a good sense of humor."

"I think so." Jay nodded his head toward pastry case in the front of the restaurant. "I thought I owed you pie."

"You'll have to pay up some other time."

Those words answered a question he had been afraid to ask. She might see him again. Excellent. A glance around the room showed it still empty enough to stay a bit longer.

"So, Hope Senior, what more can you tell me about you? You are a sophomore next semester, so that means you've already been here for one? You like anthropology, drama, and literature. What else should I know about Hope Senior who is not a senior?"

"Actually," she laughed, "This is my third semester." His thoughts must have registered in his face because she quickly added, "And no, I am not struggling with my classes."

"Third semester, still a first year... did you change your major?" His interest piqued, he leaned forward, waiting for the answer.

"No, I'm just taking my time. It's kind of a long story."

Jay accepted his plate of cherry pie and leaned back in his chair. "They don't need the table, and I have plenty of time. I

18

would like to hear this."

A shout from outside, and a car full of screaming fans, drew their attention away from the discussion for a minute. The Warriors must have won the game. When Jay turned back to her, he saw her swallow hard and take a deep breath. The slight twist at the corner of her lips as she pursed them — it looked like she struggled to control her emotions.

"If it's personal..."

"No, not that kind of personal anyway. My story has an accident too, but I wasn't the one injured. My brother was hit by a car three years ago — on his way to one of those stupid Black Friday sales. He died a few days later."

The room filled with cheering fans. Jay stood and grabbed the check. "Can we talk on the way back? We should — "

She stood, pulling on her coat. "Definitely. Let's go."

The next bus wouldn't arrive before they could be most of the way to her dorm, so they chose to walk, the cool autumn air biting at their ears and noses. Jay waited until they were a block or two away from the post-game melee before he cleared his throat, ready to find another topic. She could tell him more about her life some other time.

"Anyway..." Hope nudged his arm with her elbow, "And thanks for not asking, but I don't mind talking about it."

"I didn't know..."

"Anyway," she repeated, "Mom and Dad had saved and invested since before Con was even born. He saved too. They took all that money, kept investing it, and when I graduated, they showed me what I had to work with."

Jay watched as she tried to brush away tears without him noticing. His own throat thick with emotion, Jay chose not to ask the one question burning in him. *What kind of name is Con, anyway?*

Before he could think of anything to say, she pushed on with her story as if she had to tell it now. "The account is really big. I could pretty much choose any field and it'd be covered — or very nearly so. It'd be great if I wanted to go into medicine or law — I could almost do it debt-free, but those don't interest me."

"Not many students have such wealthy parents."

19

"They're not. They just knew how to save and invest. Dad's a principal; Mom didn't work until I started jr. high…" She stole a glance at him and flushed when she saw that he was still watching her. "So, Dad suggested I just take classes—take my time. He told me to retake ones I thought were cool, do all the social stuff that kids want to do and often don't have time for—anything." She kicked a rock as they crossed a side street. Jay watched as it bounced over the rough road and slid into the curb.

"So…"

"So it was hard to wrap my brain around that idea—seemed wasteful, you know? But man, I love the stress-free college experience."

"I think it's brilliant. I like it. You have your entire life ahead of you. Why not take your time to decide what preparation you need to live it and enjoy yourself while you do that?"

The relief on her face tugged at something in him. She took a deep breath, exhaling white puffs of air. "Not everyone understands. Most people think I'm not a good student or don't know how to manage my time." Her shrug failed at nonchalance and instead showed her vulnerability. "I'm really doing this for my parents as much as for myself. It means so much to them for me to do this. They missed out on all that stuff with Con."

"And have you declared a major?" Jay winced as he heard his words. How nosy.

"Yeah. Liberal arts with a minor in English."

"That explains the diversity of your classes." A car whizzed past, filling their lungs with exhaust fumes. He choked before he added, "Do you have a specialty in English, or…"

"I'd specialize in Children's Lit, but my guidance counselor wasn't impressed. I'm hoping to be the children's librarian in Marshfield. The current librarian plans to retire in six years, so…"

Her face glowed as she described her dreams for the job. By the time they reached her dorm, even Jay felt excited about story hours and themed book parties. He opened the door for her, aching to invite her out again. Dinner or a lecture—something.

Instead, he said, "Thanks for coming. I really had fun."

"Hey, thanks for dinner. That was great. You really should have let me pay for mine, though."

"I was happy to do it."

With a little wave, she stepped inside saying, "If I don't see you before then, I hope you'll come to the play."

Before he could answer, she allowed the door to shut behind her. The temptation to chase after her and invite her out—anywhere—overpowered him long enough to get the door open. He let it close and turned away, reminding himself that they had plenty of time. The play, however... he'd be there for that.

CHAPTER 3

The audience sat spellbound as the mythical, mystical village of Brigadoon rose and fell on the stage like the highland mists. Hope sang her way into the hearts of every person present, drawing them into the imaginary world of eighteenth-century Scotland. One word described the effect—surreal.

As the curtain fell, the applause thundered through the theater. A standing ovation kept the curtain calls coming for several minutes. The final curtain fell, leaving the audience standing, but few made any attempt to leave. Jay felt it keenly. The lights flickered and then glowed brightly—still no one moved. His eyes roamed the room and took in the scene. Most people stood, whispering amongst themselves, their hands still clasped together from their final clap.

The atmosphere changed as the cast members appeared from backstage. Those with loved ones in the cast rushed at the stage as the curtains opened again, revealing the cast mulling about and hugging one another. The rest of the audience moved toward the doors, speaking in semi-hushed tones as if not to break the spell cast by the players.

Jay stood by the side exit doors watching Hope. A middle-aged couple rushed to congratulate her, the man's arms filled with pink rosebuds and white daisies. Her delight with the flowers showed in her face, the hugs she gave, and the way she inhaled the scent.

A strange feeling washed over him as he observed the little

family interact. It took a minute or two to identify it, but once he did, his heart constricted. Although he had never met her brother with the strange name, the absence showed. The way the family moved, stood, interacted—there was always an empty place as if someone else stood there. But only three truly did.

Just as he turned to leave, Jay caught Hope's eye. He pantomimed rousing applause and laughed at her exaggerated curtsey. She beckoned him to come meet her parents, and after a moment's hesitation, he climbed the steps to the stage.

His empty hands shamed him. He should have brought flowers—it was customary. Trying to cover his awkwardness, Jay began speaking before he even reached her side. "You all did a wonderful job, Hope! Thanks to you and your fellow cast members, none of us will ever be satisfied with our modern lives again." She started to speak, but he added one last thought. "We will all leave here in search of our own Brigadoon."

She flushed, her eyes shining with tears that he knew she willed not to flow. In an obvious attempt to hide her embarrassment, she introduced him to her parents. "Mom, Dad, this is Jay Brown. He came to my rescue a few weeks ago when a term paper extortionist wouldn't leave me alone."

Jay shook hands with the Seniors, teasing Hope as he did. "She didn't need me, though. She sent the guy packing before I could get near them. I was almost afraid to introduce myself."

They liked him. He saw it in their eyes and in the way they exchanged amused and curious glances. After a minute or two of chat, Ron Senior waved off the women. "Go get her cleaned up so we can go eat." To Jay he added, "We planned on a late dinner celebration. Would you like to join us?"

Hope continued toward the rear of the stage, but Cheryl Senior turned to listen. Jay hesitated. Hope's night... her parents there. She probably preferred to have them to herself. Just as he opened his mouth to decline, her voice drifted from the stage entrance, "Make sure he comes, Dad. He's a lot of fun, and I owe him dinner. Better on your dime than mine!"

Cheryl grinned and took a few steps back toward him. "Sorry, Jay. I think we have Senior-ity on this one. You'll just have to come."

24

Their appetizers arrived just in time to give Hope something to focus her attention on while ignoring the discussion. Story after story of her childhood antics — it was worse than bathtub pictures as a baby. At least those had the decency to be cute and almost unrecognizable.

Cheryl urged Jay to take another skewer of shrimp. "There's plenty. And now, tell us something about your childhood. After all, we shared Hope's shenanigans." She speared a shrimp and added, "I assume by your accent that you were born in India?"

Hope blanched. Before she could think of some way to extricate him from the question without embarrassing her mother, Jay finished chewing his food and wiped his mouth. His eyes reassured her, stopping the hasty apology forming on her lips. "I regret to say that I have no memory of my childhood here or in India. However, my mother says that I was a model child — always helpful — and that I never cried. From what I understand, I changed my own diapers from six weeks of age and was able to prepare dinner by three."

It was ludicrous — ridiculous — but Jay's face held no trace of jest. She saw the question form in her mother's mind as clearly as if spoken — was it six weeks or six months? However, before Cheryl could speak, Hope caught an errant twinkle in Jay's right eye and snickered.

"He had me. I can't believe he had me. I was sure the six week thing must have been six months — or maybe that they didn't use diapers or something — but I've never seen someone drop a bomb like that and pull it off."

Her parents exchanged indulgent smiles. So, she liked dry humor. What could possibly be wrong with that?

"So what do you do, Mr. Senior?"

"I'm the principal at Marshfield High," Ron said.

"Do you like it?"

Before Hope's father could answer, their meals arrived. She couldn't help glancing Jay's way as they prayed, but he bowed his head with the rest of the family. She didn't know if it meant anything, but prayed it might be indicative of faith.

She intended to ask him if he was a Christian, but her father launched into a description of his job that brought a smile to her face. None of her friends' fathers ever spoke with such passion about their job as her father did. Jay asked intelligent questions — ones designed to keep the other person talking.

The two women exchanged glances and then Cheryl interjected another question. "You said you don't remember — what do you mean by that? Do you truly not remember your life in India?"

Hope waited, wondering how much he'd say. Would he tell more? Ever since he'd described his injury, she'd been fascinated with the idea of not knowing if a random memory was something he'd observed or experienced.

"That's a simplistic answer, but yes. I have a brain injury that affects my memory. It isn't that I can't retrieve the memories — I just don't know if they are my imagination, someone else's imagination, or something that actually happened."

"That is unbelievable."

"Tell me about it."

Something about such an American expression spoken with an Indian accent prompted snickers from the Seniors. "See what I mean? Isn't he hilarious?"

"Do your parents help with that?"

Jay swallowed his food, took a sip, wiped his mouth, and set his fork down. Assuming that he was uncomfortable, Hope started to assure him that they would understand if he'd rather not discuss it, but Jay leaned back in his chair, arm over the back, and grinned.

"You tell me if they do. There is one memory that I don't know is true, but I suspect it must be."

"Why?"

He winked at Hope. "Because my *amma* won't tell me if it is or isn't. If it wasn't, she'd say so."

"How mysterious..."

"Oh, Mom! She's probably just messing with his head. He

probably learned it from her too."

"Let him tell the story, Hope!"

She amused him; his eyes told her what he'd probably never say. She imagined him as the sort of man who enjoyed listening to others, asking questions, drawing them out, but not much of a talker himself. Still, he waited for her until she urged him as well. "Let's hear it!"

"Well, we lived in Chennai — big city — but my memory is of being at a place in the jungle. *Amma* and *Appa* were sleeping. I can see their feet on their mats. I went outside. It was nearly dark; I can see a couple of stars in the sky if I allow my mind to look up."

"Can't you imagine the Indian sky at night — so beautiful?"

"Yes, yes," Cheryl snapped. "Let him tell the story!"

"I don't know how long I was out there. I cannot even remember what I did; this is why I doubt the story."

He looked so apologetic that Hope felt compelled to say, "I can't remember all my childhood stories — lots of them are just snippets. People tell me about them later and I think, 'Oh, that's what happened in there.'"

"Exactly. I have thought of that, but since my *amma* will not confirm and seems to have silenced *Appa*, I still have missing pieces to the puzzle." Again he winked, this time at her parents. "I remember a scream — long and piercing. It should have meant my death, for I was holding a snake — very poisonous it seems. In my mind, it is a king cobra. He isn't large though, just having the characteristics of one, but I imagine that if it truly happened, it was probably more likely the common Indian krait."

"What is the difference? King cobras are very poisonous, aren't they?"

"Yes they are, but it seems a little too romantic to happen to be in the Indian jungle and handling a cobra. The krait is found everywhere."

Fascinated, Hope couldn't help but ask, "How dangerous is the krait?"

"Very — and very easily provoked. From what I've read, they're nocturnal. A bite usually results in death within eight hours — another reason I am not sure the story is real."

27

"People handle king cobras all the time, though. Are they that trainable, or do they milk the venom from them, or what?"

"Actually, as poisonous as they are, they're very intelligent snakes and not very aggressive. They rarely attack humans or other snakes."

"He's done his homework," Cheryl commented to her husband.

"It is the one story that confuses me most."

"It's real," Hope insisted. "Think about it. You're in the jungle, playing with a poisonous snake. Any mother would freak. You just happen to have one that isn't aggressive, so you're safe. Your mother doesn't like to talk about it, but she doesn't want to lie. If she says it's true, you might keep talking. If she ignores you, maybe you'll drop it."

"But my father," Jay protested. "*Appa* will not say one way or the other either."

"But your father has a wicked sense of humor. I'll bet he does it just to mess with you. It's real. I'm sure of it."

Jay leaned against the table, bending toward Hope's parents in a conspiratorial whisper, "She thinks it's real. I suppose that means it is so?"

CHAPTER 4

Two weeks passed. Jay hadn't seen Hope once. Busy with his own study for finals week, he watched for her as he crisscrossed the campus, going from class to cafeteria and then home again. However, as much as he would have liked to, he hadn't made a concentrated effort to see her. If he didn't find her soon, she'd be gone for the winter break.

That thought consumed him for two days until he surrendered. Foolish—he felt so very foolish for feeling disappointed at the idea of another month passing before seeing her again. "New friendships need much watering and attention to grow into something strong enough to withstand neglect," he muttered to himself as he passed the fine arts building—again.

This time, his mind traveled back to the play. That memory sparked a new idea, sending him off to try and tempt Hope to make time for him. With any luck, she would be done with most assignments and then she would feel free to agree to his plan.

Hope, almost late, rushed to her seat in anthropology an hour later. A daisy, a small note tied to it with string, lay alone and out of place on her usual desk. Frustrated, she dumped her backpack in the next seat, but her name on the outside of the note caught her eye.

She slid the flower and note aside, pulled out her laptop, and set it up. While it booted, she picked up the daisy. A glance around her revealed that she was now the center of attention. Behind her, a girl—Wendy perhaps—nudged Hope, tossing her hair over her shoulder as she pulled an already tight sweater even more taut.

"This, like, really cute Indian guy asked where you usually sit. He was like, sooooo hoooottttt. Is he your boyfriend?"

"No, Jay's just a friend."

She opened the note, confused. The words implied meaning or familiarity. She had neither. "*Thou art as sweet and fresh as a daisy.* I hope to see you at dinner this evening."

"I wonder what that means..."

Determined to put the enigmatic message from her mind, Hope tucked the note into her pocket and broke the stem of the daisy in half. As she skimmed her pre-exam notes, she tucked the daisy behind her ear and lost herself in matrilateral and patrilateral parallel and cross-cousinry. Despite her best intentions, her mind refused to ignore the inevitable. She'd be in the cafeteria most of the evening.

That is where Jay found her at dinnertime. With her back to the door and engrossed in her World Lit. book, Hope didn't notice as he sat beside her. However, as he pulled the flower from behind her ear, she jumped.

"Jay!"

"I see you found it."

"I got the note too, obviously. I just can't place that quote anywhere. It sounds familiar though..." She shrugged, giving up. "So what is it from?"

"A children's book..."

"Well, that's probably why it's familiar, but I just can't put my finger on it."

Jay took a bite of his salad before explaining. "I don't remember the name of the book, but it was about a little Quaker girl named Hannah. My parents said it was one of the first books I brought home from the school library."

"Why would an Indian boy bring home a book about a Quaker girl?" She passed him her extra packet of croutons. "Want more?"

"Thanks. *Amma* says that the librarian did it. She was always giving me books about different pieces of American culture and history. In the story, the father said that about the daisy to his little girl. My mother says I said it often when she would change clothes in the evening before my father would get home from work." Jay sighed.

"You sound sad about that, but I think it's sweet. What mother wouldn't want her son to tell her she was sweet and fresh as a flower?"

"It's a hard memory for me. *Amma* says it was the morning after I got home from the hospital; she woke me wearing one of her favorite saris. I remember how her eyes sparkled, the sunshine shining through the window; she was like a goddess—so beautiful."

"And that makes you sad?"

"I said she looked like the daisy and she cried—so happy."

"I would be too. That would be such wonderful news. You remembered."

"She thought so too. She thought something so familiar and emotional would clear away the fog, but it didn't. *Amma* couldn't accept that—still can't. She hopes that someday I will see it all clearly in my mind."

"But you think you won't."

"The doctors think I won't," Jay corrected. "There is something damaged in the neuro-transmitters." He snickered. "Or as my father says, my 'neuro-transmissions.'"

She laid her hand on her arm, a sympathetic smile in her eyes and weakly forming on her lips. "I'm sorry, Jay."

In that moment, he knew what she meant and how she could speak with such conviction and sympathy. She did know. All the well-meaning words that usually felt like insincere platitudes, despite the sincerity behind them didn't help when you felt like you'd lost part of your life. She knew that loss. It hurt to think that she did.

Jay tucked the now-wilted daisy back behind her ear. "I feel a little sorry for it. You have stolen its freshness."

"Should I be wary of the flatterer? If you want something, I'm not giving it. Write your own term papers. I don't know anything about business anyway."

"Ah, but what if all I want is a nice conversation with a fascinating girl…"

31

"Yep. Flattery. It won't get you anywhere."

Jay glanced around him, and shoved his tray back. "Why don't we go for a drive—see the Christmas lights in some of the more festive areas? Winter break will be here in a couple of days and then it'll be next year—"

Hope groaned. "Oh, why do we never quit saying that? It's like a mantra for peace and happiness in the New Year or something."

"Then you'll come? I heard of a neighborhood up in the triangle that has luminaries lining the sidewalks and driveways and in windows..."

When she hesitated, he was sure she'd say no, but her smile followed quickly. "On one condition."

"Name it."

"You let me take my books back to my dorm first."

"Sure."

At her dorm, he waited in the common room, instinctively knowing her parents wouldn't appreciate a man in their daughter's room. With a daughter as gorgeous as Hope, he didn't blame them. She must have run because she was back downstairs, a wrapped present in hand, before he could even begin to feel impatient.

"I hoped I'd see you before I went home. Merry Christmas."

He opened the door, leading her back out to his car. As they walked, he played with the ribbons spiraling over the top of the box. "Um—should I open it now or wait for Christmas?"

"Now, silly! Hurry!"

Jay waited, partly to taunt her for her impatience and partly to be inside a warm car as soon as possible. Once he started the car, blasting the heating vents on them and sending freezing air to torment them for a few seconds, he opened the package. Inside was a card taped to the top of a box, which Hope recommended he read later. Jay lifted the lid from the box and discovered that the book he imagined was a Bible was actually a box of fudge.

"Did you make—"

"Yep. The church let a few of us use their kitchen to make

32

large batches for Christmas gifts. I sure hope you like fudge."

"I do, but I am surprised. I was certain that it was a Bible."

She laughed. "Why would I give you a Bible?"

"I assumed it was what Christians gave their heathen friends on things like Christmas or Easter." He shook the box. "It's about the right size and weight too."

As Jay pulled away from the curb, Hope sat in silence. He feared he'd offended her, but then she spoke. "I've never thought of you or anyone as a 'heathen friend.' You're just a friend."

"I wasn't offended. I hope I didn't—"

"Oh, no. I think I've just always assumed that anyone in America who wanted a Bible would have one." She urged him to take a piece of fudge before continuing. "I think if I had thought of it, and I'm pretty sure I wouldn't have, I would have assumed you wouldn't be interested in reading it."

"Well, I've never read much, it's true. I know some things that people quote. 'Judge not' and 'do unto others.' Things like that."

Hope's mind still seemed stuck in the loop of buying Bibles for all her non-Christian friends. "I don't think I'd do that unless the person expressed interest in having one or something. I mean, if I wasn't a Christian and someone just gave me a Bible all wrapped up like it was a present, I'd probably be pretty ticked."

"I wouldn't have minded at all. Now that I have a friend who reads it and believes it, I should probably get one and read it someday."

Jay turned onto a street where nearly every home had some sort of decoration. The contrast between homes, however, proved comical. A house that looked like it was ripped from a Currier and Ives painting sat next to a house that Jay couldn't help but call the "Rockland Strip."

The neighborhood of luminaries, however, was surreal in its simple beauty. "You know, it reminds me of that art exhibit in Central Park a while back—remember? *The Gates* or something like that?"

Jay nodded slowly. "The orange panels?"

"Right! This is like them in reverse—the same effect of a river of beauty, but in miniature as if lighting our paths."

"But to where?"

"That's a good question."

The trek through the neighborhood took much longer than anticipated. Trapped behind a long line of cars moving at the speed of push, Jay doubted that they'd ever make it out again. At last, he turned the corner.

Just two blocks away, a small, slightly neglected-looking church caught Hope's attention. "Look! Can we stop? I want to see."

Jay maneuvered between two parked cars, skillfully avoiding a fender bender. He followed Hope from the car to the edge of the living nativity. The beauty of such a simple scene affected him, and if his observations were correct, it moved her as well. A small crowd gathered to watch as sheep snuggled next to each other, a donkey jerked at the reins that tethered him to a post, and "shepherds" gazed in apparent awe at a realistic-looking infant doll posing as Jesus in the arms of an apparently exhausted Mary.

"I'm glad she looks tired," Hope whispered.

Jay couldn't bring himself to ask why. He had never seen the nativity shown so realistically. His experience was limited to tacky plastic yard ornaments or miniature crèches in gift store windows. The impact of life-sized animals and real people intrigued him.

Someone in the crowd began singing. *"Silent night...holy night... Aaaalll..."*

One by one, the group picked up the tune, singing together with even occasional attempts at harmony. The words he'd heard and remembered, Jay sang with the rest. By the last verse, only Hope and an elderly woman sang, but the entire group, including Jay, picked up the last line, *"Jesus Lord at Thy birth."*

At her shiver, Jay nudged her toward the car. "Let's go. There's still one more street on the way back to campus."

"M'kay."

As they pulled away from the curb, Jay saw her wipe the corner of her eyes. "Are you okay?"

She sighed as she nodded. "I'm fine—really. It was just so beautiful. I always knew that Mary was young—probably younger than me. Would I have had the faith to trust that God knew what He was doing? Would I accept the rejection and shame that she must have suffered? They could have—should have—stoned her!"

Jay turned down what he thought was the last impressive street, but it wasn't much more than any other street in the city. A few houses here and there but nothing special. At last, he asked, "Do you believe that Jesus physically came to earth?"

Hope's answer came almost instantaneously. "Without a doubt."

"I mean as a baby."

"Yes, Jay. I believe that the God Who created this world came to earth as a helpless infant, utterly dependent upon a young woman and her betrothed for life, sustenance, and shelter."

The quiet confidence in her tone spurred him to ask yet another question. "Do you really believe she was a virgin?"

"Absolutely."

"Why?" He winced at his own questions. "I hope you do not mind the semi-interrogation. I am just curious, but—"

"I don't mind. Do you mean why was she a virgin or why do I believe it?"

"Well, I meant why she needed to be a virgin, but I am also curious as to why you believe it."

She didn't say a word, make any gesture, or even move, but he sensed she prayed before replying. "Well... Isaiah prophesied that a virgin would conceive and bear a son who would be the Savior of the world. One reason Jesus had to be born of a virgin is to fulfill that prophesy or God would be a liar."

"Okay..." It still didn't make sense. Why make such a prophesy in the first place?

"That's not the only reason, of course. God didn't have to do it. But you see, without a virgin birth—supernatural birth—Jesus would have just been another man, born in sin and in need of redemption Himself. Because of His deity, He had to be conceived without a man. He had to be fully human without the sin nature passed onto Him by a human father in order to also be fully God...aaaaannnd that probably makes no sense."

"It's a bit confusing, yes." Her dorm loomed ahead of them. "I guess you'll have to tell me why you believe it some other time."

"I'm sorry... I know that wasn't very helpful."

"I'd keep you out here until I understood, but it's cold and we'll freeze. You should go in." He frowned at his own words. They sounded clipped and curt. "I wish classes were over. I'd drag you to some all-night place and try again."

The disappointment on her face soothed his ego a little. At least he hadn't run her off. Then her eyes widened. "I know! Can I have your address? I know I've got a copy of a paper Con wrote for a Bible class assignment once. I could send it if you want..."

Jay pulled out his wallet and fumbled for an unneeded receipt. Reaching into his backpack, he grabbed a pen and wrote down his address, email address, and phone number. "Feel free to call, write, email... anything."

He watched her fold the paper and slip it into her backpack. As much as he hated to say goodnight, the temperature seemed to drop by the minute. He reached for the daisy still tucked behind her ear. After a gentle sweep of it across her cheek, he replaced the flower and wished her a Merry Christmas. "I'll see you after the first of the year, I hope."

She laughed. "No, Jay. I Hope. You Jay. Merry Christmas." As she reached for the door handle, Hope added, "I'll write or call or something. Thanks for the ride; it was wonderful." She squeezed the hand that still rested near her ear and stepped from the car. He waited for her to reach the doors of the dorm before he pulled away from the curb.

As Jay drove home, his mind mulled over their conversation, wondering how anyone could believe that a virgin gave birth to God. Absently, he hummed "Silent Night" as he parked his car and walked to his door.

CHAPTER 5

A store loomed ahead of them. "Dad! Stop! Please! I need to go into Covenant Books."

As Ron eased into the right lane and turned into the store's parking lot, he asked, "What's so important?"

"I gave Jay a box of fudge for Christmas, and he said he thought it would be a Bible — something about Christians always buying their unsaved friends Bibles."

"Really?" Cheryl turned to look at her daughter. "Do you think it's a good idea —"

"He actually seemed a little disappointed, so I want to get him one."

Ron waited until they'd reached the door before saying, "This is America. If someone wants a Bible, he can find one on almost any corner. Even thrift stores sell them for pennies. You'd think if he wanted a Bible he'd have one."

"I know, right? That's what I said. I also said I'd send him Con's paper on the virgin birth, so I thought I'd stick it in a Bible and ship them together."

"Well, that'll help him if he wants to look up references," Cheryl remarked as she led them to the wall of Bible options.

Her usual awe and delight at the sheer number of Bible options dissolved into a less enthusiastic awe. As she tried to choose the perfect one, her heart sank. "Is this how seekers feel when they come in here? There should be a shelf of 'Seeker Bibles' or something."

"That'd help." Ron picked up his favorite version and read a few verses. "It seems clear to me, but…"

"Well, he's an intelligent guy. It's not like we're buying a Bible for a kid or for someone who doesn't read much."

A sales assistant approached, offering help. After a long debate over traditional versus contemporary, the Seniors chose a new, unfamiliar version that promised to use modern word choices to ensure accuracy in both translation and meaning.

"At least I won't confuse him further with this," Hope said.

Never had she imagined that buying a Bible for an unbeliever could be so difficult and unfamiliar. Something as simple as whether she should have his name embossed on the cover drove her crazy. Would he be offended—feel obligated to keep it even if he didn't want it? "I don't know what to do!"

Ron passed the box across the counter. "We'll take it. As is. Can you put something in there stating that it can be embossed at any of your stores or something?"

"Sure. I'll just put a slip in the box. People do it all the time."

An hour later, she sat on her bed, leaning against the headboard and her knees drawn up against her chest, trying to decide what to write. *Lord, this could be one of the most important things that I ever write. I'm so nervous,* she prayed.

Her nerves spilled into an emotional prayer for wisdom, encouragement, and wise choice of words. With her heart soothed by the Spirit through prayer, Hope opened the Bible to a flyleaf and wrote. She struggled, determined to design each word as a magnet to draw Jay to Jesus.

Disgusted with herself, she muttered, "'Faith comes by hearing and hearing by the word of God,' not the words of Hope Senior."

Once she finished her note, Hope reread the inscription with every inflection she could imagine. Satisfied it could only be encouraging, she closed the Bible, added her brother's paper, and replaced the lid to the box. Within the hour, it sat amongst dozens of other packages in a bin at the Marshfield Post Office, awaiting the drive to Westbury.

Jay dashed across the neighbors' lawns, dodging the attempts of the neighborhood children to tackle him. As he reached the end of the cul-de-sac, a string of lights ran across the street from light pole to light pole. He threw the football over the lights, ending in a victory dance. "Touchdown!"

Seconds later, he lay buried in the snow by a pile of bundled children. "It's good that you are all so well-padded," he complained jokingly. "If this were summer, I'd be black and blue."

"Let's do it again. It's our turn!" the nearest boy, Tyler, insisted.

From the corner of his eye, Jay saw his mother watching him from the corner of their house. As usual, her face wore a mask of concern. "I need to go in now, but maybe tomorrow. Besides—here comes Mrs. Joan. You probably have packages to open, shake, and mutilate."

The kids scattered to their respective homes as Jay strolled across the street to his mother's side. "I'm fine, *Amma*. Really. I'm not even sore."

"You may be fine, but my heart is still chasing tigers."

Jay urged his mother indoors, all while he teased her for her protectiveness. "Perhaps I should wear a helmet while walking to the mailbox too..."

"And to bed, and to the table, and when reading a book!" Amala Brown winked at her son. "For all the good it did you on the football field."

The doorbell interrupted their banter. Amala went to answer it while Jay punched the TV remote, looking for something more interesting than a daytime talk show. The idea of yet another, "My husband just told me that he has four other wives," didn't appeal to him. Just as he settled into a rerun of Andy Griffith, his mother dropped a package and three credit card offers beside him on the couch.

"It looks like three want to take from you and one gives to you. Who is Hope Senior?"

Jay's eyes lit up at the sight of the name on the package.

"She's a student at the university — the one in the play I told you about. Remember?"

"The singer — yes. You said she was very good." She accepted the envelopes he handed back to her smiling. "I'll shred them for you. Do you want anything from the store? I am going to go get a few things."

Jay asked for his favorite throat lozenges and waved goodbye as he tore the zip strip from the end of the box. From inside, he pulled out a box advertising a "Contemporary translation for the modern reader." Beneath the lid was a note, the paper she had promised him, and a Bible that couldn't have been inexpensive. His hand traced the embossed cross on the cover before he opened the envelope and read the enclosed note.

Jay,

Greetings from Marshfield. We're already in the middle of Christmas traditions here at home. Mom and I have enough baking planned to feed half the town. Dad keeps interrupting us, demanding a critique on his latest change to the light display, and the neighborhood children are all huddled around our yard, dying to play in the snow. We have the only yard on the block without footprints in it.

Mom is a bit obsessive and the kids love and fear her. She bribes them with cookies and threatens them with loss of limb to keep that yard pristine. So far no kid has snuck out at night to destroy it, but I don't think it'll hold out much longer. Dad keeps to the walkways and stepping-stones. Let's hope he doesn't fall off a ladder and make an accidental "snow angel" like he did two years ago.

I kind of feel sorry for the kids. All that fresh, unadulterated snow... They just want one more snowman... just one... or a few angels. So they shuffle back and forth along the sidewalk and ogle and dream. Hope springs eternal.

I've enclosed the promised paper as well as a Bible. I figured it might help to have one while reading Con's paper. I hope that it is the encouragement and inspiration to you that it is to me. I recommend starting in Mark. It's what Con called "a man's book," full of action and strength — not to mention brief. He knew how to say the most with the least amount of words.

Every other year, our family hosts a New Year's Eve party for the neighborhood. Our neighbors take the off years. Anyway, I wanted to invite you to come to dinner and then the party. Mom says you're welcome to stay over. You could have Con's room and go with us to the chili cook-off at church on Tuesday.

Email me at hopesenior90@letterbox.com if you can come. We'd love to have you.

Merry Christmas (I hope that isn't offensive),
Hope

He read the letter twice, his plans for New Year's Day now settled. He'd email Hope after he read a little in the Bible so he could tell her about it. He would ask his mother to help him make chili to take to the cook-off. Her spices always gave chili the best flavor.

Jay set the note and the several-page paper aside and withdrew the Bible from its box. The gilded edges felt smooth under his fingertips. Near the front was a table of contents. Mark stood out against the lower half of the page; he'd start with that. Definitely. As he closed it, his eye caught writing on the flyleaf and he read.

Jay,
I'd like you to introduce you to my friend and Lord, Jesus. I pray that His words will bring you comfort and understanding. I also pray that you will learn to know and love Him as I do.
Hope

He smiled to himself. How very like her. "Mark," he murmured to himself. "I'm supposed to be reading Mark."

An hour and a half later, Jay closed the Bible both fascinated and disappointed. After their discussion of the virgin birth of Jesus, he'd expected to read about it, but Mark never mentioned Jesus' birth or His childhood. "I guess I'll have to ask her," he muttered to himself as he reached for his laptop.

Jay copied her email into his address book and composed an email.

Eternal Hope,
How are your springs? I sit with your beautiful gift beside me and am fascinated by the portion I have just read. Your Jesus is quite a

41

remarkable man. *I never thought of myself as hot-tempered, but I think I would have lost patience with some of those people. He comes, he heals, he give hope to the hopeless (Is that what he did for me when I met you?) and all those people said it was wrong and executed him.*

I am curious. Do you truly believe that all of this happened just as Mark wrote it?

Now I have a confession. I am disappointed that you did not give me the part where Jesus was born. After our discussions, I assumed it would tell me about the birth of Jesus and about Mary.

I thank you for your invitation and accept! I will bring my mother's chili for the meal at your church, and is there anything I can bring for the party? My number is 555-550-4101. Please call if I can help in any way.

I wish you and your parents a wonderful holiday (and you did not offend me with your good wishes either). I will keep you all in my thoughts, as I am sure this is a difficult time of year for you.

Until I see you,

Jay

He sent the email into cyberspace. Still intrigued by the birth of Jesus, he clicked on Google, but the sound of his mother's car in the garage stopped him. He shut the laptop, gathered his things, and stashed them in his room. He'd read more later.

CHAPTER 6

"Sweet sugar cookies in my stove... they'll taste great, oh, don't you know...Gosh oh, gee do I have fun..." Hope sang, swaying as she punched the buttons on the oven timer.

She surveyed the counters, beaming at the array of icing, sprinkles, metallic balls, and colored sugar. Did she have it all? While the oven worked its magic with the shaped cookies, Hope flipped open her laptop, waiting for it to boot. "Argh! Stupid updates! Why, when I don't have very long, must you always update right then?" She drummed her fingers, waiting for the password screen. Her fingers hovered, waiting for the cursor in the password box and then flew across the keyboard. ONE.2.THR33. Once it loaded, she clicked on her email icon.

Just as the email began dumping into the inbox, the timer beeped. She saw Jay's email as she turned to rescue her cookies from over-baking. "Drat!" she muttered.

Minutes later, as the first batch of cookies cooled on their racks and the second batch began warming in the oven, Hope returned to read her email. She chuckled at his greeting, nodded at his assessment of the Pharisees, and felt foolish for neglecting to recommend the beginning of Luke. She had just begun to compose a reply when the timer beeped again.

"Oh, this won't work," she snapped in exasperation. "I'll just call him after this batch is out of the oven."

The phone rang only once before a rich, woman's voice with an Indian accent answered. "Hello? I am answering

Sanjay's phone. Who am I speaking with?"

"Oh… um hello. My name is Hope—Hope Senior? I'm a friend of Jay's from the university."

"Yes, Hope who sings. I am his mother. How can I help you?"

How many mothers answered their son's cellphones… strange. Irrelevantly, she also noticed that Jay's mom spoke without contractions—just as he did sometimes. Did he learn it from her? He used them sometimes, though. Her mind swirled as she tried to remember when or why.

"Hello?"

"Oh, um sorry, he asked me to call him with some information he wanted. Um, is he available?"

Mrs. Brown asked her to hold, saying she was looking for her son. Feeling foolish, Hope muttered to herself, "Is he available? Really? I can't believe she didn't say, 'Yes, but not to you!'"

"My *amma* would never say anything so rude, I assure you." She could hear the suppressed laughter in Jay's voice.

"Okay, that's not embarrassing or anything. I just never expected anyone else to pick up your phone." Before he could respond, she continued, "I just got your email. Sorry about forgetting the part about Jesus' birth. Can't believe I forgot that. First, no reference and now I give you a backhanded proposition to your mom. What next?"

"You should not scare me with thoughts like that."

The doorbell rang. Hope excused herself, leaving Jay hanging. He listened to muffled sounds of her house—voices, the beeping of a timer. It was almost like a glimpse into her life. The minutes ticked past while he waited. Noises grew louder, implying that she was close. "Oh, Jay. Sorry. I forgot I had you on speaker. I was trying to take the cookies off the tray so I could pick up the phone."

Her rambling dialogue prompted a few chuckles. "Well, cookies come first—always."

"Ok, so this poinsettia cookie… I think I'll do red sugar leaves and little gold balls in the center. What do you think?"

"That sounds very tasty—and pretty." What decorated

44

cookies had to do with the birth of Jesus, he didn't know, but he felt it would be rude to ask. Wasn't Christmas about the birth?

"Have you ever made Christmas cookies?"

"No, I don't think I have. I've eaten them, though. Parties at school and stuff. I don't think I've made them, but they are very pretty."

"Yummy too," Hope said with what sounded like a mouthful of cookie. "Ours melt in your mouth. I'll send your family some. Would that be all right?"

Jay assured her that it was not necessary. "We'd appreciate it, though. We never turn down desserts."

He chatted with her through the rest of her cookie decorating and baking. She talked to him as she put away the cookies, boxing some up to send to him. He laughed at the sound of bubble wrap popping as she wrapped the cookies. "They will arrive—all twelve of them—unbroken and in a box big enough for five hundred of them."

"Not true!" she cried. "I have two dozen in a Priority Mail box. So there!"

He felt as if he could hear her stick out her tongue. "You are so transparent—even over the phone."

"Are my arteries clear? It's never too early to make sure they are healthy."

"Very funny." He shifted down on the couch, propping his feet up on the arm. "If I answered, your doctor would have me arrested for practicing medicine without a license."

She changed the subject abruptly. "So, I suppose you want me to tell you where to find Mary, Joseph, and Jesus."

"Well, I can Google it, but you're probably faster, and you're right here…"

"Do you have your Bible handy?"

"Yep, grabbed it while you were answering the door."

"Ok, can you find Mark again—the end of the book?"

"Got it." He turned the page. "Next comes Luke."

"That's where you want to read. You just need the first two chapters. They take you from conception to somewhere around age twelve."

His eyes were already scanning the words that slowly

pulled him into the story. A sneeze from the other end of the phone brought him back to the conversation. "Oh, sorry. I started reading and…"

"No worries."

The words tried to pull him back into the story. "I keep trying to read. Can I call you back if I have questions?"

She hesitated. A lump swelled in his throat as he waited for an answer. Had he said something wrong?

"Um, do you ever read aloud? Somehow, I think you'll have the perfect voice for reading it."

"Perfect voice?" What could she be talking about?

"I've always loved to hear men read the Christmas story, but your accent… you've got that deep voice and yet it's so gentle."

If you could hear a swoon—he grinned. What was it about this girl and being able to hear her expressions, gestures—all of it over the phone? Without comment, he took a drink, spat out his throat lozenge into a tissue, and began reading.

From Gabriel's visit to Zechariah and baby John leaping in his mother's womb, Jay read, his voice apparently sufficiently perfect and melodic if her occasional purrs were any indication. Occasionally he backtracked, rereading sections with care—much slower as he tried to keep his tone deliberate and confident.

As he reached the end, Hope's voice joined him reciting the last line, "'And Jesus increased in wisdom, and in stature, and in favor with God and man."

"How much of this do you have memorized?"

"I know some of it because I've read or heard it read so often—the beginning of chapter two in particular. The last verse was my favorite in my early teens. I wanted to emulate the thoughts in that verse so badly."

He laughed. "I think you failed."

"Well gee, thanks."

"Sorry, Hope. Regarding stature, you're hope-*less*."

"Ha. Ha. Very funny." His silence seemed to provoke impulsive confessions. "Okay, I admit it. I prayed I'd grow taller every night. I wanted the wisdom and the favor with God and man — really." She sighed. "But yeah, I prayed for the height thing the most."

"Just how tall — aren't you?"

"I should *so* refuse to answer that." She giggled. "Okay, fine. I made it to a whopping five feet one and one quarter inches."

"That quarter inch makes such a difference." Even as he spoke, he knew that if he were in the room with her, he'd be dodging a pillow or something.

"Hey, I worked hard for that quarter inch. Oh, the milk I drank hoping to push those bones..." She sighed. "I try to console myself by believing I would only have been four foot nine if I hadn't. Just how tall are you, anyway?"

"Exactly six feet. *Amma* says that I am too much of a perfectionist to bother with inches or fractions of inches."

"Are all Indian men that tall? Seems like most I've seen are shorter."

"Well..." his fingers flew over his laptop keys to discover the average height of Indian men. "My father is about five foot ten, I think. The Google says that the average Indian man is five foot nine." He laughed adding, "Perhaps the air in America grows taller men."

Before she could reply, Jay noticed the name on the paper she'd sent. "Hey. Your brother's name was Concord?"

"Right."

"So Con is just short for Concord. I see."

"Weird name, right?"

He agreed but kept it to himself. "It's unusual anyway."

"Since you're too polite to ask, I'll tell you. It's a family name. Skips every other generation. Con got the generational short straw — and don't you dare say that it should have been me. I can't believe I walked into that one."

"How long has it been in your family?"

"Well... the first Concord's father came over on the Fortune."

"The Fortune?"

"The ship that arrived at Plymouth after the Mayflower. They loved those virtue names back then."

47

"What does concord mean? I've only heard it applied to the supersonic jet." He glanced at the paper again. "Except that I think the airplane had an e."

"It means unity and agreement."

"And yours means that they didn't expect that unity and agreement among siblings but they desired it?"

Hope didn't speak for several long seconds before she said, "I am so going to flatten a snowball in your face."

Jay spent the next thirty-six hours engrossed in creating the perfect Christmas gift for Hope. Once complete, he used a piece of printer paper to wrap it, but the package looked rather uninteresting. "*Amma!*" Jay strolled down the hall calling for his mother.

"What!"

"Do we have any ribbon? This looks so boring."

"I have..." she answered as she dug through a pencil holder, "a gold pen. Here. Will this work? Can you draw a pattern on it?"

"No ribbon, though?" As he asked, he seated himself at the table, staring at the paper and the pen, willing himself to think of something.

"I could go—or Mrs. Jensen might have some."

"Mrs. Jensen. She'll help." He drew the elongated stars that seemed popular on Christmas cards, scattering them across the little package.

"Do you think she'll like it?"

"I think so."

"Will who like what?"

Jay and Amala turned to see Jay's father leaning against the refrigerator. Amala pulled him close to the table. "The project he was working on—this is it. It's for that girl—Hope."

"It is about time you found a girl, Jay. Who is Wish?"

"Hope, *Appa*. Her name is Hope. She's just a girl from school. She sent me that Bible, so I thought I'd do something for her too."

48

"Our son spends almost two days making a gift for 'just a girl' and thinks we will believe that it means nothing."

"Raj, don't tease him."

"If I am not teasing him, I am wasting this perfect opportunity. He is too long without a girlfriend. The men at work are telling me my son is the gay."

"Appa!" Jay flushed, failing in his attempt not to be caught in his father's jokes.

"See, you prove them wrong. I will now tell them that your Wish has come true."

"Hope," Jay growled. "Her name is Hope."

"Listen to how he is correcting me. He is protective."

Jay jumped up from the table, waving the package to dry the ink. "I'm going to Mrs. Jensen's and then to mail this. Do you need anything while I'm out?"

"I am needing to meet this Wish..."

He grabbed his jacket and escaped before his father could say anything else to embarrass him. Their neighbor answered before he finished knocking. "Hello, Jay! I wondered if you'd have time to see me. I made peanut butter cookies..."

"That sounds delicious. I actually came to beg a piece of ribbon. *Amma* didn't have any and..." He showed her the little present. "This looked a bit bare without it."

"Oh, sure. I have gold and blue. Both would look good with that. What do you think? Did you make that paper yourself? So pretty. I'll wrap up some cookies for you to take with you." As usual, the woman chattered almost non-stop from the moment he stepped inside her door.

Mrs. Jensen took the package from him and carried it to the table. From a nearby cupboard, she pulled a basket of ribbons and finally chose a complimentary gold mesh. "It'll be festive and elegant—simple."

"With that, I didn't need to put on the stars."

Minutes later, she escorted him to the door, waving as he jogged to his car. Jay hesitated at the corner—FedEx for assurance of speed, or Post Office since it was only going twenty miles? He opted for FedEx and within the hour, the package was on its way to Marshfield.

49

Oblivious to the price Jay paid at home for his gift, Hope thanked the driver for the package the next morning, eagerly ripping the mailer open. Jay's note fluttered to the floor as she unwrapped the present—a CD. As she pulled the paper away, she wondered what he might have sent, and laughed when she saw the label and cover. "Did he use Photoshop or what?" she murmured as she picked up Jay's note and read it to herself.

"Merry Christmas, Hope,

I have recorded Luke chapter two for you to listen to anytime that you like. Alas, I imagined you there, despairing over the stature issue, so I decided to find something else as well. I looked through the table of contents and only found three books that sounded like women's names — Esther, Ruth, and Ezra. I chose Ruth because I was sure it was a woman's name and it was a mercifully short book. I thought you would appreciate that. By the way, I loved the story. It was beautiful. If you will not hold it against me, I will admit that I am a bit of a romantic, and found it very satisfying. I look forward to discussing it with you sometime soon.

Until New Year's,

Jay"

A pile of crumpled wrapping paper covered the living room floor at the Senior home. While Hope inspected every pocket, section, and accessory of her new leather rolling backpack, Ron thumbed through a new biography of John Taylor Gatto, pausing occasionally to examine a picture. Cheryl played with the features of her new camera, snapping pictures of random things.

"I wonder if Jay's family exchanges presents."

Ron reached for a new roll as he said, "Probably. I read about Christmas in India last week; Yahoo had an article on it. They have trees, lights—the works there."

"Cool."

"Perhaps it is the British influence for so many years,"

Cheryl suggested.

"Con would say I missed the point of Christmas if my question was about presents instead of whether Jay felt moved by the story of Jesus."

The moment her lips formed the word Jesus, Hope wilted. She watched, heartbroken, as the joy and relaxation on her parents faces dissolved into pain and loss. Cheryl gathered her gifts, muttering something about putting things away. Ron gathered the wrapping paper and balled it up, dropping each ball into the fireplace. When all the paper was burned, he grabbed his book and gave her a weak smile before slipping upstairs.

Hope stared at the fire, her mind lost in the flickering flames. Shaking herself, she gathered her gifts, shoved what she could into the backpack, and carried it all upstairs. She climbed beneath the covers, pulled them over her head, and cried herself to sleep.

When she awoke, it was dark outside. Bleary-eyed, she struggled to focus on the clock. After five. She dragged herself from bed and began dressing for Christmas dinner. The chocolate velvet dress swirled around her knees and her hair bounced around her shoulders as she skipped downstairs. The scent of baked ham filled the lower level.

She tiptoed into the kitchen and examined the covered dishes all over the stove. Guilt stabbed her in the heart. She'd slept through the meal preparations. Her job of forming dinner rolls had been left to her mother. A glance beneath the towel that covered the breadbasket amended that thought—her father had clearly made them.

The empty living room prompted her to remove a stocking from the mantel. She curled into one corner of the couch with the stocking lying flat on her lap. Hope traced her fingers along the letters of her brother's name.

Reaching into the stocking, Hope pulled out a handful of folded notes and letters. She opened each one, the words both soothing and wounding her simultaneously. The raw pain her parents shared in their letters showed in each word on the pages. Hers were rambles through memories of past Christmases while

51

her parents' centered on the regrets of lost dreams. However, as heartrending as they were, each one ended with reminders of love and an eagerness to see him again.

As she heard her parents coming down the stairs, Hope slipped the notes back into the stocking and rehung it. Evidence of tears showed around her mother's eyes and her father's lips were tight with repressed emotion. The little family stood at the base of the stairs, hugging for several minutes before Cheryl pushed her husband and daughter away saying, "Enough of that. Let's eat!"

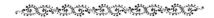

Lamb curry and cardamom rice — Jay's favorites. He took another bite and moaned with pleasure. "Oh, *Amma*. The poor children all over this city who do not have your cooking tonight."

"I suspect most Americans, even those who enjoy Indian food, probably prefer ham or turkey today."

"Still..." That comment sent his thoughts in new directions. "I wonder what Hope's family eats on Christmas. Ham? Lamb? Turkey? Roast beef?"

"The Jensens served ham the year we ate there, remember?" Raj elbowed his wife. "Notice that even eating dinner, he cannot keep his Wish out of his mind."

"Raj..."

"I am just speaking..." He waggled an eyebrow at Jay. "So will you be seeing more of this Wish next semester?"

"Well, I hope so."

"He is spending New Year's with them. That sounds interesting, do you not think?" Amala winked at her son.

"Very." Raj polished off his *poori* grinning with pleasure. "My Amala is such a good cook."

"That she is," Jay agreed. He swallowed, took a drink, and then asked the question he really wanted to ask. "So, I was thinking about inviting her to something at the RAC. How would you feel about that?"

"The RAC? Like what, a concert?" Amala's eyes

brightened. "That sounds fun."

"What about opera? They're doing *Don Giovanni*."

Raj laughed. "Well, it's not Bollywood—"

"For which you'd be grateful," Jay joked. "Bollywood isn't that bad."

"Speak for yourself. Some things don't mix. I like India. I like Hollywood. I do not like Bollywood." Raj spoke as if that settled everyone's opinion.

Amala spoke up, obviously trying to divert an old argument before it became another debate. "Why opera, Jay? Do you think she will like it? Modern young people do not like opera, do they?"

"Well, the RAC has a formal dress code, so I thought it'd give her a chance to dress up—evening gowns and all that stuff."

"No, Sanjay!" Raj's eyes flashed. "You are not that man."

Jay's eyes widened in surprise. "What man? What are you talking about?"

"Raj—"

"No, Amala! Our Jay will not. I will not allow it!"

"*Appa*, what?"

"You cannot misuse a girl like that; I do not care how expensive the opera tickets are."

"Misuse? How is taking a girl to the opera of all places misusing her? I would never—"

"You planned it. I heard you—the evening gown."

Even after a lifetime with his father's mixed idioms, Jay remained confused. Amala, on the other hand, tittered as understanding dawned. "Raj, evening gowns are very different from nightgowns. Jay means fancy dresses—like for the Oscars, not Victoria's Secret!"

Jay's eyes closed. He took a deep breath. "Oh, Hope will kill me if I tell her and torture and kill me if she ever finds out that I didn't tell her," he groaned.

CHAPTER 7

The house looked as all-American as he could have imagined. Two-storied, box hedges in front, a green lawn with a large tree—white with a red door partially hidden by an enormous wreath. What should have been a pristine white frosted lawn looked like ants in combat boots had marched in a serpentine across it—several times. It seemed as if the kids had finally won.

He glanced at the clock on the dash—early by almost two hours. His irrational hope for time to fly during those last few miles had not materialized. He had a choice. Call or return later. He punched her number.

"Hey. So, the errands I meant to do didn't take as long as expected. Before I head home, I thought maybe I could be of some help..."

"Come on over!"

"You sure?" He stepped out of the car, grabbed the pot of chili from behind his seat, and locked the door.

"Yes! I'm so glad you did! How soon will you be here?"

Jay jogged around the yard, protecting it from nothing, and jabbed the doorbell. "About half a second ago."

Hope's call of, "I've got it!" reached him even before she flung open the door, her hair piled on her head in rollers, with fuzzy reindeer slippers on her feet and mascara wand in hand.

"I'm so glad you are here! Come in." She pointed to her head. "I'm still in Medusa mode, but you can go chop veggies in

55

the kitchen with Mom. I'll be down in a few minutes."

He followed the direction of her arm and found Cheryl in the kitchen. "I have been hired as sous chef." He raised the pot in his hands. "Is there room in the fridge for this?"

"So glad you could make it. Sure—Ron! Come get Jay's chili," she called. To Jay she said, "Why don't you grab a knife from that drawer—no, that one, yes—and you can start on the celery. Just peel off the strings." She smiled, squeezing his arm as she passed. "We're so glad you came."

"I felt rude—"

"Never. Hope hasn't stopped talking about you coming."

Ron stepped into the kitchen and took the pot from Jay. "Good to see you again." His eyes traveled to the counter and the knife in Jay's hands. "And thanks for that; it'll save me butchering the poor things."

She pulled out a bag of carrots and began scrubbing. "Did you have a nice Christmas?"

"I did. Did you?"

"Absolutely. You know," Cheryl added, "we spent half of our dinner time wondering about what your family did on Christmas—what you ate for dinner, or if it was just a normal day for you. Ron said that a lot of Indians celebrate Christmas." She winked. "I think that almost disappointed Hope."

"Why would that disappoint her?"

"Because then you would already have experienced all the things she thought she'd get to introduce you to."

"Well, it's true. In India, a lot of Indians celebrate Christmas. They have lights, stars—some even have trees." He hesitated, wondering if he would offend if he spoke truthfully when he hadn't been asked. "But here in America, my father did not care to continue it. 'I am not a Christian. I will not celebrate Christ's Mass,' he said."

"That seems reasonable. I think Hope expected a more secular version of Christmas—Santa, presents, lights—if you celebrated at all."

"I think *Appa* just thought it best to skip. We do have the festival of lights and that is enough for us." He smiled as he turned back to his celery. "So you were talking about what we

56

might be doing while my parents and I were wondering what you might be eating."

"Really?"

"Yes. We wondered what kind of meal you ate at Christmas."

"Ham, green bean casserole, mashed potatoes—the usual. What did you have?"

Jay laughed. "That was my father's guess! I'll have to tell *Appa* he was right. We had lamb curry, cardamom rice, and *poori*."

"*Poori*?"

"Little fried breads—puffy. Very tasty."

Ron burst into the room, "Hey, Cheryl?"

"What do you need?"

"Where is the vacuum? The commercials are almost over!"

"I think Hope took it out to the garage to clean off the dance floor."

Seconds later, a shout came from the living room. Jay's head jerked up but Cheryl didn't seem to notice. Ron's voice blasted through the house, "Dodge him, you idiot! He's coming right at you!"

Cheryl glanced up in time to see Jay's astonishment. "Ron can get a little... intense about football."

"That's an understatement!" Hope strolled into the kitchen and immediately began pulling plastic containers of cookies from the freezer and arranging them on trays. Though he tried not to stare, the transformation that a few curls and a dressy outfit made in her captured his interest. He had always considered her long, straight hair attractive, but the bouncy curls that now hung just below her shoulders framed her face, unexpectedly softening it. As she passed, he noticed fingernails with polish—something he hadn't noticed in the past.

"Hey, Cheryl! Can you help me in here? I think I've got the drapes stuck in the vacuum!"

The exasperated woman dropped her knife onto the cutting board calling, "Oh, honestly, Ron..."

Hope grinned. "This is the best part of a party."

"Ruined drapes?"

57

"Dad always has to be rescued."

She moved to finish her mother's job. Jay watched from his side of the island before saying, "You look wonderful, by the way."

"By the way... as in, 'Oh, by the way, your dog got out and destroyed my begonias last night...'"

"It's not easy to tell a woman she's pretty," he muttered.

"Why not?"

"Because..." Answering could get him in serious trouble. Not answering would likely be worse. "Well, because it feels like that it implies you normally look boring."

"Really?" She chopped a few more carrots before saying, "How about we make a deal."

"What kind of deal?" Suspicion laced every syllable and from her expression, she noticed.

"You can tell me whenever I look boring too. That should fix that problem."

"I'm pretty sure that's not something you'll ever have to hear," he muttered.

"What?"

"I wondered if you have root beer."

She snickered, crossing her arm, the knife close enough to skin to make his own crawl. "I *so* don't believe you."

"I *so* wish you would put that knife down."

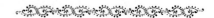

While Hope set up a playlist, Jay watched, fascinated by her selections. Big band, Christian contemporary, alternative, classical, country, pop music, oldies from so far back he didn't know the decade—she chose them all. "So what kind of music don't you like?"

"Oh, I like most—wait. Don't?" She thought for a moment. "The kind I'm not in the mood to hear. Oh, and rap—hip-hop... well most of it. I've heard a few..."

"Opera?"

"Some. I like it best when it's actually on TV so you can see the story since I can't understand it otherwise—even in English!"

That was excellent news. "So what should I expect from this party? Who is coming and what will we do?"

She hopped up from the chair, fully animated as she described the party. "Well, most of the guests are neighbors and sometimes a few friends who moved away come back. I know Dad invited one or two people from church..." She shrugged. "There'll be people we don't know well, but it's a good way to get to know everyone."

Surprised, Jay admitted, "I assumed it would be mostly people from your church." He could analyze the relief he felt later.

"Not really. This is just a neighborhood party. We'll go caroling, play some games. If the Wesleys got back in time, there definitely will be some dancing. Mr. Wesley is a great dancer — always teaches us new steps."

Dancing. That wasn't good news to a man who considered himself a terrible dancer. "Is there room for dancing in here?" Maybe it was a smaller party than it seemed.

"Oh, we dance in the garage. Dad and Con walled in the sun porch a few years back — extended the garage — and that part is all set up with a floating floor and everything."

"That seems... dedicated."

"Con was definitely dedicated," she agreed. "He was totally into swing dancing — good too. He won a jukebox once. It's out there."

The doorbell rang to announce the first guests. When he heard Cheryl call, "Hope, the Wesleys are here." Jay cringed.

The next hour passed in a whirl of introductions and sidelong glances. The curiosity level rose with each person who entered the house, but Jay opted to let them wonder. He justified his feigned ignorance to the meaning of some questions by assuring himself that he'd probably never see any of them again.

Caroling seemed strange after Christmas. One of Jay's neighbors was a retired minister, so very few years passed without carolers singing at his door. But that always occurred the week before Christmas, not the week after. However, the party divided into groups and he followed Hope as she led him to a section six blocks away.

They strolled slowly up the street singing "Winter Wonderland." One older man gave him a disturbing eye waggle at the line about Parson Brown, but to his great relief, Hope missed it. At the end of the street, they sang "Auld Lang Syne" beneath the streetlight before turning the corner.

"When we carol before Christmas, we end each street in 'We Wish You a Merry Christmas,' Hope whispered as they walked to the next street.

"Huh?"

Hope pulled his shoulder closer to her head and stood on tiptoe. "See, you're too tall. People shouldn't tower over the rest of humanity like you do."

"Perhaps it is the fault of those who do not grow enough — or perhaps you should have prayed for faith."

"Faith?"

"There is that verse in the Bible — the one about if you have faith you can move mountains. Surely, if you can move a mountain with faith, Hope can grow a few inches."

"You're a letter?" Tom Novak tried to guess Hope's word as she acted out her charade. "Maybe that song about the YMCA?"

Hope tried again. She stood with feet together and arms over her head, almost in a Y pattern — but not quite. After repeating the movement, she pushed her arms behind her head before dropping them again.

Jay recognized the motion. "A gymnast." His mother's obsession with Olympic gymnastics had finally proven useful.

"Yes!" She grinned and pulled him up from the floor. "Your turn."

Jay thought for a moment, choosing his charade carefully, and then began. First, he walked back and forth in straight lines, pretending to pick up something and put them in an imaginary bag. After a pause, he settled himself at Cheryl's feet and pretended to sleep.

"Ruth!" Ron clapped. "I should have caught it right away.

We just listened to Jay's reading of the book of Ruth yesterday!"

They set up a few card tables after the charades ended and people sat down to play poker or blackjack. Others congregated in the garage for a "Charleston contest." Jay inched toward the blackjack table, but found Hope tugging him toward the garage. "Come on, Jay. I'll show you. It's really easy."

Jay glared at her in mock disgust as his feet fought the so-called "simple pattern" of the Charleston. However, once he did make the correct moves, it wasn't so bad. He started to admit that it was even kind of fun when she said, "Now just copy me when I change steps. You'll catch on right away"

Her confidence, clearly stronger than his ability, did little to help him keep up with the music and her ever-increasing step changes. His brain injury seemed magnified as he seemed to enter a scene from *It's a Wonderful Life*. At any minute, he expected the floor to give way and everyone fall into a swimming pool. His mind fumbled with memories, but Jay was certain it was just a movie — he hoped.

When the rest of the dancers switched to a jitterbug, Jay begged off and went to sit with the other non-dancers who congregated in lawn chairs where Cheryl's car usually sat. Hope's feet flew as she matched her partner's feet step for step. She twisted, twirled, and danced with carefree abandon. So engrossed was he with the scene before him, Jay almost didn't notice when Ron sat down beside him.

"She is so like her brother. Concord was a marvelous dancer." The wistful tone in Ron's voice barely hid the man's struggling emotions. "They used to bop all over the living room like that."

Hope's hair streamed out behind her as she spun rapidly with a middle-aged man. "She sure is good. I couldn't keep up."

"You tried. That is what matters most."

At eleven fifty-five, everyone congregated in the living room. While Hope set up her favorite rendition of "Auld Lang Syne" on the computer, the senior Seniors poured glasses of sparkling cider for their guests. Mr. Wesley turned on the television and muted the volume as they waited for the ball to drop on Times Square.

"…six…five…four…three…two… one… Happy New Year!"

The group sang, some making slight dance moves in line together, each verse changing the feet just a little. He didn't know the words to the song, but he'd heard it — somewhere. The guests all hugged one another after the song ended and instantly the party atmosphere changed.

Cheryl stood by the front door, saying goodbye to each of her guests. Hope helped everyone find coats, purses, or plates of snacks or games they'd brought. Jay found himself beside Cheryl, trying to block some of the cold from her as the door opened and closed with each departure.

Once the guests had all left, Jay began gathering empty cups and plates, but Hope stopped him. "Oh, no, Jay. We'll clean up in the morning, but tonight we get to rest." She glanced toward her parents for backup and then pointed to the fireplace. "Why don't you stoke the fire and I'll change the music."

Hope's parents said goodnight and went upstairs. Hope watched them with that same wistful longing he'd seen in her father just an hour or so earlier. "They used to stay up with us and watch the tree lights. You know, last hurrah. We take it down tomorrow. They haven't done that since Concord died. I don't think they can handle it anymore."

Feeling helpless, Jay watched as she fought back tears. The instinct to comfort her was only overridden by the reminder that they really weren't close enough friends for him to do so. "You need your traditions to help heal your pain while they avoid some traditions to soothe theirs."

"Pretty much. I want them to stay, but I don't want them to hurt." She sighed. "Is it totally rude and selfish that I'm glad you're here? I'm not alone this year."

"I think it is understandable and I am pleased that I could be of service. We will sit here and do whatever traditions you are used to doing after a party."

He cleared the couch, stoked the fire, and turned out the lights so that they could see the Christmas tree at its finest. They settled at opposite ends of the couch, their feet almost touching in the middle, and talked.

"So what kind of New Year's traditions does your family have?"

"Well, it is a little different here than in India—"

"How?" Hope's eyes reflected the lights of the Christmas tree, making her look almost childlike.

"There, we celebrated New Year's— *Varsha pirappu*—in April. When we moved here, my *amma* insisted we change to coincide with the American New Year and then we combined it with *Diwali.*"

"That is so cool—kind of like the Jewish New Year is different."

"And the Chinese and many others."

"So are there traditions that go with it?"

"You and your traditions," Jay teased. "Yes. *Amma* always fills the house with the little white twinkle lights—like those on your mantel. Every table, every doorway, every window—if it can hold lights or a lamp, it has them. We get new clothes—kind of like Christians at Easter." He paused. "You'll have to explain that to me someday."

"Ok. Lights, huh? Sounds pretty."

"It is. My favorite part was always that everything is new for *Varsha pirappu* and *Diwali.* If I was in trouble for something, it was over. I was never grounded over New Year's."

"I like that..."

"My *amma* says, 'The year is new. Nothing bad has happened. We cannot bring the old bad over into the New Year.'"

"I imagine for a mischievous little boy, that must have been such a relief."

"I don't know, but I can call around to cousins and ask them. You see, I was a model child—"

"Yeah right," Hope retorted, rolling her eyes. "Do you have New Year's resolutions?"

"Yes, we make just as many resolutions and break them too."

She seemed to wander off into her own thoughts and get lost. "I think I like your traditions very much. I love the idea of the lights. Maybe next year—"

"I think you should read more about it. The Festival of Lights is a Hindu one — religious. The lights are to drive out evil. Feuds and grudges must be set aside in honor of a fresh start. I like that part, but as I said, it is Hindu…"

"But must I believe in every aspect of something in order to enjoy the beauty of it?"

"Well, no, but people might get confused."

Hope shook her head. "But there are so many Christian parallels to it. Jesus is the light of the world. We are told to let our light shine before men. If we fill our homes with lights that are symbolic of who Jesus is and how we are supposed to reflect Him, if we choose to put on the new man and drive off the old, and if we choose to forgive and 'keep no record of wrongs,' how could that be confusing or offensive?"

"I suppose it can't," he agreed.

They talked into the wee hours of the morning. Jay continually dragged the conversation back to the book of Ruth. The concept of the kinsman redeemer fascinated him. He loved the richness and beauty of the story, but the significance in the parallel to Jesus touched him the most.

As the clock struck two, he urged Hope to go to bed. She beckoned him to follow, assuring him that they had Concord's room ready for him, but Jay shook his head. "I think it'd be easier on your parents if I just sleep on the couch."

CHAPTER 8

Jay awoke to the scent of simmering meat and spices. He rolled over, nearly falling off the couch. Opening his eyes, he saw Hope standing over him, smiling. "You look like a little boy who has just woken up from his nap. Go back to sleep. It's early yet."

An hour later, when he awoke once more, Jay wasn't sure if he'd dreamed of her of if she really had sent him back to Slumberville. He stood, stretched the kinks out of his joints, and tried to appear alert. The delicious scents coming from the kitchen sent his stomach into a fit of grumbles and he wondered about breakfast. Could they afford the time to go out to breakfast? Would it be a welcome relief or a burden?

Upstairs—somewhere—Hope sang. He climbed the stairs, calling her name softly. "Hooopee. Hooo-ooope."

She stuck her head around an open doorframe and grinned. "Come in. Did you sleep okay? That couch is kind of short for you." She grinned—at least that's what his sleep-blurred vision showed. "Are you hungry? I'm starving."

He started to leave, assuming she felt uncomfortable with him in her room, but her chatter continued even as she pulled him in further and nudged him toward a chair. Early riser with an incredible amount of annoying perkiness even when low on sleep—discovering Hope's personality kept him hopping. That was for sure.

"Hey, I just wondered if maybe I could take you guys out

for breakfast. I just didn't know with the chili—"

"Sure! Go ask them. It smells like the chili is at the 'simmer until we leave' stage anyway. Do we need to do anything more with yours?"

"No. Just heat and go. *Amma* cooked it through."

Hope grabbed a couple of hangers. "I'll be down in a minute. Just have to get dressed."

He stood and glanced around the room once more before going downstairs. Her room intrigued him—frilly curtains, ruffled bedspread with hearts and flowers, pink walls—it seemed like the dream room of a little girl rather than the Hope he knew. Was there a story behind that?

Ron and Cheryl greeted him warmly. "Did you sleep okay? Hope should have shown you to Con's room."

He leaned against the island and smiled. "She offered, but I chose the couch. So…" He saw a look pass between the Seniors and hastened to avoid any further awkwardness. "I wondered if I could take you all out to breakfast."

There went the expression again—had he really been that offensive? Had he misjudged? Was it insulting not to use the room?

"That'd be great!" Cheryl squeezed his arm as she hurried from the room.

Ron crossed his arms over his chest. "It's probably rude to say it, but thanks for understanding about Con's room. When Cheryl saw you on the couch this morning, I saw her relax; it looked like she'd peeled twenty years off her face."

"Whew. I thought maybe I had offended—"

"Not at all. Let's go." Ron turned the chili down to the lowest setting, stirring well. "We'll need to go somewhere close, but we should be good for an hour or so."

Plates of steaming omelets, sausage, and pancakes filled their nostrils with wonderful scents as the server brought their orders. Jay watched as each of the Seniors paused for just a moment before picking up their forks. Contrasted with other prayerful moments he'd witnessed, it was private, unobtrusive, and refreshing.

Curious, he decided to ask about it. "May I ask a personal question?" Hope nodded, her mouth full of food. The eyes of the other two Seniors seemed equally agreeable. "Well, last night you prayed aloud for your food, but today I almost didn't notice."

He watched Ron exchange a glance with his women before saying, "So do you wonder if we're ashamed to show our faith in public? Is that the question?"

"Ashamed—no. I would never have imagined you as ashamed, but I've been out to lunch with other Christians who do. Is it not required?"

Ron shook his head. "For our family, it's a matter of how we understand Jesus' admonition to keep our prayers private."

"You are supposed to keep them private? Then why do—"

The older man interrupted him. "Jay, I don't want to attack how other Christians live their faith. I can only tell you why we do what we do."

"I respect that."

"In Matthew," he looked for confirmation from his wife and daughter. "chapter six?" Hope nodded and Ron continued, "Ok, chapter six, Jesus says not to make a public show of our prayers. In our own home we pray aloud because it's private; we're three Christians praying together. In public, we keep silent so as not to appear to make a show of our beliefs."

"You remind me of my boss," Jay said. Trying to give himself a moment to collect his thoughts, he took a drink of his orange juice. "Mike is a good man. I know he is a Christian not because of what he says or does, but because of who he *is*. Does that make sense?"

Hope beamed. "I cannot tell you what a relief it is to hear that. Too often, I see other Christians—probably do it myself and don't even know it—trashing the name of Jesus with their actions."

Jay agreed, but chose not to admit as much. He took a bite of egg, trying to give himself a moment to formulate an honest reply that agreed with them without insulting them or their

67

faith. Fortunately for him, Hope continued before he could speak. "Christians should be known for being kind, caring, loving, honest, and trustworthy—all without pretension. That old song 'They'll Know We Are Christians by Our Love' should be a truth we sing rather than some ideal out there."

That would do it. "You do." Jay gazed at each of them before adding, "Isn't that where it starts? You live your faith and encourage others. They learn from your example and it spreads."

Hope swallowed quickly and took a gulp of water. "Like that one dude said, 'Preach the Gospel, if necessary, use words' or something like that."

"Wasn't that St. Francis of Assisi? I don't think you quite have the quote right, but the gist is there," Ron agreed.

Jay nodded. "I like that. You know, I have never been interested in Christianity. I don't mean to offend, but it's true. I respected my boss' faith, but when I met Hope, I realized that he wasn't a one-of-a-kind Christian. There are more of you."

Cheryl smiled at him. "My husband will tell me that my priorities are all out of whack—that a discussion even remotely related to Jesus is much more important than something silly like chili, but if we don't go soon, we could burn down the house."

As Jay signaled for their check, Ron jabbed his wife, laughing. "I told you that you put too much cayenne in it."

The Church at Marshfield—such a strange name in Jay's opinion. As they carried their pots of chili into the building, Jay asked about it. "Why is it just 'the church at?' I mean, Marshfield doesn't just have one church; we passed two on the way."

"It's taken from the names of the churches in Revelation. 'The church at Ephesus,' or Thessalonica, or whatever."

That made sense. Before he could ask another question, a girl rushed up to Hope, chattering eagerly about Christmas and apologizing—again, it seemed—for not making it to their party. "Is this Jay?"

"No," Hope answered. "This is one of the other dozen-and-a-half Indian men I've met that you haven't."

"Ooooh... interesting."

Hope glared at her friend before taking Jay's pot and carrying it toward a side door. He glanced at the girl and shrugged. "Did I say something?"

"Hope gets sarcastic when she's feeling self-conscious. Methinks—" the girl sighed. "Methinks I shouldn't say what I thinks. I'm Kirky."

"Nice to meet you."

She tugged at his sleeve. "Come on. We can't lose the opportunity to see Hope at her finest."

"Her finest?"

"She's brilliant when sarcastic."

They found her plugging in a hot plate for his chili. Several people glanced his way and smiled, but they waited for Hope and Kirky to introduce him. The names blurred in his mind, but they welcomed him with what seemed like genuine friendliness.

Groups sat together chatting. As he passed, Jay heard them discussing football scores, Bible verses, and sometimes both in the same conversation. Small children chased each other amongst the tables and elderly people nudged one another at the sight of Hope with a man.

Jay swallowed hard. It wasn't that he objected, of course, but the wrong idea could be awkward. He glanced at her as they strolled toward a group of young people singing in one corner and caught her grin. She knew exactly what the others thought and didn't seem to mind. If she didn't mind, why should he?

Report folders—the kind he'd used in high school for research papers—held pages of song lyrics. As he listened, Jay grabbed a chair, turned it around, and straddled it. Kirky leaned over and whispered, "You're awfully comfortable for someone who isn't a Christian."

He shrugged. "They're just people, right?"

Hope's friend nodded as she considered his response. "Okay. You're officially the coolest guy to darken our doors in ages."

"What's that, Kirky? You noticed I arrived?"

69

Jay glanced over at the man behind Kirky and grinned. Without turning around, she elbowed him in the gut, saying, "Brian, go away."

"Not on your life. I want to meet your feller."

"Hope's feller."

Jay forced himself not to groan. Before he could answer, Hope rolled her eyes and nodded at the newcomer. "Hey, Brian. This is Jay."

From the other side of the room, a man called everyone to attention. "It's time to start the judging for those who enjoy watching a group of men eat. The rest of you can ignore this announcement."

Hope grabbed Jay's arm and led him to a spot near the tables. "I just know you're going to win," she hissed.

Each judge carried a fistful of plastic spoons and a glass of milk. Jay laughed with the rest of the room as the men choked on four-alarm chili, each guzzling his glass of milk after just a small bite. One judge—one of the church elders, according to Hope—refused to continue without a new glass of milk.

He had a hard time reading most of the judges, but one was as transparent as the glass he carried. The entire room erupted in laughter as the judges tasted the concoction provided by the high school youth group. One of the kids shouted, "Insta-win!"

"Not hardly," the nearest judge muttered as he gulped another mouthful of milk.

When they reached Jay's pot, his eyes automatically traveled to the judge with an easy face to read. It wasn't necessary. The judge next to him took a second bite. Surely, that was good, wasn't it?

The youth group protested as the elders pronounced Jay's Indian chili the winner. "Not fair!" cried young man. "Our chili is proof that we're on fire for the Lord!"

"Yeah, but you gave us tongues of fire," retorted the transparent elder. "That's the job of the Holy Spirit."

Jay turned to Hope for an explanation, but she shook her head. "Too complicated. I'll explain later."

"I'll hold you to that."

After games, singing songs that sounded amazing but

made little sense to him at times, and a lunch of excellent chili and cornbread, Jay discovered that there were indeed many more Christians like his boss and the Seniors—people who didn't hide their faith *or* trumpet it.

Ron dropped an arm around his shoulders as Jay approached to say goodbye and thank the Seniors for their hospitality. "We were glad to have you. I hope today wasn't too awkward."

"Not at all." He hesitated—uncertain if he should share his thoughts. Then again, who else would he share them with? "I'll admit that I'm growing interested in your faith. For the first time, I've seen religious people who seem fulfilled by their faith rather than seeking that fulfillment."

"Anytime you want to talk, you know where we are."

Hope strolled his way with an empty, washed pot. "Can I have your keys, Jay? I'll take it out before it gets lost in the shuffle."

He took it from her. "I've got it. I need to be going anyway."

She walked him to his car, silence hovering between them. At the door, their eyes met and held. Hope shivered as she said, "I'm glad you came."

"Thanks for inviting me. I really had a good time." He glanced at the building. "Those are some very nice people in there."

"Yeah... they're like family." She laughed. "What am I saying? They are family—God's family."

"You'll have to tell me about that too." He smiled at her, resisting the urge to hug her. "I guess I'll see you when classes start back up again."

Jay reached for his door handle but found himself smothered in a brief but fierce hug. "I'm really, really glad you came."

CHAPTER 9

Hope's cellphone vibrated in the backpack at her feet. She slipped it out to see the message. She kept her contact list deliberately short. Few people had her number and even fewer would call during class. As she glanced at it, she smiled—a text message from Jay.

DIDN'T KNOW YOUR CLASS SCHEDULE. HOPE I'M NOT INTERRUPTING. LEARNING THAT SPEAKING W/O SAYING "HOPE" IS NEXT TO IMPOSSIBLE—OR SHOULD I SAY HOPELESS? MEET ME IN YOUR COMMMON ROOM AROUND NOON?

Happy to hear from him again, she sent a text saying she would be there, and smiled. She missed half the lecture on the principles of archaeology, and to her chagrin, Hope didn't care. Never had a class dragged as miserably as that one.

An hour and a half later, she found Jay in her dorm common room, typing madly on his laptop. She sat next to him, but Jay didn't stir. Although she hated to interrupt, he had asked her to meet him. "Hey, you. Bad time?"

Jay's head jerked sideways, surprised. Clearly, he hadn't even noticed her arrival—not very flattering. However, the pleased expression in his eyes, and the smile that grew around the corners of his lips, told her he was happy to see her again.

"Not a bad time at all. Just trying to have everything finished for a presentation on Thursday."

She leaned back against the back of the couch and kicked up her feet on the coffee table. "So, as my grandpa used to say, what can I do you for?"

Jay pulled an envelope from his pocket and passed it to her. "Actually, it was something I wanted to do for you." He waited for her to accept the tickets before adding, "The RAC is doing *Don Giovanni* and I remembered that you said you'd always wanted to see it, so I got tickets for opening night."

"Oh wow! Thanks." As she looked for times and dates and seat rows, she asked, "So when and all that jazz?"

Jay snickered and closed his laptop.

"I said something funny?"

"I suppose not. I just had a mental picture of *Appa* when you said that. He would have wondered at your misunderstanding of the kind of music played in opera and would have tried to explain the difference between jazz and opera."

Her mind slugged through confusion as she tried to understand Jay's meaning. "Why would he have thought—oh, because I said, 'all that jazz?'"

"Yes. English idioms are fun with him around. He says things like, 'loan me your fingers,' when he needs help with something." At her laugh, he added, "Oh, and my favorites are when he interchanges 'dragging your feet' and 'pulling your leg.' I can't tell you how many times a friend has gotten confused when he said, 'I am just pulling your feet.'"

Jay painted a comical picture of his father—one she wished she could enjoy in person. "I'd love to meet him. I think I'd like your dad."

"I hope you do. I know he'd like to meet 'Wish.'"

"Wish?"

"Long story. Anyway, to answer your question, it's on Thursday. Sorry for the short notice. I tried to get tickets for over two weeks and when my boss found out, he gave me his for cost—good seats too."

"Oh cool! I don't have any Thursday classes and nothing due for two and a half weeks—well, nothing major. This Thursday or—" She saw the date and nodded. "This. Okay, what time—"

"I was going to offer to go with you if you didn't have someone else you'd rather take, but now I can't. Half an hour ago, my Friday night meeting got moved to Thursday."

So it wasn't a date. He hadn't intended to take her. Hope felt just a little relief and a whole lot of disappointment. "Well, that got you out of it easily enough."

"I didn't want an out. I just didn't want you to feel obligated to go with me simply because I bought them."

"You shouldn't have to miss it. Can't the meeting be rescheduled for next week?"

He shook his head. "Sorry, no. I'm low man on the work totem. I have to take what I'm given."

"But if you bought the tickets from your boss..."

"Mike doesn't know," Jay explained. "Take a friend. Have fun. And then let's have dinner so you can tell me all about it."

"I don't know anyone who would want to go—not that I know well. Most of my friends and even the girls here aren't really into stuff like opera." Her disappointment settled itself into her heart. Opera with Jay would have been wonderful. "Everyone I know wants to go to that traveling Woodstock thing." She stared at the tickets again. "I'll take this one. I'm not missing *Don Giovanni* for anything, but give the other one to someone else or maybe you can resell it."

"If you had a car, I might do it, but there's no way you should ride the subway alone at that time of night." Jay waved off her protest. "I'm serious. If you don't find someone, then I'll join you after my meeting. Surely I can get there by the intermission. Otherwise, I'll wait for you in the lobby."

Hope fingered the tickets before handing one back to him. It felt almost dishonest not to tell him she would have taken a cab rather than riding the subway. "Then I'll expect you there on Thursday. I'd rather."

His fingers closed around the ticket. "I'll be there."

She saw several people watching and realized that the questions would start soon if she didn't get him out of there. Defining her friendship with Jay wasn't something she was ready to do. "Hey, do you have time to go get something to eat?

Cafeteria is serving stew today."

Even as she spoke, Hope realized that Jay saw through her. Thankfully, he didn't comment. "Sure. Let's go."

She dashed upstairs to deposit her backpack and jogged back down again, her purse swinging from her shoulder. Once outside, she nudged him. "Thanks for understanding."

"People make assumptions that they cling to despite anything you say. I don't blame you."

He led her into the cafeteria and waved her toward the sea of tables. "Find us some place to sit. I'll bring food. Want a roll?"

"Yes. I'll get drinks."

"Water for me," Jay insisted.

Over lunch, their conversation settled into its companionable rhythm. "You know," Hope said after a little while, "I was about to call you. I wanted to make sure you weren't offended with the church or anything."

"Of course, not. I enjoyed it. I've been swamped with work and final semester classes and all that stuff." He winked at her. "I knew if I called I wouldn't want to get off when I needed to, so I waited for this presentation to be over."

"And that happened to coincide with finding tickets."

Jay nodded. "Convenient, isn't it?"

She stirred the last carrot in her bowl absently. "Do you feel it," she whispered.

"Feel what?"

"It's probably just me."

Jay nudged her. "Come on, what?"

"We've just always been comfortable talking—never run out of anything to say."

"That's why I waited to call… I said that."

"But I mean how often does that happen with someone right away? Even Kirky and I had those weird times when neither of us knew how to just be together without talking and yet we didn't know how to say what we wanted to say. We don't have those awkward silences." Even as she spoke, she suddenly felt the first bit of awkwardness. Why was she talking about this? "Of course, I am rarely silent so…"

"*Amma* says I used to talk a lot more."

"What?" Confused, she stared at him, wondering why he'd said that. It didn't fit. Then she grinned. Distraction. He was good. "Nice one."

"I try," Jay said. "No, really. She says I was one of those obnoxious teenagers who incessantly flood conversations with irrelevant facts about inconsequential things." He popped an oyster cracker in his mouth and added, "Now she always complains that she never knows what I'm thinking."

"Really? I didn't realize you'd had a personality change too. That must have been confusing for your parents."

"My *appa* says I dress better now, so that it is a good trade off. He likes to tease that now he can get in a joke at the dinner table." Again, Jay winked at her.

"Oh! Dress!" Hope clapped a hand over her mouth as she heard how loud she was. She tried again but quieter. "What do you wear to the opera? Do you dress up like in the movies, or what?"

"The RAC has an unofficial formal dress code, so you should dress up, but I doubt they'd turn you away for not wearing a full length gown, furs, and diamonds. Just wear a nice dress and you'll be fine."

"No way. I missed my prom, so this is going to be it. I've never owned an evening gown, but I'm going shopping!"

"Evening gown."

Her spoon dropped as she waited for an explanation of his two snickered words. Her hands folded together and still she waited. "Well…"

"I was trying to decide if you'd be offended."

"I won't. Tell me. I shouldn't get an evening gown?"

Jay laughed. "Not at all. I can't wait to tell *Appa* you suggested a 'night gown.'"

"A nigh—oh, wait. Idioms. I get it. Do you think he'll mix those?"

"He already did." Jay laughed at her obvious embarrassment. "He told me that he would not allow it—no evening gowns for 'Wish.' He insisted that I not 'misuse' you like that."

"Aww… if he wasn't married, I might fall in love with

77

him."

Jay leaned back in his chair, hands behind his head, a slow smile growing as he watched her. "Well, he is taken, but I happen to know he has a son who is intelligent, charming, ruggedly handsome, and best of all, available."

Hope spun, twirling in the dress—again. Her critical eye condemned the price, decided it was too formal, and argued against something that would require a wrap to keep her from frostbite.

Eyes riveted to the mirror, she spun in place once more. Princess seams flared from just below the hips into a wide circular skirt. Hand-sewn, scattered Swarovski crystals sparkled across the hem, growing closer together as they neared the waist. The bodice, almost encrusted with what seemed like millions of sparkles, scooped upward to a satin band at the neckline. The tiniest of spaghetti straps sparkled with more of the illuminant crystals.

Another swirl almost broke Hope's resolve. She desperately wanted the dress. She tried to ignore the protestations of the sales clerks as she forced herself to leave the shop. She wanted to cry. As she dragged herself from the store she muttered, "I'll go to a department store and get whatever they have that works— maybe something on clearance from after Christmas stuff. I should have known better than to look in a boutique. Cha-ching!"

Dreaming of a night in the dress of her dreams, Hope didn't hear her cellphone. A pedestrian tapped her shoulder and said, "Your phone has been ringing for the past half a block. That's some long ringtone."

Hope fumbled for her phone, scrambling to answer it. "Mom—you still there?"

"I was about to give up. You okay? Did you find a dress?"

"I found the perfect dress! I mean, this thing is so gorgeous!"

"Color?"

That was all the encouragement she needed. Hope launched into a thorough description. "It's just the darkest midnight-y, eggplant-y purple you've ever seen. One second it looks black and then you turn and bam! Purple again. There are about a million crystals all over it and—"

"Strapless?"

She shook her head and gesticulated the size as she spoke. "No, it's cut like it's strapless with the little facing thing folded over the top edge, but there are tiny crystals on these dinky straps. So cute."

"Go get it. I can hear how much you like it. Go."

"But it's crazy expensive. I'll never wear it again!"

"So what? Think of all the money we didn't spend on other formals. Combine them. Will it cover it? I bet it will. And even if it doesn't," Hope heard a catch in her mother's voice that cut her, "I really need you to do this for me. Please."

"But, Mom—"

Cheryl's voice transitioned from pained to stern. "Hope Elizabeth Senior, I expect to see a picture of you in that dress at the opera, or I will personally drive to your dorm and spank you."

For a fleeting second, Hope almost capitulated, but a gust of wind flung her unzipped parka open. "Oh, Mom but I don't have anything warm to wear with a dress like that. My dress coat really isn't dressy enough—"

"Then buy a new coat, a cape, a shrug—something! Get the dress and I demand pictures." The phone went dead.

Hope stared at her phone, bewildered. When had her mother ever hung up on anyone? Confused, she took one step toward the boutique again and then hesitated. After an about-face, she managed three steps away before she turned again, nearly slamming into an elderly woman.

"Oh, I'm so sorry. Are you okay?" Tears sprung to her eyes—illogical, irrational, likely hormonally driven tears.

"I'm fine, but you don't look like you are."

Her dilemma spilled from her in a rush. "My mom just told me to buy a really expensive dress. She has no idea how much it really is. Just for one night. I can't justify—oh, I'm so sorry. I...

sorry." She turned to leave but the woman touched her arm as she passed. "Buy the dress. Make your mother happy. Mothers rarely get a chance to extravagantly indulge their daughters."

Once more, Hope paused, remembering homecoming — at home. Prom night — bowling. Grad night parties — watching movies in the living room. All the things they'd so looked forward to over the years, gone — with none of the traditions and photos that a mother expects to have. She hugged her impromptu advisor. "Thank you! You are so right. I'll go get it now. Thank you so much!"

In a strange out-of-self experience, Hope felt like the star in a lighthearted romantic comedy. She dashed through the crowd, somehow managing to avoid injuring anyone, and burst through the door of the little boutique. She skipped up to the register desk with a little hop and said, "I'll take it. I just have to have it. I'll need some kind of wrap to go with it, though."

That idea failed. After trying on half a dozen that seemed worthless to ward off the worst of the cold or too overdone for what she wanted, Hope had an idea. "I'll just take the dress. I think I know what I can wear with it."

CHAPTER 1O

The house lights flickered just as Jay entered the theater. He saw a mass of golden curls and watched as Hope gave one last glance around the room before she made her way back to the grand circle. Beautiful—the only word for her was beautiful. With her hair piled on her head and the dress—*wow what a dress*—she caught the eye of half the men in the room.

He made his way to the seat beside her and leaned close, murmuring, "Enjoying yourself?"

Hope yelped. "Yikes! I looked for you, but I didn't see you." Her eyes appraised him before she added, "Wow, you look sharp! Very handsome. What is it about a man in a tux?"

"Thanks. I think my dinner appointment thought I was a little over dressed, but he felt sorry enough for me missing the first half that he closed the meeting early."

"Oh, no. Is that good or bad?"

"Well, I got the account for Mike and managed to make it before the orchestra drew the first string—I'd call it good."

"Well, there's that string," she whispered as the lights dimmed again.

A few tuning strains followed, giving Jay time to say, "And let's just say that if I look 'sharp,' you are utterly stunning."

Her cheeks flushed, but she smiled. Without turning to him she murmured, "Thanks."

A short while later, Jay dug in his pocket for a packet of

81

Kleenex, marveling at how women cry as an emotional response to anything. Beauty, sorrow, joy, heroism, relief—they dropped tears at any and all of them. Hope accepted the tissues, but seemed confused. Jay leaned close and said, "My client suggested that I be prepared."

By the time the curtain fell, Jay expected her to be a mess of makeup and misery, but apart from faint traces of red around her eyes, she looked the same as when he'd arrived. "Let's let some of the others leave before we try to get out of here. We'll have to wait either way."

She grinned. "Don't let me forget to have you take a picture of this dress. Mom promised to spank me unless I sent a picture the minute we were out of here."

"Promised, or threatened?" Jay noticed that others seemed to have the same idea about leaving and urged her to rise. "Looks like I was wrong. Let's go."

In the lobby, he found a corner that didn't detract from her dress and took several pictures. "She's going to love them."

Hope stopped a passing employee and asked the older man to take a picture of the two of them. He hadn't been willing to ask, but Jay was thrilled to know there would be one. "My *amma* will thank you."

"Oh! I'll get one of you too." She giggled. "I feel sixteen or something."

With phones full of pictures, Jay led her to his car and entered the long line of cars trying to leave the Rockland Arts Center. "So, what did you think of it?" he asked, once he turned onto the street.

"I thought it was amazing. It was hard to understand the words—not speaking Italian and all—"

"There is that," Jay joked.

"—but," she continued with a playful nudge at his sleeve, "I was amazed at how much I did understand. I mean the program was helpful and the subtitles were great, but really, when I actually understood a word, it wasn't difficult to figure it out."

She made no sense to him at all. "Remember an example?"

"One... *innocente amor*. I think I heard *illuminate* and *prepare*

82

too, but not in the song with *amor*."

"Innocent love. You're right. I didn't hear it, but I just assumed I couldn't understand, so I listened to the sounds of the voices rather than the words."

"Wasn't that tenor amazing?" Hope nearly quivered with repressed gesticulation.

He glanced at her, laughing. "Talk with your hands if you must. Who cares?"

"I can't and look through these pictures—oh, I'll send this one." As he braked, she thrust the phone into his line of vision. "We look pretty good! Mom's going to love this. She made me buy the dress and promise to send a picture."

"I'm glad she did."

Her head turned to him. "I wouldn't have taken you for a camera hog."

"No, silly, the dress. I'm glad she made you buy it. It's fabulous and you look amazing in it."

Her fingers smoothed over the skirt, lightly dancing over the crystals as she brushed them. "It does look good on me, doesn't it?"

Jay chuckled. "Yes. Definitely."

Hope stammered an explanation before she sighed. "I know that sounds full of myself, but I don't think I am—not really. I just think it's stupid to pretend like I don't know it."

"There's something to be said for that."

"Besides," she continued, "it's not like I can take credit for it. I didn't create myself."

Those were words he could understand and appreciate. "I like it. I like it a lot, actually. You don't play head games with yourself or anyone else."

The duet from *Don Giovanni* filled the car as her phone rang, making Jay smile. She lived each experience to the hilt—no holds barred. Or, as his father liked to say, "No holding in the tavern."

"I think they got the picture," she murmured before answering her phone. "Hey, Dad! Did you get the picture? What?"

A horrible silence like nothing he'd ever experienced filled

83

his car. "I'm coming home."

Jay's heart constricted.

"No way. Come get me and my stuff on Saturday. I'll withdraw from classes and pack my stuff—no way. I'm coming."

Whatever it was, he hated it already. As Hope listened to something else her father said, Jay's mind tried to sort the pieces he heard. The results depressed him. She was leaving school. She wouldn't be far, but that wasn't the point. Whatever was wrong was serious enough to prompt her to abandon school.

"—coming. Family first. She'll need help with appointments and dealing with the chemo—"

Jay nudged her.

"Wha—hold on, Jay is trying to say something."

"I'll take you home. Don't let your dad leave if your mom is sick. Whenever you want to go, I'll take you."

Hope gave him a weak, artificial smile before turning her attention back to her father. "Okay, Dad? Don't come after all. Jay will bring me home. Okay—love you. Hug Mom and tell her I'm coming."

As he wove through the streets, Jay glanced often at Hope as she stared out the window, apparently lost in some other place. From the little he heard on his end, the news sickened him. Chemo meant cancer. How could Hope and Ron manage another blow so soon after Concord?

"I'm glad *Brigadoon* was last semester," she whispered for reasons he couldn't fathom. "I wouldn't have been able to continue." She glanced at him before continuing. "Then again, Kelli was good. She was my understudy. I guess they didn't need me. I did enjoy it, though."

The play seemed an odd thing to think of at a time like that, but Jay kept quiet, allowing Hope to talk through whatever she needed to. She mentioned her guidance counselor and the two classes she thought she could continue online. Just as he thought she sounded normal again, Hope surprised him.

"I'm glad I listened and bought this dress. Mom needed me to do that. It was important. It looked good." She sighed. "I'll never get to wear it again, though, and my fur throw is now

84

chopped up into this capey thingie."

What throw? What? Unsure how to respond, Jay reached over and squeezed her hand. His heart squeezed again as he felt the ice-cold fingers beneath his. Was it shock? "I agree," he began. "You look absolutely beautiful. It'll mean a lot to her. It's good that you listened to her." He squeezed her hand once more as he added, "Look, your hand is freezing. I'm going to hold it up to the heater for a minute, okay?"

Jay turned the heat up full blast and held her hands, one at a time, up to the vents. She seemed a little distant — uncomprehending. He swallowed hard and tried again. "Hope, I need you to concentrate. You're really cold. Can you rub your hands together? Rub your arms? You need to warm yourself up."

She sat, almost unresponsive until Jay pleaded, "Please, Hope!"

His sharper tones seemed to pierce whatever had separated them. Hope turned to him, tears filling her eyes and sliding down her cheeks. "Mom is sick. They're doing surgery on Monday. Pancreatic cancer." She choked back a sob and said, "She didn't tell Dad until after she got the picture tonight. She didn't want us to know until —"

Sobs shook her for several minutes before she regained control. She stared at their hands for a few seconds before asking, "What are you doing to my hands?"

He stopped his attempts to warm her and tried to give her a reassuring smile. "You went into some kind of shock or something. You were so cold."

"Now I'm burning up. Can we turn down the heater?" She took a deep wavering breath. "Jay, what am I going to do? I can't lose Mom too. Dad won't make it if he loses her."

He hesitated for a second, maybe two, and took her hand again. "You won't necessarily lose her. Cancer is so much more treatable and beatable now than it was even five years ago. You and your church will pray. I will pray if it will help. She will be fine."

Hope shook her head. "We just saw a documentary over Christmas." A fresh sob shook her. "Oh, I think Mom must have had us watch it on purpose!" After a few long seconds, she tried explaining again. "It's like the fourth leading cause of cancer deaths and the odds even after surgery are only like twenty-five to forty percent of living up to five years. Did you hear that? After surgery... after the chemo and all that stuff. Then, you might have twenty-five to forty percent chance of surviving for another five years."

"Maybe she caught it early enough. Don't 'lend trouble,' as my *appa* would say."

It worked. She chuckled. "He has never said that, has he?"

"No, but it sounds like something he'd say."

As he pulled up to the dormitory, she leaned over and hugged him. "I'd rather go in alone, if you don't mind. If you go with me, I'm going to bawl. Keep reminding me that we'd have given anything to have five more years with Con, ok?"

"Okay, but Hope..."

"Hmm?"

"Your faith. Remember your faith."

Jay carried the last box of Hope's things from his car, up the stairs and to her room, he stacked it against the wall with the other things she'd brought home from the university. His eyes roamed around the room once more. So girly, so childlike, so pink—it made her seem younger and even more vulnerable. As it was, she'd cried all the way to her home.

At the foot of the stairs, he hesitated, torn between leaving quietly and hoping they understood or going into the living room to say goodbye. Cheryl's voice calling him in settled it for him. "I think that's the last of it..."

"Thank you for bringing her home. If she would have agreed to a car..."

"Mom, I told you. It would just tempt me to run home all the time or go shopping. I wanted to immerse myself into campus life."

The strangled choke as she finished speaking told him she wouldn't make it much longer before breaking down again. Jay wanted—needed—to be gone before then. "Well, I need to be going, but if you need anything, if I can do anything, just call."

Cheryl stood and hugged him. "Don't be a stranger."

Jay glanced back at Hope standing in the doorway and waved before he jogged to his car and climbed inside. As he pulled away from the curb, he felt unsettled—almost as if he was ten years old and moving away from his best friend. Prayer. He had promised to pray too. Did Jesus even listen to the prayers of unbelievers? Would He listen to the prayers of an investigator on behalf of a believer? What could it hurt?

The prayer came in awkward spurts, words flung out at random moments as he drove back to Rockland.

Jesus, I know there must be some proper form of prayer. A car ahead of him swerved, and Jay followed, narrowly missing a large pothole in the road. *I also know that if you really are God, you know I'm not sure that I believe it, so what good does formality do then? So, I pray for Hope*—he swallowed hard at the forlorn picture in his mind of Hope standing alone in the doorway—*for her parents, and I guess for me.*

A mile or two passed before Jay could bring himself to turn his mind back to the prayer he felt obligated to offer. *I pray for comfort—strength—and for health. Please cure Cheryl.*

As he pulled up to his house, Jay allowed the car to idle. The curtains shifted—twice. His *amma* worried about him. *Oh, and Jesus, I am not promising anything. I won't believe just because she's healed in six months or six years. I'll only believe if something convinces me to believe. I'm just praying because it's the only thing I think I can do.*

CHAPTER 11

Jay stared at his phone, willing her to call. The surgery should have been over hours earlier—several hours earlier. A sick feeling flooded his stomach and threatened to drown his heart. He envisioned many such days—waiting to hear news when he had no real claim to information.

The buzzing of his phone sent it dancing across his desk. Jay snatched it up and answered without looking—his mother. "Hello, Amma."

"Have you heard?"

"No." He smiled at the concern in his mother's voice. "I'm coming home now."

After promising to bring home a gallon of milk, Jay closed his laptop and slid it into its case. He grabbed his coat, pulled it on, and gathered his things. Just as he reached his car, his phone buzzed again. This time it was Hope.

"Hello! How are you? How is your mother?"

"Hey, sorry I didn't call sooner. After Kirky and my aunt in California—" Hope sounded weary. "Long day."

"Did surgery go well?"

There was a catch in her voice as she said, "The doctor seems optimistic." Her struggle filled him with frustration. Why this woman?

"He says we'll know more in a few weeks when they run tests."

"Did they do the full—"

She sighed. "No. I think they should have. Maybe it'd be worth it, but I guess they don't do that much anymore. They went in to do a partial and can't. It spread into blood vessels."

"Oh, Hope." He opened his car door and settled himself in the driver's seat. "What comes next?"

"Chemo, radiation, and a whole lot of prayer." A sob hung on that last word until she whispered, "Jay, we need a miracle."

"Then we pray for a miracle."

"Oh, here comes Dad. I've got to go. I'll call later."

"If you ever need to talk, someone to sit with you while you're waiting—anything. Don't hesitate to call me."

"Really?"

His heart broke at the sound of relief and eagerness in her voice. Hope had many friends and people from her church to support her; why would she prefer him? "Of course. Any time."

"You have no idea what that means."

"Mind if I ask why not Kirky or the people from your church? I am not complaining, but it seems natural…"

"It is," she agreed. "Jay, with you, I don't have to hold you up too. I mean, you know her and I know you care what happens to her, but not like Kirky. Mom is like a second mother to her. She's losing someone too and I have to be strong for her. The people at church—it's kind of the same. With you, I can fall apart and not have to feel bad about it."

He started to reply when she cut in quickly. "Dad says hi. I've got to go. I'll call you—or email. Or text. Or something." A second paused between them before she added, "Thanks, Jay. Bye."

He turned on the car, shivering as the cold air blasted him. His mind lost in their conversation, Jay passed the supermarket, passed the mini-mart, and pulled up in front of their house much quicker than he expected. As he stepped inside the front door, his mother walked past wearing one of her favorite saris. "Oh, *Amma*…"

"Where is the milk?"

The words registered, but their meaning remained elusive. "I—"

"Sanjay?" Amala led him to the kitchen and pulled out the

90

blender. "I'll make *lassi*. You tell me what is bothering my son." Her eyes widened. "Your boss was not angry that you cut short your meeting, was he?"

"No. I just talked to Hope." He turned. "Oh. Milk. I am sorry, *Amma*. I'll go—"

"I can get it myself. You tell me what is wrong with Hope."

"Her mother's surgery was not successful."

Amala set the lid on the blender and came to her son's side. She wrapped her arms around him and held him close. "I am so sorry."

"How do people stand it? I cannot imagine what I would do if—"

"Then I must not die. Problem solved."

Jay nodded. "They are Christians. I think her faith helps her."

"Good. What use is it to have a faith if it does not help you when things are difficult?"

"Do you regret it?"

"Regret what?" Amala returned to her blender, crushing the ice and yogurt together.

"Leaving behind the Hindi faith?"

"We did not—not really. We did not make a *puja*—no shrine for our deities and relics—but there are parts of the faith that we keep as tradition. *Diwali*, of course. We keep the festival of lights—just in our American way. We are here now and my Raj did not wish to continue a faith that he did not embrace."

"I love *Diwali*," he murmured.

"You always did. That first year you were so upset when we changed it. You cried for days."

"I cried?" Jay didn't remember that at all.

"How could you forget? Oh, the drama!"

"I only remember the relief of knowing that no one would think me weird for having new clothes in October or November."

"That came later."

"Did you ever consider abandoning it? At what point did tradition trump a life without faith?"

"It had meaning to us. We liked the fresh start of a new

91

year. I liked the beauty. Your father did not object as long as I did not teach you that the lights truly do drive out evil. He does not believe that."

"I think Hope believes that Jesus is the light that drives out evil."

"That is a beautiful thought."

He stood and accepted the glass of *lassi* before turning to leave the room. "I just wish I knew if it was true."

The hospital cafeteria rumbled with the noises of chattering diners who ate their tasteless food with little relish. Jay sat across from Hope, listening as his friend described the horrible weeks of chemo and radiation. Dark circles under her eyes made her look like something from a horror film.

"...told me that the tumor is growing again. I don't know what to think." She shoved aside her tray and folded her hands. "So tell me what I have missed. Did you do anything special for Valentine's Day?"

"I brought my *amma* a rose. She liked it." What kind of question was that? "Did you do something?"

"I forgot all about it. Dad remembered, though. He brought Mom a dozen roses." Her voice caught. "He's never done that before. I guess things that seemed silly before have more meaning when you might not be able to do them anymore."

"I suppose." Jay didn't know what to say. "Perhaps he never realized how much she would enjoy them before now. I hear that men are very dense sometimes."

"Maybe." She rested her chin in her hands, leaning on the table with her elbows. "I wish I had played video games more with Con. I told Dad last night—" Jay saw the lump in her throat rise and fall as she swallowed. "I told him, 'This has taught me something. I will play with my children when I have them. I won't let myself get so caught up in PTA meetings and soccer games and my job that I don't have time to spend just with them.'"

"That sounds wise."

"Do you celebrate St. Paddy's Day?" She shook her head. "Nah, that's kind of a Catholic holiday. You wouldn't celebrate that."

"Corned beef and cabbage?"

"But they don't eat that in Ireland—just here." Her smile, though weak, brightened her face. "I bought one to make. Mom says I can't ruin it. You just throw it in and boil it to death."

"Sounds delightful."

Their eyes met and relief washed over him as she laughed. For that tiny moment—a piece of time ripped from the fabric of the universe and held close—he saw the old Hope. He saw the Hope full of life, vivacity, and joy.

"You're welcome to come eat with us," Hope offered.

"I might do that. Day after tomorrow?"

"Yes."

He nodded. "I'll try."

Her phone buzzed in her pocket. "I guess Mom is done. Do you want to come see her?"

"Would she like that?"

Hope hesitated, thinking. "You're right. She'll feel pretty awful for a while. You just have to come eat with us then. It'll be a good diversion for her."

He pulled out his phone to check his calendar. "I can do it. I'll be at your house at..."

"Six, if you can make it." She stood and dumped her tray before returning to the table. Wrapping her arms around him, she hugged him. "Thank you. I needed someone to talk to."

"Always here."

"Are you okay?"

He nodded. "I am good—now that I've seen you." He brushed a limp lock of hair from her cheek, tucking it behind her ear. "Try to get more sleep. You look exhausted."

"I look horrible, you mean."

"You do not look like my Hope; that is certain. I worry about you."

Hope watched as he wove through the tables, pausing at the door to wave to her again before he disappeared out of sight. "...*do not look like my Hope...*"

The words hovered in her mind, teasing a memory. His contractions disappeared whenever he was thinking—or when he felt emotional. What emotions did he hide this time or what was he thinking? *He's probably thinking that you look awful, Hope!* she thought as she strolled toward the elevators.

If a man she hardly knew thought that, what must her mother think? She could make an effort—for her mother's sake. Hope stopped in the restroom to wash her hands and gazed at herself in the mirror. Jay was right. She did look very different.

She washed and dried her face. The improvement there alone was startling. Despite a thorough brush of her hair, it looked no better when she was done than when she started. Hope fumbled through her purse, looking for a hair tie. "Score!"

A woman beside her frowned. "Are you okay?"

"I will be. Soon. I will be."

With her hair pulled back and a clean face, she looked better—much better. A quick swipe of tinted lip gloss added to the improvement. "I'll ask the doctor about some kind of sleeping pill, maybe," she muttered.

"What?"

"Oh, nothing. Just thinking out loud... Have a nice day."

As she stepped from the restroom, she overheard the woman say, "What a weird thing to say to someone in a hospital."

Jay opened a text message a few hours later. I ASKED THE DOCTOR FOR SOMETHING TO HELP ME SLEEP. THANKS.

He smiled and sent back a text. His mind whirled. Ron and Hope needed prayer as much as Cheryl did. Who was praying for them? He punched a button on his phone and then disconnected.

Jay strode down the hall to Mike's office. "Can I bother you for a minute?"

"Sure."

"My friend is a Christian."

"Okay..."

"Her mother is dying — pancreatic cancer."

Mike nodded. "I'm sorry to hear it."

"I know people are praying for her — people from all over the Rockland area, but..."

Mike gestured for him to take a seat, but Jay shook his head. "I can't stay. I have class in half an hour. I just — I — "

"What is it?"

"I think my friend and her father need prayer too. I think it would comfort her to know that someone is praying for her."

"And you want to know if you can pray?"

He shook his head. "I want to know if you will pray for Hope and Ron Senior — that they can stay strong and healthy during this. I saw her today."

"Not good?"

Jay sighed. "Not good. She looks as ill as her mother — almost."

"Do they know how long she has?"

Again, Jay shook his head. "I don't know. I haven't asked. I thought maybe — " What did it matter what he thought?

"You thought she might be tired of answering that question."

"Right." He gazed at his shoes. "They lost Hope's older brother a couple of years ago — hit and run. To lose half the family in such a short time..."

"Are they strong Christians? By that I mean, do they fully trust in Jesus or do they go to church on Easter and Christmas?"

"Both — and all the Sundays and some other days in between."

Mike leaned back, his hands behind his head. "I'm not going to pretend that this isn't going to be hard on them. Being a Christian doesn't mean that the pain of loss is any less, but they do have hope..."

"Yes." He grinned. "And that's her name."

"Was she well-named?"

Jay thought about it, his mind sorting all the things she had said to him over the past several months. "I think she was."

"That's a good thing, then. I will pray — and I'll ask my friends to pray too."

"Thank you."

As Jay turned to leave the room, Mike stopped him. "Um, Jay?"

He didn't turn around, the tears in his eyes and the emotion choking him not something he was willing to share. "Yes?"

"You can pray, too."

"Does Jesus listen to someone who doesn't believe?"

"I don't know. It can't hurt, though. It would comfort you and her to know that you cared enough to do it."

"And how does one pray?"

"Just talk to Jesus. Just talk to Him."

He hesitated again and said, "I might. Thanks, Mike."

CHAPTER 12

On Cinco de Mayo, three Seniors sat behind Dr. Seung's massive desk, waiting for the news that none of them wanted to hear. Hope fidgeted with her phone, rereading Jay and Kirky's latest messages as if somehow they would ensure a positive result. Cheryl sat up a little straighter and spoke.

"I know what the doctor is going to say. I can feel it. So I want to tell you now that I'm going to request palliative care if he says that what we've done up until now hasn't been successful."

Hope choked back a sob. She understood her mother's decision, but that didn't make accepting it any easier. Ron held her and wept. When the doctor arrived, they sat huddled in a ball around Cheryl's chair, praying for good news and preparing for the worst.

"Sorry to keep you waiting."

"It was good for us," Cheryl whispered.

"I suspect you know what I have to say."

Cheryl nodded and tears flowed down Hope's cheeks at the silent confirmation of her worst fears. Before Hope could ask a question, Cheryl took the reins of the conversation. "How long?"

"It depends upon the course of treatment—"

"No more treatment. I just want to go home and spend my remaining time with my family without being sick all the time."

"Then," the doctor leaned forward, his hands folded in

front of him, "I'm sorry to say I would expect two to three months."

Ron's head snapped up. "That short?"

"Yes."

"Ok, then how do we plan for this so that pain —"

The words swirled in Hope's head, but she made no sense of them. As the doctor and her parents talked, she tried to imagine life — soon — without her mother and couldn't. At one point, her mother commented on wanting to make it to August — "For Hope's birthday," and she wept.

Heaving sobs shook her as the finality of it all smothered her. How could that doctor sit there with that same placid look on his face that he always had? Did he have no heart? How could he deal out death sentences, every day, without losing his sanity in the process?

When she left the office, Hope didn't know. She followed her parents down the hall, out the door, and into the warm May air. She felt disconnected from life as her parents discussed trivial and commonplace things like having the lawn reseeded and what to have for dinner.

As their car sped toward home, Hope punched out a quick text message to Kirky and then another one to Jay. Minute later, she sent him one more.

TODAY IS WORSE THAN A MONDAY ON STEROIDS.

Hope watched as her mother slowly turned the pages of the photo album. Her weak movements told a stronger tale than any of her protests that she felt "remarkably well." One week until school was out and her father could be home. She needed to make it one week — two or three would be better, but at least one week.

"Holly?"

Hope blinked. "Mom?"

"Hmm?"

"Who is Holly?" She watched the confusion flit over her mother's features.

98

"Did I call you that? Strange."

"Who is it?"

"I always dreamed of naming a little girl, Holly," Cheryl explained. "But your dad refused to name an August baby, 'Holly.'"

"I like it. Maybe I'll name my daughter Holly. Maybe I'll have a girl in July so that I can argue it's 'Christmas in July.'"

"You get that in writing before you marry someone. It'll be nice to know that there's a Holly baby coming someday."

"It's got to be better than Hope—fewer Jokes. Jay is always teasing me about my name."

"How?"

Hope's throat constricted. Her mother had fallen a little in love with Jay. *"He brings a little of Con back into the home,"* she'd said several times.

"The last email I got said that life on campus without me is 'Hopeless.'"

"My grandmother was Ruth. When she died, my uncle said, 'And now we're all just Ruthless!'"

"Sounds like something Jay would say."

Cheryl shoved the photo album onto the couch and laid her head on the arm, pulling a blanket over her. "You like him, don't you?"

"Yeah. I mean, it's crazy. I've only seen him a dozen times or so, but we talk a few times a week, and he was really good about being there when you were having treatments." Hope sighed. "It's weird. I know him, but I don't."

"Does he still ask about the Bible?"

She nodded, remembering the random texts that she got at all hours, asking about this idea or that. "Yeah. If he doesn't become a Christian..."

"I think it's a bit soon to assume that. He might just need time."

"I wish I could ask him to talk to Dad or maybe Kirky. Maybe one of them could get through where I can't. I mean, he asks these questions," she complained, "and I think, 'Oh, good. He finally gets it,' and then he just goes on, asking some other random thing."

99

Her mother did not reply. Hope gazed at the woman sleeping on the couch and tears splashed down her cheeks. So much pain—so little time. How would they get through these next few months? She moved the photo album, helped stretch out her mother's legs, and tucked the blanket around Cheryl's shoulders. The woman hardly stirred.

Cheryl needed hours of sleep every day—hours of disconnect from the world. Hope carried the photo album upstairs, lost in memories that caused as much pain as joy now. How long before the memories included another funeral—another home-going?

Her phone buzzed. A smile tugged at the corners of her lips. Jay. "Hello there."

"Am I interrupting anything?"

"Just a pity party."

"Well, are there balloons, streamers, and noise makers?"

"Nope."

He chuckled. "Then I'm not coming."

How did he know exactly the right words to say? "If I make cupcakes, will you come?"

"Oh, you drive a hard bargain—what kind?"

Her mind whirled as she tried to remember his favorites. "I'm thinking strawberry shortcake."

"Oh… now that is tempting."

"Come on. I've got everything to make them, even. You come and I'll have them ready."

He demurred, but she heard that certain something in his voice. He would come. As he asked her to hold to answer a work call, she hurried downstairs and began assembling everything for making the cupcakes. By the time he returned, she had already separated egg whites.

"You have to come now. I just cracked my eggs."

"Well…"

She had him. "I think Dad is bringing Chinese. Mom seems to devour it these days."

"I'll be there. You drive a hard bargain. Or, as my father says, 'Your bargain is driving me hard.'"

"I've got to meet this man."

100

Hope tortured him throughout the baking process. She mentioned the sugar, the strawberries, the whipped topping that would make them melt in his mouth. By the time he had to go, she had ensured that Jay wouldn't consider backing out of a meal with the Seniors. "Hey, stop somewhere and bring a movie — anything that has been released in the past six months. I haven't seen anything."

"Will do. I've been wanting to see that spy thing with Frank Waylon."

Just as he began to disconnect, Hope added, "Jay?"

"Hmm?"

"Thanks. I needed this."

"Hope?"

"Hmm?"

Jay laughed. "I think we both did."

CHAPTER 13

The entire experience felt surreal—unfamiliar. Although he was certain he had attended a funeral a time or two, Jay didn't remember them. Furthermore, he was also certain that any other funerals had been nothing like the service taking place around him. It had started with triumphant sounding music and spiraled from there.

A man stood before them, offering the mic to anyone with a memory of Cheryl that they wished to share. Jay sat in fascinated horror as one by one, people climbed the steps to the mic and told stories that produced more tears, more sobs, and to his astonishment, laughter—much laughter. It made no sense.

He choked as he tried to offer his condolences as the guests filed past the Seniors. A group nearby told him that the family had come from California. No one could look that much like Cheryl and not be family.

He hugged Hope and shook Ron's trembling hand. His heart heavy, Jay walked to his car, leaving the others to offer the words of encouragement that he so longed to give—and couldn't. But Hope followed.

She reached his car just as Jay removed his jacket, tossing it into the back seat. Her eyes glistening with unshed tears, she smiled up at him. "Thanks for coming. Dad appreciates it too. Not everyone would come for someone they hardly knew."

Grief stricken, he watched her, marveling at the serenity he saw in her eyes. She was sad; no one could mistake that.

However, it had been less than a week, and she already missed her mother, but serene—Hope was serene. Hope Senior had hope.

"I prayed for her," he choked. "I prayed for your *amma*—several times, actually."

She smiled. "That means a lot to me—and to her, I'm sure."

"I didn't bargain with God. I did not tell Jesus that I would believe or not if He would cure her." Jay leaned against the door of his car. "I just realized how much I hoped. I really wanted Him to call my bluff and make her well."

Hope blinked back a few tears. She reached into her pocket and pulled out a handful of tissues. Handing Jay several, she wiped at her face. "Jay, He did. Jesus made her whole again. She'll never get sick now—never hurt. Cancer can't touch her now. She's with Jesus, rejoicing with the angels." A hiccough followed as she added, "I miss her already—miss her like crazy—but she has everything you prayed for and asked for her."

"And you got nothing." Jay knew his voice sounded bitter. He *was* bitter.

"I got almost twenty-one years with the most wonderful mother ever. Some people get a lifetime with hard, mean mothers and others grow up without one at all."

"But—"

"But nothing. I don't want her to go. I selfishly want her there when I get married—you know, adjust my veil and pray with me. She won't be able to sit with me during my first labor or rock her grandchildren and sing to them in her horrible off-key voice."

Tears poured down his cheeks as he listened to her describe loss he couldn't fathom. "Hope…"

"But my mom is at the feet of Jesus. I can't begrudge her that."

He shook his head and squeezed her hand as he opened his car door. He slammed the door shut behind him and rolled down the window. Gazing up at her, Jay groaned. "I don't know if Christianity is the most wonderful thing ever to happen to mankind or if it is the most cruel." He reached through the

104

window, squeezed her hand again, and added, "Write when you feel like talking. I'll understand if it takes a while."

She watched as he backed out of his parking space and drove past. A new form of grief filled her as Jay pulled out of the parking lot and drove toward the freeway. He was gone. Graduated—no longer a student at her university. Even if she returned in the fall, she wasn't likely to see him again. Somehow, she felt that the flick of a blinker in a church parking lot had changed their brief friendship to a friendly correspondence.

The familiar ping of metal preceded the whoosh of cold air as the air conditioner blasted on again. Hope glanced at her father. Ron sat with his book lying open on his chest, untouched. He didn't eat, read, or sleep as far as she could tell, but he must have—at some point. Decisions about the simplest things became her responsibility.

Things she had never expected to do became imperative as Ron fell apart at the sight of a blouse, a bra, or a sock. She packed up all of her mother's clothing, tossed her untouched magazine collection, and wrote hundreds of thank-you notes. Every day she drove to a local nursing home and dropped off another flower arrangement—when would people stop sending them? Her days were busy, but her heart felt empty.

As her father dozed, she stared at her mother's dinky little netbook. It was time to clear it out—remove all personal items, and wipe it clean. Surely, some girl at church would like to have it.

The moment she saw the desktop picture, Hope knew she'd never be able to wipe the computer clean. The four of them—how had three years reduced them to two? The Thanksgiving service—Con's cheeky grin, her mother's beautiful smile, her father's pride. She rarely looked closely at herself in group pictures, but Hope couldn't help but see the difference in her. That Hope was gone. That carefree person—gone. She choked.

Hope carried the laptop to the downstairs bathroom and compared the pictures in the mirror. It was as if she saw another person in the mirror—an unhappy version of her old self. Could pain be erased from eyes? Could she ever be that person again?

Those thoughts swirled in her head as she carried the laptop back to the couch. A glance at her father told her he still dozed—anything to keep the pain at bay. She called up her mother's email and quickly realized her mistake. As hundreds of emails dumped into the inbox, Hope found the dashboard and searched for a way to remove it all.

Deleting her mother's email account felt as though she'd deleted part of her mother. She would never again have that email address pop up in her inbox with some silly joke or heartwarming story that had already circulated through the internet a few million times. The finality of it seemed unbearable.

While on the website, Hope signed into her own email and watched as a few dozen new emails rolled into the box. Emails offering condolences and spam from every corner of the planet made up the bulk of her email, but one email address was noticeably absent. It seemed strange not to see one from Jay. "This is where it ends, then, huh?" she murmured to herself.

"Did you say something, Hope?"

She glanced up and found her father watching her. "I just said that I'll probably never hear from Jay again."

"Why not? I've been wondering when he'd be by again." Ron frowned. "Did something happen?"

"He just stopped asking questions and kind of left the friendship ball in my court. I took that as a sign that he's done with Jesus."

Ron sat up and leaned forward, his arms resting on his knees. "So you can't be friends with someone who isn't interested in Jesus? Since when?"

"You know it's just going to get awkward. He's going to ask me out or I'm going to want him to and of course, I can't go, and then everything is just going to get all icky. I don't want to lose anyone else in my life. It's just better if it dies here."

"I've never been more ashamed of you."

Tears flooded her eyes. "What?"

"You should know better than most how important people

106

are. How can you treat something as precious as friendship so lightly? Where is your faith, Hope? Where is your faith?"

"What does faith have to do with—"

Her father crossed the room and sat next to her. "You have to decide if you trust the Lord with everything or just some things. Who brought Jay to you? Do you know that he isn't interested in learning more about the Lord?"

"Well, no... he just said he'd wait for my email..." She swallowed hard. "I thought—"

"You thought that a simple act of courtesy toward a grieving girl was his rejection of Jesus? Really?"

"Well, when you put it like that..."

Ron pulled her close, holding her, shaking with repressed sobs that she suspected were unrelated to their discussion. "Don't leave Jay to wither like the seed sown on the rocks. Keep watering that seed with truth from the Living Water, Hope. You'll never regret that."

"I guess even if things did get awkward, knowing Jesus would make it worth it."

"Do you trust the Lord?" Ron tipped her chin and gazed into her tear-clouded eyes. "Do you trust that the Lord who gave you this friend can handle the friendship that follows—even when you can't?"

He stood and took a few steps toward the stairs before he added, "I almost didn't call your mother for a second date. Did you know that?"

"No..." she whispered.

"I knew her friends didn't like me and that she'd probably dump me, but we had fun—she had fun. I knew it. She was so beautiful—" He swallowed hard and grabbed the post for support. "You look so much like she did then."

"Dad—"

He continued as if she hadn't interrupted. "I called because I had to risk the rejection I expected in order to have any chance at a relationship. I felt so stupid, but I've been thankful every day of my life since." Ron stared at his feet as he struggled to control his emotions. That small movement reminded her of Jay at the funeral. At last he raised his head and said, "On our

107

second date, when your mother got in the car she said, 'I was afraid you wouldn't call again after the way Carol snubbed you.'"

Her own sobs welled up in her heart, but all Hope could say was, "I'm so glad you did."

"Me too. She wanted me to call, Hope. She wanted *me*."

"What if she hadn't been a Christian, though? Could you have stood to discover that, watch her move on to someone else, marry someone else…"

Ron beckoned her to his side, pulling her into a hug. "We weren't friends first like you and Jay, but I'd rather have a friend and lose her than never to have had the friend at all."

After weeks of wondering if he'd ever hear from her again, seeing her name in his inbox turned a lousy day right side up. "Ahh, the lovely Miss Hope," he murmured as he opened the email.

To: sanjaybrown@finchinvestments.com
From: hopesenior90@letterbox.com
Subject: Forgive Me?

Jay,
I'm sorry for not writing. It was stupid and immature. I'm so sorry. Have I mentioned that I'm sorry?
So, dropping the subject of my apologies, how are things since graduation? Is working fulltime cool, or do you miss college?
I had thought I'd be back next semester, but Dad just isn't ready to be alone. It's weird. I feel like we're reliving Con's death but without Mom to keep us balanced. Which, of course, makes no sense.
Next time you have time to meet for coffee, I'd love it. Kirky is gone for the summer, half the college group are gone on mission trips, and I could use the distraction.

Hope to hear from you soon (I can just imagine the jokes you'll have for that),
Hope

He clicked reply and then closed out again. Punching her contact on his phone, he leaned back in his chair and waited for her to answer. "Hey there..."

"Jay! Did you—of course you got my email. Dumb question."

"How are you really? You sounded a little..."

"That's exactly how I feel... just a little—something."

Jay grinned. That was the Hope he knew. "Ok, so there's a juggling exhibition in City Park on Saturday. I have to meet with my realtor at eleven, but after that, we could go see what's up over there."

"What's up... funny." He waited for it—there it was. "Wait, realtor?"

"Mmm hmm," Jay murmured as an aide stopped in to see if he wanted anything from the deli truck. "Just a chicken sandwich and some chips," he whispered as he dug out his wallet. "Thanks."

"What?"

"Sorry—lunch run. It's Loni's turn." His eyebrows drew together as he tried to remember. "What were we talking about?"

"You mentioned a realtor. I thought Indian men lived at home until they got married."

So, she'd been reading up on Indian culture. Interesting. "Many do, but my parents and I agree that the market is going to start going up soon. I want to buy while it's at or near bottom."

"Cool. You going to buy in Westbury?"

Jay sighed. "No, I think the eastern outskirts of Rockland if I can find something affordable, or maybe Hillsdale. That new line out there makes the commute only twenty minutes."

"So I could meet you at the park around, twelve-thirty?"

A slow smile overtook him. She wanted to see him—was almost eager. Hope was back—sort of. "Yes. I'll wait by the gazebo."

"Ok, thanks." The phone went silent for a few seconds, but

he didn't think she had hung up yet. "Jay?"

"Yeah?"

"Thanks."

CHAPTER 14

A call came on a Wednesday afternoon. The request: simple. Plan and execute a surprise party for Hope's birthday — that Saturday. "I'll have her gone by three." Ron promised. "Just do something that'll keep her distracted."

"You've got it. Where can I get phone numbers for the people from your church?"

Only the sounds of clicking fingers on a keyboard answered him until Ron spoke again. "Okay. There. I just sent you an email from Hope's account... just have to delete from the sent folder..." As he worked, Ron talked his way through the steps. "Got it," Jay assured him.

Jay's original plan had been a dance, but immediately he nixed that as too much of a reminder of her losses. "Is there something she's always wanted to do? One of those reality TV shows or..."

"She likes paintball. We don't have enough equipment for a good game, though, and it's awfully expensive. She likes those talent and dance shows but —"

"I doubt I could stomach it; I'm sure she couldn't. I'll figure it out. Who on this list is the best co-conspirator?"

"Kirky and/or Brian Donaldson."

"Got it. I have an idea. We'll see."

"Jay?"

He knew what was coming. "Glad to do it, Ron. See you Saturday."

As Hope and Ron turned out of her street, Jay zipped around the corner and pulled into the driveway. The key was at the bottom of the mailbox as Ron had promised. He carried in food first, then party décor, and finally, several huge armloads of uniformly sized gifts. The gifts he piled on the dining room table, but the rest he carried out to the backyard and out of sight.

The doorbell rang, sending him running to answer it. People, whose faces seemed familiar — whom he couldn't identify if he tried — filled the doorway, the entryway, the house. A woman who introduced herself as Claire Novak thanked him for setting up the party and put him to work on streamers and balloons outside. "I'll get the food and punch."

Once the party was ready, the guests assembled, and the wait begun, people grew antsy, eager for Ron and Hope's return. A neighbor boy was recruited to dash inside and over the fence at the sight of Ron's car. Travis jumped the fence hissing, "They're here," and Jay dashed inside and tried to look relaxed in Ron's chair.

As the door opened, he heard Hope's voice. "...tell me Jay was coming!"

He jumped up just as she entered the living room. "Happy Birthday. Sorry I couldn't get here earlier — work and such."

"On a Saturday? I need to meet this boss of yours and give him a piece of my mind." Hope hugged him whispering, "Thanks for coming. I think Dad could use the company."

"It's a busy time for us — last quarter and all." His words sounded inane, even to himself.

"Well," she said, pulling him toward the kitchen, "Dad says we're going to put on some great music, dance like fools, and bake a monster-sized cake that we couldn't eat if we tried."

Jay raised one eyebrow and dragged her through the kitchen to the dining room. "Presents first. I hope you like them."

With wide eyes, Hope circled the immense stack of gifts. What would she say? Would she balk?"

Hope gave him a sly glance. "What, no hand painted

wrapping paper this time?"

Laughing, he shook his head. "My pen ran out?" Jay winked. "No, actually my neighbor insisted on wrapping them for you. She likes to pretend I'm her grandson or something. *Amma* says she pampers me mercilessly."

"Mercilessly? A bit overbearing in her enthusiasm?" Ron mocked as Hope tore into the first package. Paper flew behind her in fluttering streams as she flung it out of her way. Ribbons littered the carpet.

"Not unlike your daughter and presents, I'd say."

"Shut up. A girl has the right to enjoy every minute of a great—laser tag! Cool! I hereby—more? Wow." She stared at the three open boxes and the pile of unopened ones on the table. "Are they all laser tag?"

"Yep."

"Dad, can you start calling people from church? There are enough here for a couple of armies!"

Delighted, Jay watched as Hope freed every laser tag gun found in the greater Rockland area from its wrappings. He winked at Ron and tugged on Hope's arm. "C'mon. You put on a vest and let's go practice in the backyard while your dad calls and cleans up this mess."

Ron's mock protest might have given away the plan, but the roar of "Surprise!" stunned her enough to cover his deficiencies as an actor.

Hope hugged her friends and church family before announcing. "I want an epic battle. Two people per team. Um… if your teammate gets killed, you can join forces with another orphan… um, last person or team standing wins."

"You're on," Jay retorted.

Hope leveled a look that he couldn't decipher and said, "I choose Nate Jorgenson."

"Consider your challenge accepted." Jay turned to Ron and said, "Are you with me?"

The group suited up and loaded their laser guns with batteries from the only square box in the bunch. Teams fanned out into the neighborhood, barely giving others time to duck behind bushes before opening fire. The last team out of the house narrowly missed being the first team eliminated. The game commenced.

How it took ten sweltering minutes of dodging fire before the first person went down, no one quite understood. Shouting triumphantly, Mrs. Wesley jogged slowly down the street, arms in the air, allowing everyone to shoot her. She taunted them with calls of the air-conditioned comfort in store for her while they melted in the August evening air.

Ron saw Hope aim for Jay and dove into the path of the beam, taking himself out of the game and saving Jay. "Go find Jack Wesley. I think he's two streets over."

At that moment, Jay realized that they weren't playing a simple game of tag. It was war with "living" casualties. He'd have to fight for every minute of life before someone sent him back to what they now called "the graveyard"—the Senior home.

Determination slowly overtook him. He'd win. He had to. He would be the last man standing even if it killed him. He saw a beam hit the wall next to him and flattened himself beside a garage.

"I saw that, Hope. You missed."

"I won't miss next time!"

Jay's laughter rang out across the street. "Yeah, like I'll give you a next time."

Several people walked slowly past, pulling their vests off. The oppressive heat and humidity made wearing the tag vests miserable. Their loud talk about strategies and people's positions made no sense to Jay. From where he sat, he could see that several things they said were all wrong. Understanding hit him hard. Fake—these people were good.

"Gotcha!" Jay and Hope stood face-to-face, guns on each other, triggers ready.

Hope's eyes narrowed. "Standoff. If either of us even blinks wrong, we'll shoot each other and be out of the game. Solution?"

Jay eyed her warily. "Where is your partner?"

"Got shot ten minutes ago." Sweat poured down Hope's temples.

"How do I know this is true?" The desire to wipe his own

face was only slightly less overwhelming than the desire to stay alive. If he moved, Hope would shoot.

"Because if he wasn't gone, you'd be dead."

"Good point," he agreed. "As I see it, we have two choices. We either team up or we both concede and shoot each other to get out of the heat."

Hope's face became a study in disgust. "Quit? Never! I never quit. I'll lower my weapon if you lower yours."

Jay trained his eyes on her, trying to tap into his peripheral vision to see if anyone was coming. "I—"

Before he could finish, Hope tackled him, sending both of them into a ditch. Hope's hair tie caught on her gun, and as she pulled it away, her hair tumbled around her in a jumbled mess. Jay brushed dirt out of a nasty scrape and scowled at her.

"Did you have to skin me alive?"

"Look, either I shove you over and dive after you or one of both of us get shot. Now we have to figure out where Christy is."

Jay glanced up and down the ditch, looking for some place to creep up unseen. "There. Be right back."

He ran, crouching to avoid being seen, to a bush about fifty feet away. Using it for cover, Jay peeked out at the road and took a quick survey of the area. He tried giving a birdcall—pathetic as it was—and caught Hope's attention. He waved her back down the ditch about twenty feet until she was almost even with Christy and signaled for her to stand and fire. Christy went down.

"Yes!" Hope pumped her fist and raced to Jay's perch.

"Well done. Now look over there," he said. "See that knothole in that fence?"

Hope's eyes, almost fierce in their intensity, zeroed in on the spot in the fence. Seconds later, the knothole turned bright pink before showing empty again. Hope bounced. "It's Malia. She was wearing her favorite t-shirt, 'Grumpy is in the eyes of the beholder.'"

Jay nodded. "Okay, you cover me and I'll run across the street and use that gate there to shoot her and run back. Can you do that?"

Hope grinned but shook her head. "I'll do you one better. I'll cover you on the way over. You shoot her and then we duck behind that old car. I see Jim Bradley up in the Timmons' tree house. He's picking people off on Walnut Street. If we're quick, we can get her and him almost at the same time." She gave him exactly half a second to absorb the information before she added, "Ready? Go!"

Before Jay knew what had happened, Hope half-dragged him across the street at breakneck speed. He jumped into the yard, shot Malia, and then dove behind a decrepit '63 Chevy. Blood ran down Hope's neck, but she was gone before he could try to mop it up.

Jim Bradley caught sight of her as she dashed into the Timmons' backyard. Jay tried to get in a shot, but failed. As a last resort, he charged up behind Hope, pushing her out of the way, and scrambled behind a bush. Hope followed, panting.

"We're trapped," she gasped.

"I know. He is too, though. If he comes to get one of us, the other will pick him off, and he knows it."

Frantically, Hope glanced around her as if some brilliant plan hid behind some bush or rock. He saw the light in her eyes, the expression on her face, but before he could stop her, she kicked two fence boards out of the fence and squeezed through. "Come on!"

Amazed, Jay followed. They grabbed the boards and pounded them back into the fence, using the buts of their guns. "Remind me to make sure the Timmons' aren't upset. I doubt it. The fence loses half a dozen—"

"Can we talk about this somewhere that we're not exposed?" Jay hissed.

"Right. Ditch. Go!"

They dashed between trees and behind cars before crossing the street and jumping into the culvert. One of the guys from Westbury sat in the ditch, tying his shoes. Jay managed to shoot him before he could even grab his gun.

"Good job, Jay!" she cheered as she gave him a high-five. "Sorry, Chad. Feels almost like cheating to take you out for a shoelace."

"That's okay." Chad handed over his gun. "Take it. I've hardly fired it." Despite his nonchalance, the guy looked disgusted with himself. "I'm dying to get something to drink. I'm parched."

Hope stopped Chad from climbing out of the culvert. "Go down that way about forty yards. See that bush? Climb out on the other side, dash across the street, and then try to make it look like you came from that way."

Chad winked and took off in the indicated direction. Hope grinned. "Helps to be the birthday girl."

Amazed at her ability to keep her mind in the game, not to mention her extreme competitiveness, Jay said, "Hope, you're hopeless."

"I'd say I'm hopeful."

His laughter rang out loudly. Hope clamped her hand over his mouth. "Shh! Do you want to give us away? Oh, great! Hear the feet? Get ready."

Jay couldn't believe her persistence—her determination to win the game at any cost. He stifled a laugh as she rigged up one gun ready to shoot and then moved several feet away. She waved him back to one spot and hissed, "Over there! You shoot, I'll shoot, and then I'll actually get him from this one. He won't expect a third."

Her glee amused him. Shot one fired, the beam missing by a wide berth. Jay shot almost immediately after it. Mark Franklin whirled back to where the first one had been fired and waited, hiding behind a tree. Jay felt sorry for him. It was almost too easy. Hope stood, took quick aim, and then took Mark out of the game.

"Hey! Three guns! No fair!" Mark cried as he jogged across the street. He grinned at Hope and tossed her his gun as well. "Get someone else. Get him good. I'll go get you guys some water. There are at least three teams left. If you win, I'll buy the batteries for the next game."

"You're on." Hope passed the second spare gun to Jay and nodded her head in the other direction. "Thanks for the water. We'll meet you down by that tree at the end of Ash."

Hope and Jay deliberated over their options. They had to

leave the ditch or they'd never win. However, the relative safety of their present position was tempting. "I just don't want to win by default," she grumbled.

"Okay, so what if we work our way back to your house, picking people off as we go that way?"

"Let's go!"

They dodged, with relative stealth, between cars, behind fences, and beside garages, as they worked their way up the first street. Residents peeked out of windows in air-conditioned comfort and watched as Jay and Hope, sweat soaking their clothes, searched for their last opponents. Streetlights flickered in the twilight as the commando pair peeked around the corner at Cottonwood Lane.

"Clear. Let's roll." Hope raced for the next parked car. Jay followed, stifling a guffaw that would surely get him clobbered. She sounded like an actor in a television crime drama.

Just as she moved to race for the next car, Jay saw a reflection in a nearby house's window. Instinctively, Jay grabbed her and pulled her back, clamping his hand over her mouth. "I see long dark hair in that window there." He pointed to the house. "Is that inside the house or behind us?" he whispered in her ear.

"That's Kirky—definitely a reflection," she whispered back. "Good catch."

"You take the back of the car, and I'll take the front. Count to ten and come out blazing." Jay crept to the other corner of the car, counting slowly.

On ten, they came out shooting. Kirky stumbled, spun wildly, clutched at her chest, and as soon as she stood on soft grass, collapsed to the ground, gasping, "Tell my mother—I—love—" Her head dramatically flopped over before she finished.

Mesmerized by the scene played out before him, Jay didn't notice that Hope wasn't watching. He felt himself jerked back behind the car and winced as his tailbone connected with the pavement. "Pay attention," she hissed. "You're gonna get us killed. Kirky is just playing it up to distract us."

He stared at her. As he mentally tallied her injuries and his own, Jay realized that he should have added a jumbo-sized first-aid kit to the pile of packages. Her arm now sported a fresh gouge from the car's license plate holder. "Do you have to take it so seriously? You're going to get one of us permanently maimed!"

Hope ignored the question and gestured for him to repeat their last kill. She dashed out behind the car, taking out Kirky's boyfriend before Jay could react. As she retreated to their holding position, she grinned at him wickedly. "I may be maimed, but at least we'll win."

Jay shrugged and prepared himself for what he expected to be a brutal last few minutes of the game. After seeing what she was willing to endure, he decided that if they managed to avoid breaking bones, he would consider it a successful conclusion to the day. Something caught his eye. "Over there. Behind that tree. I'll get him."

Too late. Hope raced behind cars and had the player down before Jay could take a single step. Within minutes, they had everyone down except for Brian Donaldson. While Hope scoured streets and yards for some clue, Jay could do nothing but fantasize about the water they had been promised.

Jay spied a hose trickling water onto the base of a small tree. He dashed to it for a quick drink. Hope followed. "Oh, this is good. Where is Mark with the water?"

"We left Ash. I bet he doesn't want to give us away."

Hope nodded and replaced the hose. "So where do you think Brian went? Last I saw, he was hiding behind that minivan up there, but I don't see him now."

Before Jay could respond, sprinklers clicked on, sending them running for cover again. As she dashed behind the car, she tugged at Jay's sleeve. "He's over there. Behind that motorcycle, see?"

They strategized. Jay was tempted to put himself in the line of fire in order to give Hope a clear shot, but he didn't like that idea. Quitting was distasteful, and he knew instinctively that she'd lose respect for him. She'd fight until she won or went down fighting.

Brian crept along the garage and ducked behind a pillar near the door, the garage blocking their aim. Hope's eyes widened and pulled him close. "That's Mrs. Wrigley's house. She'll let me come in through the back door and nab him. Go around the other side of the garage and wait in case he moves before I get there."

A bit dazed, Jay followed to the other side of the garage and watched, amazed, as Hope jumped the fence. What wouldn't she do to win the game? He heard a shout and footsteps coming his way. Just as Brian rounded the corner, Hope and Jay shot simultaneously.

"Yes!" Hope pumped her fist and did a little hop-skip-jig. "We did it!"

Jay followed Hope and Brian as they strolled toward her home, discussing who took out whom and how. He still marveled at the intensity with which she played the game. Matted with mud, twigs, and leaves, her hair looked horrible. Her clothes were torn and stained with grass, mud, and blood. She stumbled over her shoelaces. Dried blood marked several cuts and one nasty gouge still oozed.

As they reached the drive, an idea formed in Jay's mind. He smiled. He jumped in his car and drove off into the night without a word. Hope stood, hands on hips, watching him — bewildered.

CHAPTER 15

The crowd slowly dispersed, leaving plates of partially eaten birthday cake stacked in trashcans and on the counters. Half-empty punch cups littered every possible surface. Jay stepped into the living room just as Hope started to clear away the muck.

"Hope?"

She glanced up at him, smiling into his eyes. "Where'd you go earlier? One minute you were right behind us and then bam! Gone."

"You'll find out later." He took the cups from her hands and motioned for her to go upstairs. "Take a shower and clean those wounds. I'll take care of this."

He saw her start to protest, and glared pointedly at the gash on her arm that had started oozing again. Exasperated, she nodded. "Okay. Be down in a few."

"Bring some antibiotic cream and some bandages with you. That looks nasty."

Ron entered the kitchen as Jay bagged up the garbage and took the bag from him. "Why don't you go take a shower in that bathroom in there? I'll get you my robe. Oh, I've got a pair of swim trunks with a drawstring. Those and a t-shirt should work."

"I'll wait until she's done. I don't want to take all her hot water."

Hope's father pointed to the bathroom behind the stairs.

121

"This floor has its own water heater. Towels are in the cabinet to the left of the shower. Leave the door unlocked, and I'll put clothes in there in a minute."

Jay hesitated before hurrying to the bathroom. He could be in and out of the shower faster than Hope could. As he stood under the hot stream, the grime, sweat, and fatigue washed down the drain and out of his life.

He dressed quickly and hurried out to vacuum before she came downstairs. It worked. Jay finished just as she crept down the stairs, her arms full of a large basket of what looked like medical supplies. As he wound the cord around the vacuum, he pointed to the couch. "You, sit."

"Yessir."

Ron laughed as he dug through home movies. "How did you get that kind of respect out of her?"

"I earned it through blood, sweat—"

"Yeah, yeah. Whatever." Hope nudged him. "Here's the misery basket."

He dabbed peroxide on Hope's cuts and scrapes, wincing with her with each dab of the cotton ball. She sighed. "I feel silly."

Jay smiled into Hope's eyes. "Why, silly?" They winced as he worked to clean around the biggest gash.

"In movies guys always get hurt and have to be patched up, but I'm the one with all the cuts and bruises," Hope sniffed with a mock-injured air.

"Not all," Jay insisted. "I'm still sitting gingerly, thanks to you. I think you cracked my tailbone!"

"You were going to get us shot! I had to!"

Jay rolled his eyes. "Had to. Right." He reached beside the couch and passed a large gift bag to her. "Here."

Hope fingered the gift bag and its wads of tissue paper packing the contents. She looked at him, surprised. "I thought the laser guns were my gift."

"They would have been, but everyone contributed so much that I doubt I had to pay for a package of batteries. This is my real gift."

Hope pulled fistfuls of crumpled tissue paper from the bag,

revealing a modest-sized baby doll. Dressed in a sleeper, the doll sported a bottle and a pacifier as this season's hottest doll accessories. Hope stared at him, and asked, "A doll?"

"I thought you needed a safer toy—one less likely to leave you scarred for life."

Ron's laughter that began at the words "safer toy" fizzled into a choked sob. He stood and left the room, leaving Jay confused and Hope near tears. "Wha—"

"This one might not scar me," she whispered, "but a real one would."

That surprised him. "You don't like children?"

"Of course, I like children. Who doesn't?" The spark was back in her voice.

"I don't understand the part about scarred for life with a real child, then."

"I'm sorry, Jay. It… it was a saying of Mom's. She would always say, 'A woman's children scar her for life. Once she feels that first kick in her womb, they are indelibly etched on her soul.'"

Her smile—the playful punch she gave him almost convinced him that Hope was okay talking about this. However, her stoic façade disappeared as tears welled in her eyes. She tried to blink them away, as she reached across him for a tissue. "I'm sorry," she whispered. "I thought I was fine."

Jay glanced helplessly at the stairs, seeking help from the man who disappeared up them just moments earlier. Deep wrenching sobs shook her as the pain of the past few weeks exploded in a torrent of tears. He'd listened to her talk about having the blessing of a mother like hers for so many years, but these tears told him she needed the release. He took a deep breath, stuffed aside his own discomfort, and wrapped comforting arms around her, holding her as she sobbed out her loss and sorrow.

Ron crept down the stairs at the desperate sound of her cries. He sat across from them, his own tears streaming down his face. Hope felt heavier and heavier until she grew limp. His eyes questioned Ron.

"She's asleep," Ron mouthed.

It took him thirty seconds to decide to carry her to bed. If she woke, so be it. He scooted off the couch before lifting her and struggling up the stairs. She hardly shifted as he laid her on the bed, but she looked cold and vulnerable despite the August heat trying to press in from outside. He pulled a throw from the end of the bed, pulled it over her, and crept from the room.

Downstairs, he sent Ron an apologetic glance. "She's still sleeping. I'm sorry. I didn't—"

Ron interrupted him. "You couldn't have known, and it's probably for the best. Hope is a little too levelheaded for her own good sometimes. She needed the release."

"I understand that," Jay said. "I've worried about her."

"She tries to be so strong for my sake, but she misses her mother terribly." Silence hovered until Ron continued. "You know, she didn't want to go to the university. I mean, she was excited about the experience—classes, dorm life—but she knew she'd miss us and it was so soon after Con's death..."

"That would be hard, but the school is close—only what? Forty minutes?"

"Yeah. As it turns out," Ron murmured, "maybe I should have let her stay."

As Jay thought about it, he shook his head. "I think you did the right thing, urging her to go like that." Ron started to protest, but Jay continued. "No, really. Just think about how much your wife enjoyed Hope's experiences—the play, preparing for the opera, everything. They made memories that can't be duplicated. You can't put your life on hold because of the 'what ifs.'"

Several seconds passed before Jay added emphatically, "You did the right thing."

Hope padded downstairs in the wee hours of the morning. She didn't remember falling asleep or climbing into bed, and her disorientation left her feeling vulnerable and alone. A huddled mass on the couch—one with black curls on top—brought everything back to mind.

124

Despite a growling stomach, she sat in her father's chair and watched Jay sleep. He'd been so comforting—even with the awkwardness of comforting her. Still, he handled the situation with the grace of a nineteenth-century gentleman. She started as the thought occurred to her. *That* was Jay's appeal. Being a gentleman was second-nature to him—so much so that it never seemed affected.

Jay rolled onto his back in an awkward position. She wanted to try to rearrange him so that he'd look more comfortable but knew he would likely awaken if she did. Instead, she smiled as she watched him sleep. He shifted, snorted, and then snored lightly before rolling over onto his side. Something about his features reminded her of a picture of an Indian orphan that had once hung on their refrigerator.

Hugging her knees to her chest, Hope prayed fervently that Jay would come face to face with Jesus, and, like Jacob, that his life would be preserved. She prayed for his parents—that they too would learn to love her Savior as their own. New tears slid down her cheeks as she poured out her heart to the Lord.

Jay awoke and saw her crying. "I'm so sorry, Hope." His voice, husky with sleep, broke as he struggled to speak.

"I'm not crying about Mom anymore."

He raised himself on one elbow and cocked his head, looking curious, boyish, and, if she were honest with herself, utterly adorable. The urge to tease him welled up in her heart but she stamped it down again. It didn't seem appropriate. "I was praying."

His eyes softened. "Praying for what?"

"For you… well, you and your parents."

She watched the emotions flicker over his face. Was he always so transparent? She didn't think so. Perhaps interrupted sleep was the difference. Regardless, she saw in him curiosity that told her he wanted to know but wouldn't ask. "Thank you."

Her soft laughter scattered through the room. "You want to ask why I prayed for you, but you don't know if you should."

"It seemed like a personal question."

"It is." Hope laughed again as Jay tried to rearrange his features into nonchalant acceptance. "It's personal to you, not to

125

me. Some people don't want to know what you prayed."

He nodded slowly, glancing at her face and then down at his hands before meeting her eyes once more. "Do you mind sharing? I will understa—"

"I don't mind at all," she said, interrupting. "I prayed that you and your parents would see Jesus in all His majesty and humility—that you'd see Him as your Creator and your Savior." His eyes, curious and unoffended encouraged her to continue. Almost in a whisper she added, "I prayed that your knees would bow and your tongue would confess Jesus Christ as your Lord—soon."

"That sounds familiar." His eyebrows furrowed as he tried to recollect the verses. "It's from one of those books after Acts—about the return of Jesus to Earth, isn't it?"

Hope tried, rather than succeeded, to mask her surprise. "Well, I was using it in another context, but yes, it was written as a description of the second coming of Christ."

She watched as he digested her words. Disappointment battled with exultation as she saw that he did not believe—yet. "You want to believe." Hope spoke simply, as if stating the color of the sky or grass.

From his place on the couch, Jay watched the emotions flicker over Hope's face. If he told her—if he tried to explain his doubts and questions—she might try to persuade him like the official in Acts. He did not want to be "almost persuaded." He wanted full understanding or none.

"Hope, I just—"

"It's okay, Jay. You have no pressure from me. Keep reading when you want to, and we can talk when or if you're ready."

CHAPTER 16

As he pulled out his ringing phone, Jay glanced at the clock on his laptop. Noon—did she want to go have lunch? That could be interesting. Her voice sent ripples through him that he didn't dare examine. "Hope…"

"Hey, are you busy?"

His heart plummeted. Something in her tone hinted at trouble. "Not at all. Let me ask Greg to bring me back something from the deli—hold on." He used the time it took to walk to Greg's office and pass the man ten dollars to collect his rational thoughts. As he turned, he said, "Okay, what's up?"

"Dad wants me to go back to school—apparently he and Mom even re-enrolled me in the classes I missed last semester so I wouldn't have that as an excuse."

Jay settled into his chair and propped his feet on his wastepaper basket. "I think you'll have to explain the problem. The idea sounds good to me, but that could be because it means you'd be closer to me," he hastened to add. "It could possibly be pure selfishness."

"Very funny."

"What's wrong with the idea, Hope?"

"It's this house—our life. I had no idea how much work it takes to run a home."

"Okay… I don't quite follow. What does that have to do with you and school?"

"I—oh, I don't know how to explain it. You know, when I

was a kid, I woke up in a clean room with clean windows, fresh sheets, and vacuumed floors. I put on freshly washed — sometimes ironed — clothes and shoes. Heck, until I was, like, ten, Mom bought most of my shoes while I was doing something I'd rather do than shop."

"Those days are long gone," Jay joked.

"Perhaps. I might learn to hate it soon." She sighed.

"I still don't understand your point."

"The point is that this isn't all. Downstairs, we lived in a well-decorated and ordered home, ate food prepared and procured for us by Mom. I went to school, and while I was gone, Mom bought more food, cleaned the bathrooms, washed the clothes, vacuumed the carpets, shopped for everything we needed, and that is just the beginning — "

Jay interrupted, hoping he didn't sound obtuse. "Still not following you. Can you tell me what this has to do with Hope Senior and college?"

"It's just that every day I wake up and it takes most of the morning to do everything. I don't have that work rhythm thing that people get where they go on autopilot and get things done in half the time as others. If I don't start dinner by noon, we don't eat on time. I don't have the skills to know that this thing and that thing work together. I have to follow every recipe to the letter."

"Ok... so maybe you eat simpler foods that don't require so much effort — bake a chicken, steam some veggies. Or, maybe you let the cafeteria cook for you and your Dad can eat what he likes."

As if he hadn't spoken, she continued her rant. "Don't even get me started on bill paying. How can he possibly do it all?"

"Maybe," Jay tried again, "everything doesn't have to be done every day. If no one is home all day, who is there to make things dirty? Maybe his bathroom gets cleaned twice a week or whatever, but the other one not until the weekends, or maybe it won't need so much vacuuming. Is that even good for carpets?" Her workload did seem exhausting, but he wondered if all of it was even necessary.

"It won't work, Jay. Dad has severe allergies. If he'd get rid of the carpet, sure. We could cut the work, but he wants his carpets. That means daily vacuuming of the whole stupid house. Laundry, meals, clean up after meals — and not doing the bathroom every day — gross! He can't just not eat or wear clean clothes."

Jay rumpled his hair and tried again. "Well, outside of meals, can't he do most of the work on weekends? Aside from vacuuming and wiping down the one bathroom he uses every day — of course."

"Would you want to come home to more work after spending all day dealing with teen angst?"

He could not say it. The temptation was right there, taunting him. If he kept quiet, she would not get angry. His honesty forbade him from hiding it. "I'd say that a grown man should be able to decide for himself how he wants to spend his off time. Not to mention, the outlet might be helpful and preferable to dealing with an empty house."

"What about my being able to — *as a grown woman* — decide if I want to return to school or not?"

He laughed — really couldn't help himself. "Hope, I have bad news for you. Until you are married with half a dozen kids and at least as many gray hairs, your father will be incapable of considering you a grown woman. It's genetically impossible."

Thankfully, she laughed. They'd maneuvered through that minefield safely enough. As long as she didn't open a new playing field, he'd be fine. A new thought occurred to him. "Hey, hire a housekeeper — someone to come in three days a week and do whatever needs to be done. You can go home on weekends and cook and freeze meals for him. I'll drive you and help."

Her silence unnerved him. How could that be offensive? Just as he was ready to apologize, she spoke. "That might work. He could even sell Mom's car to pay for it. Maybe I could take on a more traditional school schedule and finish earlier — "

"Don't, Hope. Don't kill another of your father's dreams. Don't do that to him. I don't think he could take it." The words were out before he could stop himself. She'd be angry — furious. He wouldn't blame her.

129

"Jay?"

"Mind my own business?"

"Not quite. I do want to go pray about this, though. I'll talk to you later."

Jay stared at the phone, wondering how far over the line he'd pushed her. He shoved his doubts and concerns for Hope from his mind and concentrated on the reports he had to finish for the next day's meeting. As he stared at the blurred letters on the sheet before him, pen poised to do absolutely nothing, he muttered, "Do guy friends send girl 'friends' flowers when they are sporting athlete's mouth from a recent foot invasion?"

A female colleague walking by his desk stopped and glared at him. Jay sighed. "I take it that's a no?"

The woman reached over and handed him the phone. "Just don't send red roses."

Hope still nursed her irritation with Jay when the doorbell rang. The sight of yet another bouquet of flowers did nothing to improve her mood. She wanted to scream, *The woman has been dead for two months already, give it a rest!*

Her frustration and discouragement must have shown, because the delivery woman nodded sagely, "I told him you'd rather have red roses."

A small smile grew into a grin as she accepted the bouquet. "Thank you!"

The vase full of sunflowers brightened the dining room as she dug into the vase for the card. She had no idea how enjoyable it would be to get flowers that were not accompanied by a "With Sympathy" card. She tore open the tiny envelope and stared at the three words:

Forgive me?

Jay

The delivery woman's comments prompted her to pull out her phone. She punched his number and waited for it to dial, praying he hadn't left work already. It'd be an hour before he got a chance to return her call once he pulled away from the office. Relief filled her heart as she heard him answer.

"Jay? Oh, I hoped you'd still be at work."

"No, I believe Hope is at home; Jay is at work."

"Ha, ha. Very funny. They're beautiful, though. Thank you. I love them."

"I am so glad. I thought I'd have to drive up there and do the prostrate begging thing." The relief in his sigh made her giggle. "They're all right, though? I had to go by what the woman described on the phone. I wasn't sure…"

"Oh, that reminds me—funny story. When I opened the door and saw the same gal who has come here weekly since Mom died, I didn't even notice what they were. I just didn't want to deal with another sympathy bouquet." She sighed. "I guess I must have looked disappointed because she said, 'I told him you'd rather have red roses!' Isn't that funny?"

Two hours after their conversation, Jay sat alone in his room, remembering. She had been so forgiving; or wasn't she truly offended? He didn't know. She had wanted to nurse her pain, though. That had been obvious.

Frustrated, he called. "Hope, I have a question."

"A question?"

So she hadn't expected him. Perhaps that was good. "In this book, um… Eh-fe-SEE-ens?"

"Ephesians?"

Jay nodded absently as he tried to formulate his question. "I really like this book, by the way." He found the verse he sought. "Ok, in chapter four at number twenty-seven, it says to be angry but do not sin. Those two things seem contradictory to me. Is it not wrong to be angry at all?"

She answered without hesitation. "I think it's kind of like the word love. There are many uses of the word angry just like there are many instances of the word love. I say I love pizza, but it isn't the same as if I say 'I love you' to my parents or my friends."

His mind followed her direction easily. "Okay, keep going.

I think I understand."

"Well, it's the same with anger. Selfish irritation and rage are obviously sin. It's never right to blow up over spilled milk—so to speak."

"My *appa* says, 'Pour it,' instead of 'Spill it,' when he wants you to speak."

"I really gotta meet this guy," she said, snickering. "Anyway, Jesus got angry, right? I mean, He got royally ticked at the moneychangers and their abuse of the temple. He was angry! He threw them out, overturned tables. He let His indignation show."

"Yes, I liked that part. It showed His humanity. I think I have read too much about a meek and gentle guy who had no backbone."

"Jesus definitely had backbone. Anyway, I think there's one more kind of anger that is justified—even if it's personal. Someone steals your property, lies to you, or maybe they ruin all the work you just did, or harmed your reputation. I think that's the kind of anger Paul talks about there." The line went quiet for a moment before she added, "I don't know for sure, of course. It's just how I've always seen it."

"It does make sense. So how are you 'angry' in that situation but not 'sinning?'"

She answered in a rush. "Well, it says, 'Don't let the sun go down on your wrath.' That kind of implies to me that it is talking about anger that isn't sin. I mean, you can't resolve all righteous indignations before bedtime, but you *can* resolve your personal issues before you let too much time go by—if you're willing to die to self."

This Jay understood. Relieved, he asked, "So can you go to bed tonight anger-free?"

Her chuckle told him the answer would be yes long before she said, "Jay, I have a confession, but I have to tell you that, confession or not, you're not getting the flowers back."

"Tell me."

"I wasn't angry with you. I was angry with me. I knew I was wrong and it irritated me. It was easier to take it out on you than to deal with it. I'm sorry."

132

"Hope," he whispered, feeling very vulnerable but unable to stop himself, "that is what I like about you. You are who you are. There is no guessing who you will be today. If we can't take you as you are, well, that's our problem. I love it."

She chuckled and murmured, "Goodnight, Jay. I think you're getting tired. You sound sappy."

CHAPTER 17

A pair of brown boots appeared in his line of sight as Jay sat thinking.

"Hello, they told me downstairs that you could analyze me."

Jay dropped his pile of papers, grinning. "Hope! What are you doing here?"

She pretended to be affronted and turned to leave in a huff. "Well!"

"Get back over here. You know what I mean."

Hope dug through her purse and offered him a breath mint. "Want one?"

"Do I need one?"

"Very funny," she muttered. "I just had to come see where you work."

Jay accepted the mint and smiled at her. "What do you want to know?"

"What do you analyze and why?"

Jay watched her as he explained the basics of market analysis and why they paid him to do it. Her fascination with the global implications of a single product on the market spurred him to continue. "Retirement funds can be made and lost based upon the success or failure of that one product."

"Mind-boggling."

He grinned. "Isn't it?"

"How did you choose this? I've never heard of it before

now. I mean, I think I've heard the term, but not really heard about it."

A frown creased his face as Jay paused to answer her question. "Well, actually, I had never heard of it either. In my senior year—high school—my parents took me to a career specialist to figure out what I would be good at."

"You didn't have any interests?"

"Well, before my accident, I was really into computers. I spent hours working on graphics, playing games, recording things, but I don't know how to do that anymore."

"Wait," Hope looked confused. "You said you just had jumbled memories. You said your skills and information were fine—most of them."

He tried again. "What I mean is that I lost whatever used to give me the ideas of what to do. I was so confused between fact and fiction that they had to restructure my whole life so that I could find things and know what to do next." Jay studied his hands. "When I told the specialist about the high level of structure required for me to manage a basic existence—back then anyway—she suggested market analysis for those reasons. It's highly structured and organized."

"And you don't like that."

"I actually do like it most of the time," he tried to explain. "I just wish that I didn't know there was a part of me missing. I wish I didn't catch my mother looking at me and longing for the son she used to have." He felt the heat rising to his face and was grateful for dark skin that would hide it—or most of it. "I'm sorry. How morbid of me. Do you want me to show you around the offices? Meet Mike?"

He started to rise, but Hope reached across the desk, covering his hand with hers. "Whoa. This isn't morbid; this is you. Talk to me."

A glance around the office made up his mind. He had no desire to talk about his personal life in a room full of now curious onlookers. "Let's go get some lunch."

Jay mulled her words for days. Over enchiladas and the best pico de gallo he had ever eaten, she had stripped down his insecurities and refit them into a new package—one he wasn't afraid to open anymore.

"It's simple," she had said. "Your new structure didn't leave room for creativity. You need to take time to do things you did before—even if you don't do them well. Who cares? You started off doing them like a beginner and got good at it because the skills and interest were there. Just do that again."

Simple words—she was right about that. They were simple. They were also true. He just didn't know if he had the courage to try it. Knowing he once had a skill that he lost was discouraging enough. Discovering that it was irretrievable would feel like failure.

His phone buzzed, snapping him out of his self-pity. "Jay?"

"Hey, how's it going?"

She sounded breathless and hurried as she said, "Can you do something for me?"

"Sure. Anything."

"Oh, wait." She paused, as if for effect. "I may have to rethink my request with that answer."

Jay opted for laughter and a little flattery to keep him safe. "If it was anyone else, I would be nervous now, but I think I can trust you not to abuse my generosity."

"Yeah, yeah. Whatever. Look, some of the media-broadcasting majors are using our debate as a group project. They're filming us live on WRAC in..." The panic in her voice rose three notches. "Four minutes. Can you tape it for me? I have to go. Thanks if you can. I'll figure out your punishment if you can't—later. Bye!"

Jay dashed out of the office, dodging the mail guy and his boss, and into the media room. One hand fumbled with the remote, scanning channels as he tried to find the local PBS station while the other hand tried to work open the cover to the stack of blank DVDs. A voice from the doorway startled him.

"What are you doing?"

"Trying—hold on." He stopped at the PBS station and grabbed the DVD, slipping it into the recorder. "Sorry," Jay said as he turned to Mike. "Recording something for my friend Hope."

"Recording what?"

"If it's what I think it is, it's a debate for her philosophy class. You might want to see it." He tried to squeeze past. "I'll be right back. I'm going to get those reports to look over while I watch."

Mike waved him back into the room. "Sit down. The reports will wait. What's this about?"

"Hope has been preparing for this presentation in her philosophy class. She is trying to prove that you can't prove the existence of God."

"I thought," Mike began, his forehead wrinkled with concern, "that Hope was a Christian."

Jay nodded. "She is. That was the problem initially. The professor pitted the most outspoken Christian and atheist against each other. They each have a team behind them, but Hope says that the others have pulled back and are letting them duke it out alone."

Hope and another girl appeared on screen. Once the professor introduced them, the girls took their seats in director's chairs at the front of the lecture hall.

"Wait, the blonde is Hope?"

Jay grinned. He had expected Mike to assume the other girl was Hope. They couldn't have been more opposite. Petite, blonde, bouncy as a tied-down Tigger, Hope struggled to repress little jumps as she answered questions. The other girl, tall and dark-haired, sat looking nervous and miserable."

"She's animated, isn't she?"

Laughing, Jay nodded. "Isn't she, though? She speaks more eloquently with her body language than she does with words. She's always moving—talking. She's so full of energy."

"Whew. I was afraid I'd just insulted your girlfriend."

Jay let that slide as Hope made her opening speech. The room slowly filled with others who made themselves comfortable at tables, on the floor, or leaning against nearly every surface. Riveted to the screen, Jay hardly noticed the press of the people around him.

Hope spoke first, confidence oozing from every inch of her. "I kind of feel guilty. I kind of have the upper hand, which makes this a little unfair to my so-called opponent."

The professor interrupted and asked, "So-called?"

"Well, Dena and I ended up working together on most of this project, and we came to the same conclusion for opposite reasons. You cannot prove the existence of the God of the Bible."

Mike leaned forward, concern written across his face. Jay nudged him and murmured, "Trust me; her faith is stronger than ever."

Hope gave a brief introductory speech on what constitutes proof and how one arrives at a conclusion. She added particular emphasis on her point that proving part of a statement does not mean that the rest of the statement is not without flaw. "Where Dena and I deviate from our agreement is on the issue of faith."

The other girl nodded. "Exactly."

A snicker rippled through the media room. "That one's eloquent," someone remarked.

"I contend," Hope continued with an out of place bounce, "that we all have faith in something. For example, macro evolutionists require faith to believe that things evolve from one kind to another. I find it more logical to believe that we were each created by an Intelligent Creator to reproduce within our own kind. Dena," Hope added, "disagrees."

Hope went on to explain the difference between how she and Dena perceived creation and concluded with, "So, I believe it requires faith on anyone's part to explain how man came into being, and that premise is the foundation for my assertion that you ultimately cannot prove that the God of the Bible is real. At some point, it becomes a question of faith."

The discussion exploded from that point. While the two teams on the screen hotly debated the topic, the media room at Finch Investments sizzled with energy. The employees around the room took sides, with Hope drawing much more support than Jay would have expected.

Although students from each group rebutted arguments and fielded questions, Hope and Dena dominated the discussion. The professor seemed to delight in asking loaded questions clearly designed to fluster the girls. A surprising intellectual dynamo, Hope rarely fumbled. She shattered any expected stereotype of a weak, insecure, simplistic mindset. Her hands moved as consistently as her tongue as she eagerly accepted each challenge tossed her way.

Her concluding argument arrived all too soon for Jay. She clasped her hands in her lap for a full three seconds as she said, "So in conclusion, if it requires faith to prove the existence of the God of the Bible, and I believe that I have demonstrated that it does, one must use the Bible to ascertain how one obtains that faith. The Bible says it comes from itself. 'And so faith comes by hearing and hearing by the Word of God. Romans 10:17.'"

The professor interrupted her closing argument with a question. "But why should one give any credence to anything within the Bible? You seem to have reverted back to a faulty premise."

"Well, I was getting to that," she teased. "I'm a girl. I talk a lot." With a grin at her friend, Hope continued. "We can prove almost everything in the Bible — everything except for the deity of Christ and that His death was a sacrifice for sin. At that point, we must yield to faith. Why would anyone accept the proofs of the fall of Jericho, the existence of Jesus, and the foretelling of the destruction of Jerusalem in A.D. 70 as proven statements of historical fact recorded in the Bible and yet refuse to accept the sacrifice of Jesus? I believe Ephesians 2:8 and 9 answers that question. It says one must be 'quickened' by God and given the faith to believe. If this can be done by proof alone, then the faith that Scripture requires of us is unnecessary."

Jay jumped as the office erupted in cheers. As the room slowly emptied, he overheard one woman say, "It was refreshing to hear an argument that did not insist that simply because something was written in the Bible, everyone must take it as truth."

"But if you believe in the Bible," a man countered, "then you do have to accept everything in it as truth, so it only makes sense that Christians would do that."

"It makes sense for them," the woman argued. "What doesn't make sense is for them to expect it of me."

This set new thoughts swirling through his mind. If he accepted any part of the Bible, because of the rest of the content, he would have to accept it all. Although he'd known it—argued it even—until that moment, he had not embraced it. In the space of a few words and a few seconds, reading the Bible changed from an exercise in understanding a friend and curiosity in comparing religions. His Bible reading, and ultimate acceptance or rejection of it, would soon become a catalyst in his life. His stomach clenched.

His friend and racquetball buddy, Erik, paused as he left the room and said, "Interesting. Was that *the* Hope?"

"Yes."

"She's a little fanatical, but at least she's not obnoxious about it."

"She is a believer. I wouldn't respect her if she was halfhearted about her faith."

Erik threw up his hands in mock defense. "No foul! I'm not attacking her. I believe Jesus lived—was a good man and all that. I just don't believe He was 'God.'"

Jay tried not to wince as Erik's hands made air quotes as he said the word God. Although he knew it would open himself up to more than he wanted to discuss, he couldn't let it go. "I disagree."

Mike and Erik exclaimed simultaneously, "What?"

"I just meant," Jay almost stopped himself right there. He glanced at each man and shrugged. "Well, I do not believe that it is possible to believe that Jesus was a good man and not believe that He is God."

"Why not?"

Jay smiled at Mike. Mike knew exactly why not. "Jesus said he was God. He claimed deity. If He wasn't who He claimed to be, then He was a liar." The next words felt dragged from him. He didn't want to admit it, but he found himself saying, "If Jesus was not God, He was a fraud. I don't consider a lying fraud to be a 'good' man. You can't have it both ways. He's either a God or He was despicable."

"Have you been reading C.S. Lewis?"

Jay frowned at Mike. "Who?"

141

"Jay," Mike said, shaking his head. "You have a grasp on spiritual matters that some Christians haven't attempted to understand." He nudged Jay toward the door. "Go congratulate your friend. Just be sure that you're ready for the ConTemp presentation in the morning."

CHAPTER 18

"Did he really like it? I was so surprised that I wasn't nervous with that camera practically shoved in my face."

Over coffee, Jay and Hope hashed out the weaknesses in her arguments and discussed some of the stronger points. Jay pressed her about the archeological proofs of places and possible events. "Like Jericho. You said that they found the city and that the walls fell exactly the way it says in the Bible. Where do I read about that?"

"I don't know which chapter, but I know it's in the book of Joshua."

"And where is Joshua?" Jay pulled out his phone and paused, ready to type a note.

"It's about the sixth book of the Bible... yeah. Sixth. Just a couple before Ruth."

"Ahh, Ruth. I haven't been in that part of the Bible since I finished reading about Ruth and Bozo."

"Boaz!" Hope corrected, indignant.

"But Bozo sounds much more contemporary, don't you think?"

Once he began reading Joshua, Jay found himself lost in the Bible. The Old Testament stories were exciting, and he considered them much easier to take at face value. Jay read into

143

the wee hours of the morning until the troubles of Job were behind him.

His reading slowed during lunch the next day. He sat at his desk, munching on a burrito and struggling to get through the Psalms. Most were beautiful and easy to read, but some taxed his imagination. "It's like reading poetry," he muttered to himself.

"What?" Mike stopped beside his desk and glanced at the open book. "Oh, you're reading Psalms. There's a reason they call it one of the 'poetic' books."

"I see David in this. He must have written it because I can tell he's talking about Bathsheba. Some of these others, though. They're odd. Like this one a few chapters ahead—every other line is about God's everlasting mercy. You need it just to get through the chapter."

Mike's laughter sent the few remaining employees glancing their way. Jay looked up at him, apologetic. "Sorry, Mike. That was rude."

"It was honest. I suspect that there are quite a few Christians who have thought the same thing." He flipped a few pages. "When you get here, I think you'll like it better. Think *Poor Richard's Almanac* but inspired by God."

By the next day's lunch, he was through most of Proverbs. He reread the description of a virtuous wife. So much of it reminded him of his *amma*. She would like it.

The next book worried him. "Song of Solomon. I bet that's like Psalms. At least it's shorter," he muttered as he started into the book.

His eyebrows rose slightly as he read the first two sentences. At the end of the first chapter, Jay loosened his tie. Minutes later, he got up for a fresh bottle of water. Each sentence increased his discomfort until he found himself tempted to double check that his Bible hadn't morphed into a shady book of Hebrew erotica.

"You're telling me you're lovesick. Ugh." Jay read on,

144

occasionally glancing around him to ensure that no one could see the content of his reading. He felt like an adolescent, hiding in the bathroom with a lingerie catalog.

"What kind of woman wants to hear that she has fuzzy teeth? Hope, what is this thing?" he muttered as he read about teeth like sheep.

He grabbed his phone and punched Hope's number. Her chipper voice told him to leave a message at the tone. "Call me. I'm sitting here with my tie off, I should look like I have a sunburn, I feel guilty every time I hear voices, and I think my innocence is shattered. What kind of smutty book did you give me? I'll never look at a palm tree the same way again."

As he waited for her to return his call, Jay continued reading. Upon reading the verse following the first reference to a palm tree, Jay groaned. "Oh man!" Mortified, he wove through the office to Mike's door.

"Do you have any idea of a way to get back a voice message?"

Mike shook his head. "No, why?"

"Didn't think so. Be right back." He went to retrieve his Bible and returned, laying it on the desk. "I've been reading. Proverbs was good. You were right, but now…"

Even before he quit explaining, Mike's laughter filled the room. "What did you tell her?"

"I uh, asked her what kind of book she'd given me, told her about how embarrassing it was, and I um —"

"Oh, this is gonna be good. Spill it."

"I kind of said something about not being able to see palm trees innocently again."

"And…"

He shoved the Bible across the desk. "I think it's verse seven." As Mike read, shaking his head, Jay added, "Then, when you're done with that, keep reading verse eight. I thought Christians believe that sex is bad. Is this why they think that?"

Jay jumped up and shut the door as curious onlookers edged close to the office at Mike's fresh burst of laughter. "I can't believe I did this. How will I ever look her in the eyes again?"

"It's not that bad, Jay. The second she hears your message

145

she'll know what you were reading and why you're embarrassed."

"Why didn't she warn me?"

Mike shrugged. "She probably didn't think about it. I know a lot of people don't read it because it's just out of their comfort zone."

"It's erotic, that's for sure. Who knew there was something like that in a religious book? Doesn't it say in the other half that sex is bad?"

"How could it be bad, Jay? God designed it."

"People sure treat it like something nasty or an evil necessity."

"Then they're either wrong," Mike said, "or they are referring to its misuse. When removed from the protective boundary of marriage, sex becomes defiled and often degrading. Within marriage, Song of Solomon is a beautiful expression of sexual intimacy." He shook his head. "Or it's supposed to be. For a lot of Westerners, it's too Eastern for us to appreciate, hence the fuzzy teeth."

"It's a cultural nightmare, definitely. I can't imagine how provocative it would be if someone wrote it with imagery of today's ideas and described with our pictures of beauty."

Mike nodded, his eyes thoughtful. He leaned back in his chair, folded his hands behind his head, and observed Jay. "That's incredibly insightful."

"Thanks — I think."

"No, really. The purpose of the book — the main one anyway — is to demonstrate the subtle message of the love of Jesus for his bride — the church."

"Subtle? More like a ravishing embrace!"

Once more, Mike's attempts to contain his laughter failed. Jay eyed the door nervously. Mike choked down his mirth and took a swig of water from his bottle. "Sorry. You know, you're right. Jesus' love for us is similar to a man who would go through any tortures — anything — just to protect and save His beloved from danger. Song of Solomon tries to show that and debunks the common misconceptions of the world about what the Bible says on the subject."

146

As they discussed the subject further, Jay gained a new respect for Mary's virginity and spun his mind off on a new tangent. "I knew Christians respected virginity, I just thought it was because of the whole, 'sex is bad' thing."

"Just the reverse. We are supposed to respect and treasure virginity outside of marriage. These days, too often people ignore purity."

"So if a Christian isn't a virgin and wants to get married, what happens then?"

Mike waved his hands to stop Jay. "If you're concerned about past relationships, I need to assure you that Jesus washes that all clean."

"That wasn't exactly my question, but it helps. I can't be sure if I am or am not—stupid memory thing. It wouldn't be out of any great virtue if I am, though."

With a gentle push, Mike slid his Bible back across the desk. "Then the answer to the question I think you are asking is yes. Christians will marry those who did not wait. My wife will tell you that she regrets her past, but even more, she wishes she hadn't spent so many years focused on her failures instead of embracing her cleansing in Christ."

"So you married—" he stopped midsentence, embarrassed. It was none of his business.

"Yes. She doesn't hide it or care if I share it. Before Jesus, she was a very lost and lonely girl looking for attention. She's beautiful, so she got it."

Jay stared at a pen on the desk, his mind mulling Mike's comments. "And now," he sighed, "I've insulted Hope because I overreacted to a silly metaphor."

"I've seen worse—trust me."

"Worse than—"

"Trust me. Did you meet Nolan—yeah. You met him and Grace, right? Before they were married..." Mike grabbed the Bible again and drew it close. He flipped through it, stopping at a verse in Proverbs. "Here. This one." Mike slid the book back across the desk and chuckled. "He put that reference on the card when he meant another one."

"He sent her a Bible verse about breasts—before they were

147

married?"

"Before they were even interested in each other—total accident. Her brother slugged him. Eventually, after everyone settled down, it was hilarious."

"So what you're saying," Jay interjected, anxious to change the subject, "is that if I become a Christian, I'd be fortunate because my past would be wiped both from my mind and my soul—so to speak—whereas, most people still have their memories to drag them back into the pit that Jesus pulled them out of?"

Mike shook his head. "You amaze me. Are you sure you don't believe? You grasp the truths of Scripture in a way that explains them clearly."

"You read Song of Solomon."

"You think?"

She tried again. "I—I spent fifteen minutes trying to figure out what you were talking about. I kind of remembered something about cedars, but not palm trees. Pomegranates and pears but not—"

"You could have warned me," Jay teased, trying to stop her before the conversation got any more uncomfortable.

"I'm sorry. I tend to skip over that book."

"I've learned that is a common thing among some Christians."

"Well, I just thought it might be better to save it for if I get married. I—oh let's just pretend that I told you it's a lovely metaphor—or something."

Jay, ready to leave the land of embarrassing Bible books, decided to move onto safer topics. "Well, now that we've exhausted that subject, I wondered if you would help me with a project."

"And what kind of project would that be?"

Jay teased her about the wisdom of refusing to agree without specifics before he told her his plan. "My *amma's* birthday is coming. She likes folk music, and," he sighed. "I

148

wanted to make a CD for her. I thought maybe if I had someone singing with me that maybe I would focus on the experience and less on the technical side of things."

"So like karaoke but recorded?"

He shook his head. "I can play the guitar. We can harmonize. We'll be Paul and Mary."

"Funny. Sounds great. When do we start?"

"I brought my guitar. I thought we could practice..."

"How long do we have?"

"About two weeks."

Hope pointed to the door. "Go get it. We don't have much time."

It took about a dozen notes before she clapped her hands and squealed. "Oh, your mom is going to love this! So what are her favorite songs?"

Jay sagged. He wasn't sure. "'Blowin' in the Wind'... I think. Not sure about the rest." She started to list anything she could remember, but Jay pulled out his phone and dialed his mother. "*Amma.* Hope and I were just talking about folk music and she asked what your favorite songs are. I know you like—"

Hope stifled a giggle as his mother's excited voice came through the phone loudly enough for her to hear. Jay punched the speakerphone button and placed the phone between them. Eyes closed, he shook his head as Amala interrupted him. "Oh! Hope. Why have you not brought her to meet us? I almost think she is a filament—no figment—of your imagination. Your father is rubbing off on me. I am so excited that I cannot speak properly."

"Well—"

"I know! You bring her home for my birthday present." Hope snickered at the mental picture and then laughed aloud at Jay's rolling eyes. Amala didn't seem to notice as she continued. "I will make *parathas* for dinner. I am so excited. You ask her and I will wait."

Jay raised his eyebrows. Hope nodded her answer and hopped up, doing a silly jig. "Well, from the crazy little dance she just did, I think she's coming and looking forward to your cooking."

149

"Oh, this is so exciting. I must go tell Raj—"

"Can you tell *Appa* after you tell us the songs?"

On the drive to Jay's house, Hope found herself uncharacteristically nervous. Her animated movements and natural exuberance seemed intensified—she even managed to scratch his cheek when her hand got a little too out of control while gesturing. Uncertain of what to expect at his house, she naively prepared herself for extreme culture shock.

"What if your mom doesn't like me?"

"Well, then we'll throw you out." Hope stared at him, her eyes never wavering. Jay glanced at her. "What?"

"I'm waiting for your eyes to twinkle or your lip to twitch or something to ascertain if you are joking or not."

"Ascertain? You are nervous! I'm joking. Laugh now."

She smiled at how just the right words could be so reassuring. "I feel stupid, but I guess I just really don't want your mom to think, 'Gee, I thought Jay had better taste in gir—friends.'"

Hope hadn't known what she had expected to find at the Brown home, but Jay's house was certainly not it. Her imagery of "little India" fell flat as she glanced at the tract home, underwhelmed. Hedges framed a simple walkway and well-manicured shrubbery kept the windows free of horticultural blockage.

Roman shades hung in the windows instead of the rich, exotic curtains she had imagined. As they stepped into the living room, it looked like any living room she'd ever entered—generic. There wasn't even an interesting figurine of Kali on an end table or wall shelf.

Just as a vague feeling of disappointment filled her, a petite Indian woman rushed down the hall to meet them. "She's adorable," Hope whispered to Jay.

Before Jay could introduce her, his mother enveloped Hope in a brief but enthusiastic hug. "I am so very happy to meet you. Jay speaks of you often. I am Amala and I hope you will feel

150

welcome in our home."

Jay strolled down the hall with her overnight case and pillow. "I'll be back in a minute."

"He can take care of it. Come talk to me while I finish dinner."

"Can I help?"

Amala pulled out a chair for her at the small kitchen table. "You sit and tell me about you. What do you study at the school?"

"That's kind of hard to explain." As Jay arrived, Hope threw him a silent plea for help, but he seated himself and leaned back, listening. "I was working on a Liberal Arts degree with a minor in English. I'm also enjoying taking unrelated classes that interest me."

"That is an interesting approach to school. Are you considering a change, or..."

"Not really. I want to be the children's librarian in Marshfield, but I like some of the fine arts classes and a bit of the journalism— Oh, and I am considering a videography class after the—" She stopped short as Jay dropped his head on his arms on the table and laughed, his shoulders shaking. "What?"

"It's just so very... you. The way you bounce from idea to idea, experiencing everything to its fullest."

"Well," she swallowed hard, "I guess I've learned that life really is too short to put off what you really want to do in favor of what you *think* you should today."

"Mrs. Bro—"

"I would be pleased if you would use my name—Amala. I want to be your friend. If you are comfortable with that, we would like to be friends, Raj and me."

Raj's eyes twinkled so like Jay's. "Comfortable! Who cares for comfortable? Wish is already our friend. She will be comfortable or she will be very trying."

Jay, Hope, and Amala snickered over Raj's twisted idioms. Between chortles that threatened to morph into full-blown

151

laughter, Hope choked, "I thought Wish was good, but very trying—aaak!"

Raj threw his wife and son an expression of exaggerated irritation while he nudged Hope. "You appreciate great wit and wisdom. You are a wise Wish. Jay makes many good jokes about your name, doesn't he?"

"I've heard a few... a day... for about a year..." She winked.

Amala interrupted the joking by standing and beckoning the rest to follow her. "Let us go open my presents in the living room. I know Jay has one. He has that look on his face when he is trying to hide a surprise."

Jay shrugged and went to retrieve the gift. His mother smoothed her hands over the wrapped CD case. The contents were obvious to anyone, but still she didn't open it. "Is it from the family? Did they make a DVD?" Something in Hope's expression made her eyes grow wide. "The phone call!"

She rushed to plug it into a stereo system and seconds later, the sounds of guitar strings filled the room. Hope hadn't heard him play the song that opened the CD. It sounded Indian, but played on the guitar, it had a more Western flavor. Mid-song, Raj stood, tears in the corners of his eyes, and left the room. He returned moments later with Jay's guitar in hand.

Jay reached for it, but Raj murmured, "Not now. Now we listen. Later you play."

Through each song, apart from the three instrumental solos, Hope relived the hours spent in the recording center—the silly jokes she'd made to get him to relax in front of the mic, the goofy outfits she'd worn. It all flooded back to her. She had enjoyed two weeks of relaxed fun in every free moment. Her eyes widened as she realized that Jay had twice managed to distract her from her grief without searing her heart in the process.

When Jay picked up his guitar to play one song before they all turned in for the night, Hope watched his parents as covertly as possible. Jay had been right. His mother missed the son she lost on the football field half a dozen years earlier.

"Jay, I will go get her towels, you show her the guest

152

room." To Hope, Amala added, "I hope you will not fall over the treadmill. It is a bit awkward in that little room, but—"

"I'll be fine, I'm sure," Hope interrupted.

As she passed a room with mats on the floor, she wondered why the exercise equipment wasn't in there. She stepped into the room Jay showed her and saw Raj enter the other room, closing the door behind him. "Um, Jay? I can sleep on the couch. They don't have to give up their room for me."

"They didn't."

She pointed to the room with the closed door. "There's no bed in there—"

"It was in there for about a week before *Amma* dragged it across the hall."

"I don't be—"

"Really," he insisted. "When I came home from the hospital, she practically bubble wrapped the entire house. She bought me a larger bed and bought their first western mattress too."

"They lived here for eight years without a mattress?"

"Yep. And they did try. They climbed into bed every night and out of it again by morning. *Appa* says his bones cannot take it."

Eyes wide, Hope murmured, "Mine couldn't take the floor!"

Amala strolled toward them, chiding Jay as she approached. "You leave her alone. She doesn't want to discuss mattresses. She wants a nice, long, hot bath. You go to bed."

Jay laughed. "She asked, *Amma*!"

"Hush." To Hope she said, "Jay will wash his teeth and then the bathroom is all yours. Just relax and take your time. Take a bath, relax—oh, and there are bubbles under the sink." With an indulgent smile, Amala hugged her son, waved at Hope, and disappeared into her room.

Hope stared at Jay. "Bubbles?"

"*Amma* watches a lot of movies. She must have been watching ones where women take long, luxurious bubble baths or something."

Amused and touched, Hope managed to avoid a smirk

153

when Jay handed her three candles from a nearby closet saying, "I don't think she noticed that they usually litter the surfaces with candles too. These will have to work."

"I so wish I could short-sheet your bed before you get in there."

Jay pointed to the bathroom. "Go soak. I'm going to read for a bit. I'll brush my teeth when you're done. Night," he whispered. "Thanks for coming. You made my *amma* very happy."

CHAPTER 19

Hope groaned as the doorbell rang again. "Coming!" she called as cheerfully as she could muster. With her hands held away from her, she hurried to the door. Through the door's side windows, she saw Jay holding two boxes in his arms. "Jay! Come in. My hands are covered in chicken marinade."

She didn't bother to wait to see if he heard. She rushed back to the kitchen as marinade dripped down her arms and into her sleeves. "Yuck!"

Oblivious to Jay's inability to open the door with his arms full, Hope went back to packaging her chicken breasts. She smiled as he stepped in the room carrying one box, and then frowned as he left again. The door shut and he reappeared with the other.

"Sorry."

"You have been busy."

"Way to state the obvious," she joked as she sealed each piece of meat separately and piled them on the counter by meat type. "Can you put that index card on top of those breasts — um chicken br — pieces."

"Sure." A glance at Jay told her he tried not to snicker at her embarrassment. She relaxed as he ignored the awkward moment and read the rest of the piles along the counter. "Chicken thighs, chicken legs, pork chops, lamb chops, ribs..." He stared at her. "This will last him for months!"

"That's kind of the idea. Okay, not months. But maybe two.

I think I have thirty pieces of meat and then I'll have about thirty dishes so that he's not eating casseroles every night."

As he watched her organize the food into small baskets, Jay shook his head. "I am afraid that what I brought isn't as well organized, and the serving sizes are probably too big."

"We can repackage it. No problem. I want Dad to be able to come in at breakfast, grab meat, side dish, casserole, vegetable — whatever — and pop them in the fridge until he gets home. He can come home, stick it all in the oven, and in an hour, bam. Dinner."

It took half an hour to reorganize and repackage Jay's food and cart it off to the freezer. Hope stood with the door wide open, talking to herself. "Okay, meats here… can I have that basket of lamb chops?"

Jay passed it. "Do you want the pork too?"

"Yeah,   okay   and   now   where   are   the   side dishes…vegetables, hey should I have added bread?"

She felt Jay's hands on her shoulders as he turned her around. "You're done here. Let's go."

"Wha—"

He led her to the living room and pointed to her favorite spot on the couch. "You, there." Without waiting to see if she complied, he rifled through their DVD collection and pulled out two boxes. "Which do you prefer?"

"*Captain America*, but—"

"No buts. Where's your dad?"

"He went to get dinner. He said it was silly to cook again after cooking all day."

"Okay, I'll get the rest of the stuff in the fridge and clean up." He preempted her argument. "No, really. Please. You're exhausted. You've had a long week at school, two busy weeks helping me, a late night at my home, and now a full day cooking. You need rest."

"But—"

"Did Jesus not tell people to serve each other? You served your father. Now it's my turn to serve you. You can't have service if someone doesn't let herself be served. Watch the movie."

156

Unable to argue against Jay's logic, Hope relented. Of course, she couldn't decide if he truly made as much sense as he seemed to or if she was just so tired that she couldn't refute faulty logic. Regardless, she appreciated the help and looked forward to dinner.

That thought sent her mind whirling. Her father didn't know Jay was coming. Would he order enough food? As quietly as she could, Hope climbed the stairs to call her father.

"Hey, Dad. Jay's here. Do we need to order a bit more? Maybe more fried rice and some beef lo mein?"

Jay came around the corner to ask where to find trash bags and found an empty living room. He started to call out for her when he heard the shower come on upstairs. Despite the awkwardness of rifling through someone's house, Jay began a general search through the kitchen. What he didn't find became more obvious than what he did. Trash bags, paper towels, dish soap, and cleanser were non-existent or on their way to extinction.

"If I hadn't just bought it all for *Amma*, I would never have noticed," he muttered to himself.

Just as he dumped the last pile from the dustpan into a giant leaf bag, Ron burst through the door with bags of Chinese food. "Hey, Jay. I heard you brought me enough food to last me until Christmas."

Hope entered the kitchen with her hair in a towel and looking much more refreshed. "I am *star*ving. That smells so good."

"It does," Jay agreed. "Sit down. We'll bring it."

"Oh, come on — "

"I agree with him. Sit."

The two-men-against-one-woman battle raged through dinner, but afterward, they settled into a relaxed recount of the dinner at Jay's home. "I wish you could have heard Raj call me 'Wish.' It was funny just because of how he said it."

"I *wish* I could have heard that CD. I imagine it was wonderful."

"Ha, ha. Very funny." Hope's attempt at indignation fizzled with a snicker.

"Well, I really would like to hear it someday."

Jay grabbed his jacket from a nearby chair and pulled a disc from the pocket. "I made a special copy for you. This one is longer than *Amma's*. I added some of our goof sessions as well as the finished pieces."

"Oh! Dad, put it on. Those sessions were an absolute riot."

As subtly as he could, Jay watched Ron as the CD played and Hope explained the recording process. The pain that seemed hardened around Ron's eyes slowly peeled away. How could a man endure such loss? His son—how he must ache for Concord. Even his daughter was gone much of the time. Who would not miss a daughter like Hope? But his wife—how he must long for his wife.

What did their God plan for them? Why such hardship? It felt like a small version of Job played out before his eyes. That thought prompted a question.

"I wondered about Jonah—"

Ron stood, bade them goodnight, and disappeared up the stairs. Hope's eyes followed, concern clouding them. "He doesn't like to talk about the Lord these days. I think he feels betrayed."

Jay nodded. "I imagine you are correct."

"I just wish he would talk to me."

"Hope, if anyone understands betrayal and how it feels, it is Jesus. He can take it until your father comes around."

Her eyes filled with a new sense of purpose—one he would have called hope. At that moment, she seemed a personification of the word. "Thanks. You're right. He's just hurting. He'll come around."

Ready to change the subject, Jay asked, "So what about Jonah? I understand him. I think he got a raw deal."

Hope pulled her knees up to her chest and wrapped her arms round them. "Really? He always seemed like a spoiled brat to me."

This sparked a new debate. Jay felt that the Lord God had not kept His Word. Hope focused on God's mercy displayed to the unworthy. They did both agree that Jonah was a selfish coward.

Round and round their argument went. Jay insisted that if criminals receive only mercy then there was no retribution for crime. Hope shook her head. "It's not that. We are fallen and sinful. We are not like a Holy, Righteous Judge. God has the right to pardon where we do not. James says, 'Judgment will be merciless to him who has shown no mercy; mercy triumphs over judgment.'"

"Okay, that makes sense. The condition of the judge determines the worth of his judgment. If he is a blameless judge, he alone can determine the fate of those who are not." Jay leaned back, his hands locked behind his head. "I still understand Jonah, though. I know I would have felt the same way.

They made quite a stir entering the Seniors' church the next morning. Those who remembered Jay smiled, their eyes darting toward Ron as if to ask the significance of his arrival. Jay did all he could to keep Hope ignorant of the mounting conjecture around him and only succeeded in making her assume he was uncomfortable. "It's ok. They remember you. They don't bite."

"I'm sure they don't, but I'm not taking any chances on you..."

"Very funny."

Jay had only attended one church service—the baccalaureate in high school—and only then because a friend was the main speaker. The service at Marshfield was much less formal than he had expected, but the order kept it from seeming irreverent to him. He enjoyed the music and the prayers fascinated him; they were much less formal than he expected but also much more intimate.

At last, the minister opened his Bible and began his sermon. Each second that passed ripped at Jay's soul. As the story unfolded, he grew edgy—unsettled. He was familiar with it—the tale of Saul and the prophet Samuel. His logical mind agreed with Samuel, but his heart felt that perhaps the prophet was a bit too hard on the king. After all, the spoils of war were given to the Lord.

The minister, however, spoke strongly against Saul, his disobedience, and how he deserved death. "Like we all do," he insisted. "We all deserve hell. I've learned to hate the word 'deserve.' I hear it daily. I go get ice cream and some woman is debating whether to get one scoop or two. The other woman with her says, 'Go ahead. You deserve it.' A commercial comes on the TV or radio and urges me to buy a new sound system because I 'deserve it.' That is a lot of excrement. I don't deserve it. I deserve hell. Every last one of us in this room deserves hell."

Jay squirmed.

"Our righteous and holy Father demands purity — something we cannot give. He demands blood for sin, and that we cannot give. We don't deserve heaven. We never can. Our righteousness is as what?"

The room around him murmured with the preacher, "Filthy rags." Jay wanted to vomit.

The sermon continued. Despite the uplifting assurance that Jesus had covered those impurities and made the Christian whole and pure again, Jay couldn't drag his mind from the distasteful assertion that he deserved nothing but hell. He had no trouble with the idea that he did wrong. Each time he came across the word sin in his reading, he had no doubt. The person did wrong. The idea, however, that one could not atone for that wrongdoing by upright behavior had eluded him.

Jay understood Jesus — respected Him. A small part of Jay resisted the idea of Jesus controlling his life, but sin had not been an issue — not until a sermon rocked his half-built foundation.

As he grew more rigid with each word Pastor Shatternmann spoke, Hope knew Jay was truly listening. She also recognized his resistance. She had seen the same look of utter panic and refusal in Kirky's face a few years earlier. While Jay braced himself for each piercing word from the pulpit, Hope prayed.

Hope waved from the curb as Jay drove out of the parking lot, down the street, and away from the church. He didn't return

160

the wave. Instead, he watched as she grew smaller and smaller and finally disappeared as he turned the corner.

Could she be friends with an unbeliever? He shook his head, disgusted with himself for the thought. Of course, she could. She had so far. She had been his best friend for the past year, but would she *remain* friends with an unbeliever?

Jay liked Jesus. He respected the Galilean who had turned the world upside down. He believed in the God who sent His Son as a helpless infant to save humanity.

Emotion welled up in him, forcing him to the side of the road. The picture of Jesus' crucifixion, now burned into his mind by the morning's sermon, made him shake with repressed tears until he could hold back no longer. Jay wept.

As he struggled to regain his composure, he wrestled with his thoughts on the sermon. He hated the idea that no one deserves recognition for his or her achievements. He despised the idea of hell regardless of the logic he saw behind purifying sin from existence in some fashion.

The sight of the off ramp to his boss' house gave him an idea. He took the exit and as he waited at the first light, he punched Mike's number on his cellphone. "Hey, it's Jay. Look, I'm sorry to bother you on a Sunday, but I need help. Who can I talk to about Jesus—someone I don't have to be afraid of offending?"

"Come on over."

"Are you sure? I'm close, but I'm probably going to be very antagonistic. The last thing I want to do is offend someone who has never offended me."

"Trust me. I can handle it. Nolan and Grace are on their way for lunch. Is it okay if they join the discussion?"

"Yeah. I guess. Be right there."

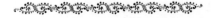

Jay sat with Mike, Nolan, and Grace in the Finch's living room, his head in his hands, defeat clouding his voice. "I'm afraid of losing my friend."

"Hope?"

Jay nodded back at Grace. "It sounds ridiculous, but I knew from that first day we talked—I had found a new best friend. I understood her. She understood me. She didn't put demands on me to change into someone else. That's pretty big because I'm still learning who I am and Hope is the first person I've met who truly understands *and* is okay with that."

Grace nodded. "I can understand your concern, but do you really think a person like you just described is going to dump a friendship if you reject Jesus?"

Jay groaned. "How can I reject Jesus?"

"Most people do, Jay. You wouldn't be the first," Mike said.

"You didn't answer my question," Grace reminded him. "Do you think Hope would abandon your friendship if you openly reject Christ? Be honest."

He shook his head. Hope wouldn't, but he knew that if their roles were reversed, he might. "No, I don't think so. I just think that in her place, my heart would be tempted away from Jesus. I would want to remove that temptation. If she had the same trouble..."

Nolan shook his head. "I'm confused. I thought you said this was a platonic friendship. Are you saying that you and Hope are romantically involved?"

Jay's head snapped up, giving him a sense of what whiplash must be like. "Of course not! Hope would never—and I would not treat her or her religion with such disrespect."

"Then I don't understand." Mike and Grace nodded their agreement with Nolan's confusion.

His head dropped back into his hands. "I don't either. I just know that the sermon I heard is making me crazy."

The discussion turned to sin, its consequences, and the penalty. These things Jay understood. He simply resisted the concept of man's depravity. He understood it—believed it—yet he fought it with a fierce intensity.

"The minister said that we do not deserve anything but hell"

"I agree with him," Mike said promptly.

"If a man works hard, saves long, and finally retires in relative prosperity, does he not deserve the fruit of his labors?"

Grace shook her head, smiling. "You are confusing earning and deserving. The man deserves hell. He earned his retirement."

"What about a man who has turned his life around. He was a drug addict, he stole, and he spent five years in jail. But he gets out of jail, goes to school, makes something of himself. Doesn't he deserve to get a second chance? Why should his past always overshadow him?" Jay was certain they would understand.

Grace's smile grew wider as she shook her head. "He earned a second chance; he deserves hell."

The debate raged. For an hour, two, they rehashed every aspect of sin, redemption, and man's utter dependence on the mercy of God. From the way that the trio of mentors before him reacted, he knew that at each moment, they expected him to relent. He never did. Dejected, he left the Finch home even more broken than when he came.

CHAPTER 20

Hope stared at her phone, willing it to ring. "Yeah, like Jay knows that you need help." She sighed. "I just need to call him, but—"

Disgusted with herself, she punched Jay's number and waited for him to answer. It had been almost two weeks since he drove away from the church—two weeks since she'd seen or talked to him. One email—he'd sent one telling her he was okay but struggling.

She'd given him all the space she could stand. She missed her friend, and now she needed his help.

His voicemail picked up, much to Hope's relief. "Hi, Jay. Sorry to bother you. I need help with my creative writing paper. Do you have time to have dinner or something and answer a few questions about your accident? I'll explain everything later. I'm on my way to class, so I'll turn the ringer off—just text something. Um, thanks. Hope you're okay. Bye."

Five minutes into her Classical Lit class, Hope's phone flashed. The message brought a smile to her face. I'LL BE AT YOUR DORM BY 6. CAN'T WAIT.

Hope finished her class with a lighter heart. The day dragged as she worked on the assignment, watched the door, and waited. At five-thirty, she gave up. She pulled on her jacket and rushed outdoors, her laptop bumping her hip uncomfortably.

The minutes ticked past even more slowly in the cool

autumn evening. "Two weeks until Thanksgiving," she murmured.

While she made plans for upcoming weeks, Jay pulled into the parking lot and saw Hope waiting for him. A lump filled his throat as he realized just how much he had missed her. He pulled up to the curb, leaned over, and opened the door. "Get in!"

Hope crawled into the car, shutting the door behind her. She held her hands up to the vents, letting the warm air defrost her fingers. "You're early."

"You're crazy. It's freezing out there. I would have come to the common room."

"I'm fine, really. I was hidden under the stairs. You wouldn't have seen me."

He drove her to the same restaurant they had visited almost one year ago. Once they were seated and waiting for their orders, Jay nodded at her laptop case. "So, what's up?"

"My creative writing paper." Hope explained the assignment, before moving onto her idea. "So, I thought about your accident and the memory — well, loss, I guess. I wondered what my life would be like if I had to start over like that. So I'm writing a fictional account of my own life with your accident."

Jay waited for her to open her laptop and then pulled it toward him and read. Although Hope had a good grasp of the extent of his accident, certain particulars were inaccurate. "Okay, see here when you don't know how you feel about your brother's death? That's not right. I would still remember him — still feel the loss even if the particulars of what happened are fuzzy. The more people confirm any memories I call up, the more I will remember and it will affect me."

"Oh, okay... so..."

"And the blessing part? That's partly correct. I mean, it would be a blessing not to have the awful memories that I know are true, but sometimes you feel lost all over again when you can't put things into proper perspective. Does that make sense?"

Hope pulled her computer back toward her and began to delete and make notes for corrections. "I wish I had brought a copy with me for you to go over while I make corrections. It'd be

166

so much faster."

"I've got a thumb drive in my laptop bag. I'll go get it." Jay took the last bite of his soup and stood. "Be right back."

They worked together for a good half hour before Jay finished his reading. "I like it. You have a good grasp on how it actually was. I mean, there are a few spots that I highlighted and made notes on how I actually felt in that scenario or what I did. You'll be able to tell if the difference between it and what you wrote is because of different direction you'd planned, a personality difference, a man versus woman difference..."

"Oh, that's perfect," Hope said, accepting the thumb drive. "I'll stick them up parallel and make some changes. This is great."

"One thing feels false, though. It seems like you're trying to turn it into a good thing that happened to you rather than the bad thing it is. It was an accident. It took away part of my life. You can't make that a good thing."

Hope's dejected expression made him wish he hadn't spoken. Before he could assure her that the story was good, she spoke. "I was thinking of that verse in Romans that says 'All things work together for the good of those who love Him' or something close to that. I wanted to show the beauty that God can bring from the ashes in our lives."

Jay pulled his Bible from the pocket of his laptop bag. He ignored the tears that sprung to her eyes at the sight of him having it close and tried to hide his embossed name on the cover. He didn't want to give her false hope. "Do you know where in Romans?" He began skimming from the first verse, but Hope stopped him.

"No, look. Back here is a concordance. It lists major themes such as love, faith, Malachi, etcetera. Maybe try good..." That failed, as did works. However, looking up "called" gave her the reference. "Romans 8:28. There."

Jay read the verse. Then he read the verses above and below it. He looked up several cross-references and then slid it across the table. "I think we understand this differently. You seem to believe it says that God will turn the bad into good. I think it says that God will take the bad and work *a* good through

167

it in your life—sort of a blessing for having to deal with the bad in the first place."

She nodded as his words sank into her heart. "I was trying to show a life that was better for having lost all memories—which is kind of an exaggeration of yours—rather than showing that blessings did come from it, despite the bad. I know how to fix this."

Her fingers flew across the keyboard as she made corrections and added to her story. Jay watched, fascinated by her intensity. She typed as though compelled. The server came; Jay paid the bill. The restaurant employees cleaned around them; Hope wrote. Jay spoke several times; Hope gave vague answers, proving she hadn't heard him.

"Hope, we need to let them close."

"That's a good idea." Hope continued to type.

Jay stood and moved behind her chair. She didn't stir. He reached around each side of her, grabbed a hand in each of his, and murmured close to her ear, "We need to go home."

The stilling of her fingers seemed to stop her mental wheels from spinning. Hope turned to Jay, his face still very close. "Have I been ignoring you?"

He stepped back, unable to resist smiling at the picture she made. Hope looked utterly charming as she tried to reinsert herself into the world around her. "A bit. But they want us to leave."

She glanced around at the empty restaurant, taking in the chairs hanging upside down from tables. She rolled her eyes. "How long have we been here?"

He glanced at her laptop screen. "It's five after ten."

Her eyes widened and then she cocked her head as she looked up at him. She crooked her finger, beckoning him closer. Jay bent a little, wondering what embarrassing food he had dribbled on his chin.

Hope now scrutinized him even more closely. "Jay, I have just discovered something."

Jay backed away, his tongue running over his teeth nervously. "Oh?"

"You are awfully handsome. Why didn't you ever tell me?"

She gave him another once over. "Why don't you have a girlfriend? Do your parents have some girl picked out for you in India? Do they still do that kind of arranged thing?"

Jay ignored the question about girls from India and hit control and S before closing her laptop. "We're leaving. You're punch drunk."

"Yeah, I may be punch drunk, but you're embarrassed. How cute is that?"

Jay eyed Hope as he slid her laptop into her case and handed it to her. "If I didn't know you were above it, I'd swear you were flirting with me, Hope Senior."

The cold night air blasted them as they left the restaurant. "You said it wrong," she teased. "You have to use my middle name."

"I don't know your middle name," Jay countered, grateful for the cool air on his warm face.

The drive back to her dorm was quiet, but not strained. As they neared, Hope spoke. "You're not offended, are you?"

"Offended?"

Hope tried again. "I mean about me commenting on your appearance. I can be kind of blunt when I'm surprised."

Jay felt both flattered and a little insulted. "You really have never noticed what I look like?"

"Well," she said after a few seconds, "I could have described you accurately—you know, height, hair color, eye color, approximate build, and stuff. I just never noticed how dreamy your eyes are!"

"So did I ask you if you were available to come to Mike's Christmas party with me?"

Hope snickered. "Are you changing the subject?"

"It depends. Did it work?"

"Well, no, you didn't ask, but if you'd like me to come, I'd love to. I even promise not to spend the evening telling all the women how handsome you are."

Jay growled and threatened fists of snow down her back after the party if she didn't quit teasing him. "I know how you play, Hope. I will not be merciful. Do not call what you think is a bluff." He pulled up to the curb. "I'll text you day and time. Are

169

you sure you don't want me to walk you in?"

"I'm good."

"I would say otherwise."

Hope grinned, thanked him, and climbed from the car. She waved back at him, cheerfully unaware of the turmoil she'd begun. He watched until she opened the common room door, thankful that she had refused his offer to walk her to her room.

He had managed to enjoy a friendship—without much thought of anything else—for almost a year. Any attraction that he felt from time to time, he had managed to squelch, reminding himself that it was wrong to consider her anything but a friend considering the religious differences between them. Thanks to Hope's sudden revelation at his supposed "dreamy eyes," he now knew he'd have to work harder in the future.

As he pulled onto the Loop, Jay remembered her saying, *"'Gee, I thought Jay had better taste in gi—friends.'"*

The abrupt change from girls to friends... Was it indicative of how she preferred him to perceive her? Could it be simply that she didn't want him to think she assumed that bringing her home to meet his family meant something—personal?

His phone rang. She waited impatiently, praying that he would pick it up. Hope grinned at his light Indian accent as he said, "Hello?"

"Jay! Dad and I would like to invite you and your parents to our house for Thanksgiving. Can you come?"

"I'd love to, but my parents won't be here. They leave for India on Thursday."

"India! Wow. Are they going to see your family?"

"My grandparents and some distant relatives."

She wondered if Jay minded being alone over the holiday, but didn't care to ask. "How long will they be gone?"

"About six weeks. They'll get home the Thursday after New Year's."

"So you'll be alone on Christmas?" Hope welled within her.

"Not if I don't want to be. Mike and Traci invited me to

spend the day with them, and our neighbor always invites us."

"Oh no. Nuh uh. You're coming here."

Jay laughed. "I'd like that too. Will you invite me for New Year's too so that your father can be fully sick of me?"

"No… but I'll invite you for New Year's so that my father and I don't spend the day missing Mom and Con."

"But you aren't hosting the party this year. I was just teasing you, Hope."

As he spoke, Hope realized that they might never host another New Year's party. "We always invite a few people— some of the elderly people from church or something. It's perfectly okay."

"So now I'm an old man?"

Hope gave a weak laugh and ended the conversation before the tears that welled up in her heart reached her eyes. "I'll see you at our house on Thursday—or Wednesday night, either one—feel free to come for the weekend. We eat at six on Thursday, but come much earlier. I think I'll need help if I want to avoid destroying this turkey."

CHAPTER 21

A strange scent slowly crept into the room. Ron's upper lip curled unflatteringly. "Hope, is there plastic on the stove? Maybe something in the bottom of the oven?"

Hope dashed for the oven, abandoning her game with Jay. A strange chemical smell overpowered her as she opened the oven. Ron came around the corner and groaned. "You didn't take out the giblets, did you?"

"Giblets? What are they?"

"Kidneys, liver, neck and all that stuff in a little plastic bag inside the turkey…"

"But there wasn't anything like that in there when I stuffed it. Just the neck and not in plastic. It's in the trash. I smell it, though. Eww."

Jay pulled the bird from the oven and set it on the stove. With the aid of oven mitts and a large knife, he slit the other end of the turkey, revealing the smoldering plastic bag. "*Amma* complained once about how they put them on opposite sides of the bird. I don't get that."

"Oh, no. What do we do now?" Hope wailed.

"We bake the little one I bought for sandwiches and have a late dinner."

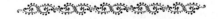

Stomachs stuffed and hearts full, Ron, Jay, and Hope

173

relaxed after their late dinner, watching the news without much interest in the projections of upcoming sales and the terrible economy. Hope reached up, pulling her hair from the ponytail she'd worn to keep her hair out of the food, and shook it out. Her hands massaged her scalp as she reached for a brush on the end table.

After two ineffectual swipes with the brush, she sank to the floor and scooted in front of Jay. "Can you brush this for me? My arms are exhausted."

Ron watched the scene, curious to see how Jay would handle something that for some men, would be quite intimate. The awkward way that Jay grasped the brush confirmed that Jay was indeed one of those men. Ron was torn—risk embarrassing their guest or potentially torture him?

Jay met Ron's eyes and gave a sheepish smile. Though he tried to work quickly, to Ron's amusement, a snarl on one side of her head prevented him as he worked to free her hair without removing half of it. With each brush stroke, Hope relaxed and Jay stiffened. Had Jay's distress not been so acute, it would have been comical.

Twice Jay offered her the brush and Hope shook her head, murmuring, "Not yet. That feels so good."

When Ron couldn't take watching Jay fight himself anymore, he spoke. "So, are you done with the hair? Can we play a game of hearts?"

Hope reached up and took the brush from Jay. As she stood, she said, "Thanks. Dad tried to brush my hair once. I still have hair left—proof that miracles still happen."

The game began almost as a study in their personalities. Hope played with a diabolical grin and a knack for avoiding the queen. Ron, on the other hand, played like a seasoned gambler, never giving away his position. Jay shot the moon.

"Hey! How'd you do that? I passed Dad the queen. That was smooth."

The game intensified. After a fierce battle, Jay won. Hope pretended to sulk and pout, but Ron saw that she recognized and respected Jay's marvelous game strategy.

Hope stood and shoved the cards to the middle of the table.

"You guys duke it out over war or something. I'm going to go take a shower." She winked at Jay. "Or would your dad say 'steal a shower?'"

"Probably."

"Well, my hair stinks like plastic gizzards, so I'm going to steal that shower."

As Hope ascended the stairs and sequestered herself in the bathroom, Ron met Jay's eyes. "I'm sorry. I never imagined that she would ask a man to brush her hair. I almost stopped her, but—"

"It's okay." Jay gathered the cards into the deck box. "I don't really think she would have asked just any man. She considers me a friend. You know, one of the girls she would invite for a slumber party while they brush each other's hair and make goop for their faces, or whatever girls do. She just seemed to really notice me last week."

"Does she know you love her?"

Jay's head snapped up and his eyes widened just a little. "I—"

"You didn't know?"

"No..." His head fought his heart for a moment before he sighed. "I guess if I had thought of it—really let myself think, I would have known. I just couldn't let myself go there," Jay admitted.

"She respects you, Jay. In my opinion, she couldn't find a better man..."

"But?"

"She won't even think about it if you don't believe in Jesus," Ron said.

"But I do."

Ron blinked. "You do?"

Ron listened as Jay explained how he wanted to accept the reality of hell but fought it. "I just can't reconcile the idea that I can't ensure I deserve more than hell. I know it in my head, but I guess I've embraced more of the American individualism than I realized."

"You're thinking about this all wrong. You believe Jesus is God?"

175

"Yes."

"You believe that He lived, died, and rose again for us?"

Jay nodded. "Absolutely."

"Then if you can believe — logically believe — without the help of the Holy Spirit, where does faith come in?"

Ron's words echoed in Jay's mind, bringing his own arguments to a screeching stop. He had been prepared to discuss his problems, his fight, his discomfort. He was not prepared to be challenged to accept on faith. "Is faith that powerful?" he whispered.

Ron nodded. "Definitely. But I think the real question you should ask is, 'Can I trust Jesus with this?'"

Jay pondered that thought and new questions sprung to mind. But just then, Hope bounded downstairs, wet hair dripping all over her, and talking a mile a minute. "I have an idea! I'll teach you more swing moves for the party. We can try to win the jitterbug contest this year."

"Should I be worried?" he asked Ron as the sounds of Big Band filled the room.

Ron nodded. "Very worried."

Despite Hope's best attempts to teach him, the moves failed — utterly. Ron snickered and Hope didn't even attempt to hide her mirth. Jay's feet scattered in every direction but the right one in his attempt to mimic her movements. Every twist, every turn, created a chain of subsequent moves, resulting in dance moves no one has ever seen — or should see.

"Can you have dyslexic feet?" Jay asked, collapsing on the couch.

"Come on, one more try."

Jay waved her off. "No way. I need sleep if I'm going to be up in time for the sales in the morning."

"Oh no! Traitor!" Hope mocked. "This has to go on the friendship application form in the future."

Ron snickered. "Well, have fun, Jay. I'll be nice and warm in my bed."

176

Black Friday sales seemed like exactly the kind of challenge Hope would love. Conquer the crowds, find the widget, save the money! Then again, Concord's accident had occurred on Black Friday. Maybe…

Hope interrupted his thoughts. "It's just lunacy to go out in the freezing cold to buy things you normally wouldn't just because they're cheaper than they were the week before."

"What about for Christmas presents? Isn't that the whole point?"

"But do people plan their presents around the sales or do they scour the sales for something that will suffice as a Christmas present? Are you truly giving what you would have at a better price? Or are you settling for just anything simply because it's cheap?"

The debate only continued for a few minutes before Hope conceded. "Well, I guess they call it 'Black Friday' because it's the day that puts many businesses 'in the black' for the year, I suppose it's good for something."

"Good for me. My realtor says I can move in early—next weekend. So, I intend to be one of the crazies in the cold tomorrow morning and I will buy myself several five-dollar appliances to get by until I discover what I want or need. I'll also buy those lamps that we saw—I liked those. Oh, and the microfiber bedspread."

"You're crazy."

"Yeah, but when I get back, this crazy guy will take you guys to breakfast. Sound like a plan?"

"Decent plan, but I've got a better one. I'll come with you and whine the whole time. I've never gone, so it'll be an experience."

Jay quirked an eyebrow at Ron. "She attacks that which she has not experienced."

Hope crossed her arms. "And she will remedy that."

177

CHAPTER 22

Jay and Hope shivered sixty feet from the door. Twenty people stood ahead of them in line, all waiting for the employees milling about the front of the store. Hope, teeth chattering, tried to complain about the situation. "I wish God were here."

"I'm ashamed of you. I thought you knew that God is always with you."

"I mean in the flesh. I want those everlasting arms that Isaiah spoke of. With God doing the wrapping, I'd be warm and toasty."

Jay swallowed hard and tried to think about his shopping list as Hope prattled on about the presence of God in their lives. "I wonder if the reflected light that enveloped Moses after he saw God had any other properties. I mean, did it have heat? They were in the desert. That could have been miserable!" She sighed. "A desert sounds good right about now."

"It wouldn't be that much warmer. Not this time of year."

A nearby teenager made a crude comment. Jay laughed at Hope, before giving the teenager a look that clearly said, "Mind your own business."

A woman behind them chatted with Hope about her shopping list. "I've been waiting for this for a month."

"What are you buying?" Jay loved the note of genuine interest in Hope's voice.

"A TV. Mine died last month. I'm going to be able to get a better set for a lot less money if I can manage to get one before they're all gone."

Hope strategized with the woman. She wrote out a list of what her new "friend" wanted and agreed to meet her in the front of the store in half an hour. "If we get duplicates, we can find someone who needs them."

"Thank you! Are you sure your husband won't mind?" The woman glanced at Jay before adding, "Oh, and I'm Mabel, by the way."

Jay rolled his eyes at the silly eye waggle she gave him before saying, "Oh, Jay's not my husband, poor unfortunate man that he is. He's just a friend. He won't mind." She glanced at him again. "Will you?"

"Not at all. I'll keep an eye out for anything I see too."

Mabel shook her head. "Oh, the line is moving. Good, my bones..."

Jay leaned close and murmured, "Don't compete for your place in line. It's not a game. You can't lose."

"You know me too well," she laughed.

Once inside the doors, she dashed for a cart and zoomed for the pallet of flat-screened TVs marked to a price that couldn't possibly make the store any money. Jay helped her put one in her cart, added one to his, and waved as he took off to find the items he wanted.

Half an hour later, every item on Mabel's list was in Hope's cart, along with a few things she decided she had to have as well. The principled part of her mind sneered at the impulse center until the sight of Mabel seated on a bench, assisted by paramedics, silenced both sections.

"What happened!"

Mabel glanced up at her as if a bit dazed and then said, "I reached for a cart when I came in and some man shoved me out of the way. I landed on my ankle and here I sit."

With fire in her eyes, Hope whirled to face the manager. "Did someone do something about that jerk? She could have been seriously hurt! She's on a fixed income! She depends upon

180

this sale. Oh, I hate this day!"

As Hope dissolved into tears, the manager assured her that they had ejected the offending customer from the store and offered to do her shopping for her. "She said someone else was doing it. Was that you?"

Hope attempted to gain a little self-control but barely managed a nod and a wave to the overloaded shopping cart near them. "I—" a stifled hiccough made her sound drunk. "I got it all." *Sniff.* "I—I'm sorry."

Deep wracking sobs overtook her, frightening Mabel. The older woman patted her shoulder and assured her, "I'm fine. It's okay. It's probably just a sprain."

When the paramedics called for a gurney to take Mabel to have an x-ray of her foot, Hope's feeble attempts to regain self-control fell apart. Her shoulders shook as she wept harder than ever.

Jay arrived and worked his way through the crowd to Hope's side. "Hey, are you—Mabel? What happened to you two?"

The manager groaned and pointed to the cart Jay had abandoned. "Can someone keep an eye on this man's cart?" he called to no one and everyone as a customer attempted to confiscate the comforter set piled on top.

An employee offered to ring up Jay's purchases at the customer service counter. Jay nodded. "That'd be great. Can you get the other one—is that yours, Hope?" At Hope's nod, he pointed. "That one too, on a separate receipt?"

To the others, he asked, "What happened?"

Hope, Mabel, the manager, and a paramedic all tried to explain at once. After sorting the tangled stories, Jay had a decent idea of what had happened. Given the memories associated with the day, he also thought he knew Hope's true problem. He reached for a box of holiday Kleenex from a nearby display and pulled out several tissues for her.

"It's just an accident," he murmured, trying to keep his voice as quiet as possible. "You're upsetting Mabel. Let's just get through this, and we'll go later where you can deal with this."

"But—" Her eyes slid across to where Mabel sat confused

and ready to be carted off for her x-rays. She mopped up her tears and choked back a fresh sob with strength that Jay suspected was the last she possessed. "I'm sorry. It's been a long week and — well, I just lost it."

With Mabel's keys in hand, they rushed to fill her car with her purchases, and then hurried back to the ambulance before it drove off. Hope wrote down their cell numbers and insisted that Mabel call if she needed help. Standing by a Salvation Army kettle as the bell ringer jangled the bell, they watched as the ambulance crept through the parking lot, the lights flashing oddly against the dark pavement.

"Let's go."

Jay drove aimlessly around town, coaxing Hope to talk. "I didn't mean to be insensitive back there. She just seemed unwilling to go unless she knew you were ok. I think you scared her."

"It's okay," she sniffed. "I appreciate it. It's weird. I don't usually think of this as being the 'bad day.' I leave that to Monday. But when I saw that poor woman surrounded by paramedics over a shopping cart — I lost it."

"Understandable."

"Well, duh. My brother died because he wanted a good deal. That infuriates me. I lost my brother to the desire for a fifty-dollar video game."

He pulled over to the side of the road, shaking his head. "That's not true. That's a lie. You lost your brother because bad weather conditions made it hard for an unprincipled man to see where he was going. It could have been any morning. He could have been riding to the store at four in the afternoon. He died because for some reason, he was done with this earth."

Hope sobbed once more. Jay didn't know how to comfort her. He rubbed her back, passed fresh fistfuls of tissues, and waited. Every few minutes she would regain control long enough for him to feel hopeful. At last, she glanced up at him. Jay wiped a tear away with the back of his hand, and the deep sobs that had filled the car ceased. Softly falling tears flowed freely then.

At that moment, Jay realized that she had never allowed

herself to grieve fully. She lost control only long enough to release tension in order to regain that control again. Grief in check, she took on the world — until the next time.

He held out the ridiculous box of Kleenex with its dancing snowman on the cover. "Do you want another tissue?"

"No," she shook her head violently. "I want ten."

Jay recognized the underlying steel in her voice and pushed Hope's hair from her face. "You need to get it all out. Let's go home where you can relax."

"No!" A terrible tone entered her voice. "I can't lose it there. Dad can't take it. Trust me," she added as he began to protest, "he cannot handle it."

He made a quick call to Ron, drove through McDonald's for breakfast, and zipped onto the Loop. Within half an hour, they pulled into the parking lot at Finch Investments. Jay ushered her inside, waving at the maintenance crew. "Who's in?" he asked the crew chief.

"No one. I think Drew said he'd be in later today, but no one is here. Was someone supposed to be?"

"No. We'll be in the media room."

"I'm done in there anyway," the crew chief assured him.

He led her to the couch and pointed. "Sit." Once she complied, he sat at her feet and passed her the Kleenex.

"I don't need to cry anymore. I think I'm all cried out."

Jay felt skeptical but nodded. "It's possible, but I doubt it. What you aren't, is all talked out. It's time to talk about Concord and your mother, and we're going to sit here until you've said everything you've thought or wanted to say during these past few years."

"But I—"

Jay took her hands and tried to pray. His inexperience and discomfort made him stumble and stutter until Hope's eyes met his. "Oh, Jay…"

She took over. He listened closely to the words and found them often jumbled or disjointed. She confessed her lack of faith and her attempts to make it through hard times in her own strength. With each falter and each sentence that came out backwards, he learned that prayers didn't have to be well-spoken—that one could speak to the Lord even without knowing what you wanted to say.

"That was beautiful," Jay said as she choked out an "Amen." Hope couldn't have heard him. Once again, she sobbed. Between her choked back tears and poured out emotion, she grieved lost dreams, lost memories, lost hopes.

"I wanted cousins for my children. Con and I had an agreement. We promised to do our best to have at least four children each so that Christmases and birthdays would be delightful exercises in cacophony. Now my children will be like we were—except at least we knew there were cousins in California—we just rarely got to see them."

Jay slid up on the couch beside her and held her as she sobbed through each of her dashed dreams. When she seemed ready to listen, Jay talked, knowing that she might not be ready for what he had to share. He just hoped to plant new ideas to ponder when she was ready.

"You know, you can still have all those cousins. Marry someone with a dozen siblings, and you'll be overrun with nieces and nephews. Your holiday celebrations will be different than you had planned, but they don't have to be antithetical. Just adjust them."

"How? Some things can't be replaced—like a mother at important days."

"No, not replaced, but how many groom's mothers are left out of the wedding process? You will have her to do those special things with you. Your God will help you forge a new relationship with her that will be a balm to your heart. I know it. She might even be what I once heard my father call a 'twice-mother.'"

Hope's face screwed into concentrated thought as she tried to decipher Raj's mangled idiom. A grin split her face, wavering as it might be, as she chortled, "A second mother to me. He's just so funny."

Jay waited for her to say more, but she didn't. The silence grew until he realized she felt heavy. She slept. He rearranged her on the couch and went out to the car to find the comforter he'd purchased that morning.

When Jay returned, he half-expected to find her sitting on the couch, ready to take on the day with her grief fully corralled and hog-tied. Jay snickered to himself over the scrambled metaphors—exactly the sort of words his father might have mixed.

Hope lay still sleeping, an occasional sob shaking her. It frustrated him. He wanted to fix the problem, but he couldn't and he knew it. He draped the comforter over her and balled up his jacket, tucking it under her head for a pillow. Leaving the door wide open, he strolled down the hall to his desk to call Ron.

"Hey, we're at my office now. She's…"

"Is she okay?" Ron's voice cracked.

"She's better anyway. I'll let her tell you about the store incident. She fell apart when a woman got hurt."

Ron groaned. Jay didn't know how to comfort Hope, much less her father. The entire experience was new territory—one he hoped never to enter again. "Ron?"

"Hmm?"

"I think there is something I should mention."

"What's that?"

Jay took a deep breath and said, "Well, she's grieving both her mother and her brother. I think she's so strong—or forces herself to be—that she only deals with her pain when it overflows. She hasn't figured out how to empty the bucket to an amount that is reasonable to carry."

"That sounds about right."

"The thing is," he continued before he found an excuse to keep out of their private lives, "she seems to grieve most over things she expected that now won't happen. Plans for vacations, businesses, her wedding, babies…" He waited for some kind of response, but it never came. "I mean, she is just realizing how much disappeared when her loved ones died. She truly did accept their absence, that they are in heaven, and that it was her loss and their gain. She just hasn't accepted the results."

Ron's voice wavered as he spoke. "You missed your calling, Jay. Actually, since you aren't a Christian, I guess you just haven't gotten it yet. You should have been a pastor or a counselor. I've never met someone who understands people and situations so clearly."

As Ron spoke, Jay's head shook. "I appreciate the thought, but I absolutely disagree. I get impatient and frustrated with most people. You can't organize them into perfect little boxes and expect them to stay there."

"True, but still… you have a gift."

"Perhaps. I don't know if I agree, but thank you. You're wrong about one thing for sure."

"What's that?"

"I'm either a Christian now, or I will be once I figure out Acts."

"What about Acts don't you understand?"

"If baptism comes before or after salvation. It seems to say both." Jay pulled up an online Bible as they spoke. "I mean, it talks about washing away sins. You can't be a Christian without them being washed away. But the blood of Jesus does that—and then it says that—"

"Jay. Stop. Question for you."

"What?"

Ron's laughter—joy-filled in a way Jay hadn't heard in months—filled the phone. "Who cares? You want to be baptized?"

"Yes, but I don't—"

"Get to the church. I'll meet you there and call Dan Shatternmann. It'll be fine. Trust me."

"But I don't want to wake Hope," Jay protested.

"So don't. Come when she wakes up. We'll be waiting."

The phone clicked in Jay's ear. He stared at it before pocketing it and turning back to the computer screen.

Acts 2:38 practically shouted at him, *"'Repent, and each of you be baptized in the name of Jesus Christ for the forgiveness of your sins; and you will receive the gift of the Holy Spirit.'"*

As they pulled into the church parking lot, Hope frowned. "Why are we at the church?"

Jay didn't know what to say or how to say it. "Well, I—"

186

"What's going on?" As he hesitated, she added, "This isn't funny. I didn't ask for—"

"I'm not pulling some stupid intervention thing, Hope. This isn't about you. I'll let your dad explain," he said as he stepped from the car. He moved to open her door, but she was already out and on her way to blast him.

"Jay—"

Ron arrived and hugged Jay. Hope's eyes bounced from father to friend before demanding, "Will someone tell me what is going on?"

"You need to have patience, Hope. Go sit down in the auditorium. We'll be in soon." Ron softened his words with a quick hug and a gentle shove toward the door.

She stumbled into the church ahead of them, but Jay didn't see her again until the curtains to the baptistery opened. His heart swelled as she squealed and jumped up from her seat. Several people sat behind and around her, but Jay hardly noticed them.

He had expected to find baptism solemn—almost reverent in its seriousness. The joy in the room, the overwhelming emotion in his heart—he hadn't expected either. The group burst into song as he came up out of the water, weeping for reasons he couldn't define.

As he stepped into the changing room, dripping water all over a spread-out shower liner, Hope stood there, ready to hug him. "I'm so—how—why didn't you tell me!"

"I didn't know how," he murmured. "I didn't know the right words to explain, so I thought maybe just coming. I was sure you'd know—"

She interrupted, excitedly. "Your parents! We have to tell them. They'll be so—oh wait, maybe they won't. What will they say? Will they be upset?"

Ron burst through the door with a towel fresh from the dryer. "The baptistery was still pretty cold, Hope. Let him change."

She hugged him once more, shivering at her own wet clothes, and went out to sing with the others while he changed. Mrs. Shatternmann brought in communion, and all gathered

187

around when Jay and Ron emerged. The minister prayed and the small group of celebrants joined together in communion with their new brother.

Ron hugged him again as they started to leave the building. "Welcome to the family, Jay."

Alone in his bed, with the comfort of privacy and darkness around him, Jay closed his eyes and allowed himself to relive the day. So many thoughts—so many emotions overwhelmed him until it seemed as if he would burst. He had never felt more alive.

The utter joy from everyone stunned him. He had emails in his inbox, welcoming him to the family. Mrs. Shatternmann had cried. Strangers had wept tears of joy for him.

Hope. So much emotion in that word—that name. Hope. He had a new Hope now—one in Jesus. Baptism had not made sense to him—not until that moment when he rose from the water. How had something so simple made such a deep impact on his heart?

As he stood there dripping in the baptistery, he had felt such a release. Even in his bed, hours later, that same sense of *gone-ness* washed over him anew. Resistance—gone. Clinging to his old self—gone. He had expected to miss it. He didn't.

CHAPTER 23

Hope and Kirky scoured half a dozen department stores until Hope wailed that she would go crazy. "Is there not a single semi-formal dress that doesn't shout 'trollop on board?'"

"Trollop? Really, Hope?"

She winked and sashayed to the next rack. "Hey, what can I say? I keep my vocabulary options varied."

"Maybe we need to try a boutique. These things look like they're designed for high schoolers for the winter formal or something."

Hope nodded absently. She picked up another long, shapeless dress of questionable material. "Or, I could choose one of these incredibly modest and retiring numbers. What do you think? I could call it 'Amish chic.'"

"I think that dress should be retired. Let's go back to the boutique where you found that dress for the opera. Surely they have something less formal that will work."

"I can't afford—"

"Even boutiques have clearance racks. We'll pray. You're the one always telling me to pray for everything from open gas pumps to the right gift for Mom. We'll pray for the right dress for a party."

"Go ahead. Throw my words back at me." She hesitated. "Okay."

A week later, Hope swirled in front of her mirror, still amazed at the dress she'd found. Though clearanced for barely more than the cost of one of the department store rejects, it couldn't have been more perfect. Matching shoes, on the other hand, hadn't been quite as inexpensive.

She gave one last turn, eyeing her loose curls with a critical eye. Should she have put it up? It was a little casual for the dress, but she liked the effect as they bounced when she moved. Her mother's solitaire earrings sparkled whenever her hair moved away from her ears.

Satisfied with her appearance, she slid on a velvet shrug, grabbed her velvet clutch, and rushed downstairs. She felt like a princess. She looked the part.

In the common room, Jay fidgeted as he waited. His phone buzzed. He glanced at the text. COMING DOWN. SORRY TO KEEP YOU WAITING.

He turned in time to see her skipping down the stairs to meet him. The sight of her heels made him cringe. How did girls stay upright in those things much less, run, dance, or skip? The lightheartedness he'd seen in her over the past couple of weeks was magnified as she beamed up at him.

"Were you waiting long?"

"Not long at all."

"I couldn't decide on up or down, smoky or natural..."

A smile twisted the corner of his lips. "Does that make sense to you?"

"Of course. My hair—up or down. My eyes, smoky or natural..."

He glanced at her and shrugged. "I get the hair down, but since your eyes don't look red from smoke, I'm assuming you went natural?"

"Very funny. I went for a mix... just a light bit of smoky but not quite natural."

He started to tell her that whatever she'd done, she looked more beautiful than he'd ever seen her, but the blast of cold air as he opened the door made her squeal. "Cold?"

"Just surprised." She stepped close, allowing him to block the icy wind. "Tell me your car is close."

"Very. Parked illegally too, so we should hurry."

As he pulled away from the campus, Hope shifted in her

190

seat as if trying to see him better. "You look different."

"I took a shower, I shaved—no smoky jaw for me…"

"Very funny. No, it's around the eyes."

Jay laughed. "I hear that they are 'dreamy.'"

"Hush. I'm trying to figure out what is so different." A soft gasp filled the small space between them.

"What is it?"

"Jesus," she said. "The difference is Jesus. It's that joy that new Christians have and too often lose."

The words made no sense. "Why would anyone lose their joy in Jesus? That can't be!"

"It happens, though. People let the world creep back into their hearts, life is hard and beats them down until they can't find the Lord anymore—lots of things."

"Don't let that happen to me, Hope. I couldn't stand it."

She sighed. "I needed to hear that. You watch for it in me too, okay?"

Jay nodded. He started to ask more—hungry for discussion with someone who understood his insatiable appetite for more of Christ—but Hope's head turned as they passed the City Park ice rink. "Oh… I haven't been there in ages. I love ice skating."

"Do you spin and jump and look like a blur when you do?"

"I can…"

He snorted, hoping to keep her talking. "As in, spin wildly as a blur while you crash across the ice?"

"No really. My friend Marie in the sixth grade was training for the Olympics. I used to watch her and then on her breaks she'd show me how to do sit spins and other disciplines. I am particularly good at scratches and laybacks…"

Impressed, Jay made a note to tell his mother and asked, "Did you ever go into regular training?"

"No, Mom and Dad knew they couldn't afford to pay for regular training, and we weren't going to uproot our family if I got really good. Marie's coach thought I could be, though," she added with a hint of wistfulness to her voice. "But it wouldn't have been good for me. Not really."

"I suppose it is a sacrifice…"

"Yeah. Have you ever been skating?"

191

Jay nodded as he turned onto Mike's street. "A few times, anyway. *Amma* says we went when I was little, but I liked hitting a hockey puck around more than 'real skating,' as she calls it."

"She likes figure skating?"

"And gymnastics. You now know what plays during the Olympics at our house."

Hope bounced in her seat. "Then let's go!"

"Now? In these clothes? Are you crazy?"

"Not now, silly. Although," she added, that same wistfulness creeping back into her voice, "I would so love to skate in this dress. It'd be so pretty with spins… oh man…"

All Jay could picture was the sight of her sliding across the ice on her backside. "I'd be afraid that your legs would freeze if you fell."

Hope wrinkled her nose in disgust. "You paint such a flattering picture of me. Tell me, after I lose my backside to frostbite, do I fall flat on my face where my tongue connects irrevocably with the ice?"

"Ok, so I'm projecting my own fears onto you. In a skirt, they're even scarier."

"Yes," she laughed. "The mental picture of you in a skirt is very scary. Ice skaters fall, Jay. Often. In shorter skirts than this. And they don't freeze."

"That is disturbing, but I agree that your dress would look lovely floating across the ice. It's incredible, and you look absolutely beautiful in it."

"Nice cover, Jay. Now if only I could believe you…"

Jay pulled up to Mike's curb and saw one of the receptionist's sons offering valet service. He scrambled from the car, dashed around it to open Hope's door, and tossed the keys to an acne-infested boy serving as a valet for the Finches.

As he reached to press the doorbell, Jay murmured in Hope's ear, "Okay, so I tried to dig myself out of an unfortunate hole. I admit it. However, I was also waiting for an excuse to tell you how beautiful you look."

Hope's answer disappeared in Traci Finch's enthusiastic welcome. "Come in. Is this Hope?"

"Saved by the answered doorbell," Jay whispered before he

introduced her to Mike and Traci.

During the next hour, half his office stepped up to meet Jay's girlfriend. He wanted to apologize for the constant assumption, but that seemed worse — as if the idea offended him. From the way she smirked each time, he suspected she was laughing at him inwardly.

Hope and Grace spent much time chatting by the piano, where Nolan played gentle background music. As glad as he was for Hope to meet Grace, Jay felt as if he'd lost the best part of his evening. Mike nudged him. "She's gorgeous, Jay. I thought she was cute in that debate, but this girl is stunning."

"Fun too."

"Don't let Grace monopolize her."

He shook his head. "She's having fun. It'll be fine."

"This is your date, Jay. It's okay to monopolize the girl you brought. It's kind of expected." Mike glanced at his watch. "I'd better hand out the bonus checks and get Traci to do her door prize thing."

"Door prize?"

Mike laughed. "She's always finding these cool things that she wants to buy, though she can't think of a recipient. So, she gets them, saves them all year, and hands them out at the party. I write them off as a business expense, and voilà. At least we don't go broke."

"That's...different."

"That's life with Traci."

He leaned against the post, exchanging occasional glances with Hope. Beautiful was an understatement. Hope's vivacity managed to avoid being showy — somehow.

When the guests dwindled to half a dozen, Jay crossed the room and smiled at the ladies. "Will you be ready to leave soon? It's getting late. I wouldn't want to drag things out for Mike and Traci."

"I'm ready when you are. You know Grace, right?"

He nodded. "It's good to see you again."

"I was so glad to hear of your baptism, Jay. I think I bawled for an hour — stupid thyroid," Grace said.

"Thyroid?"

193

From the piano, Nolan called, "My wife blames everything on her thyroid. Silly woman."

At the door, Hope and Jay thanked the Finches for a lovely evening before stepping out into the cold. At the end of the walk, Jay's car sat idling with great puffs of smoke rising from the exhaust pipe. "Wow, great thinking. It won't be freezing in there."

"As nice as your dress is, it's not very warm," he said as he opened her door.

The moment he seated himself behind the wheel, Hope sniffed at him with mock imperiousness. "I'll have you know that this dress is perfectly comfortable."

Jay's warm hand on Hope's chilled arm was all he needed to prove his point. He laughed at her indignant assertion that it was just residual cold on the outside of the fabric from the trip to the car. "You think that if it makes you feel better."

With apparent eagerness to change the subject, Hope said, "Grace is an interesting woman."

"Why do you say that?"

"She's never had a job."

Jay couldn't see the fascination. To his knowledge, neither had Hope. "Is that a bad thing?"

"No, but she's been married for less than a year. She lived alone before she met Nolan—without a job. She has a degree in Physics but she has never used it."

"Her father probably left her financially stable." Jay still did not understand the relevance of the conversation.

"That's the thing—he didn't. She thought it was fun to try to find a way to live without having to work outside her home. Isn't that bizarrely cool?"

Jay, noting that her arm was now warm, slid his hand under hers and wrapped his fingers around it. "She sounds like a 'Suzy Homemaker,' but I don't see what's so unusual about that."

Hope didn't answer. She glanced at Jay, trying to read his features in the light of the streetlights as they passed. He smiled down at her curious expression. "Do you mind?"

Her head shook in answer. She squeezed his gently and

194

then returned to her discourse on Grace's lifestyle before marriage. After another minute, she wrapped her other hand around both of theirs and relaxed. "I just think it's so cool that she knew she wouldn't want a career so she decided not to have one. I've never heard anything like it. I mean, my mom became Dad's secretary the day I entered seventh grade. She knew she'd be good at it and she would enjoy working with Dad. Me, I chose a job I thought I wanted and then found classes to help me get that job."

"That's what most people do. There's nothing wrong with that."

She nodded. "Grace didn't though. She had scholarships, so she got her degree. I suppose it didn't hurt to have something to fall back on, but she never intended to use it to get a job." Her head shook as if to clear it. "I'm sorry. I'm totally obsessing over this and ruining our date."

She'd said it. Date. Whew. He hadn't been sure if she saw it in the same light as he had begun to, but there it was. He pulled to the curb in front of her dorm and parked in the temporary spots. As they strolled to the doors, Jay smiled down at her. "Thanks for coming. I saw how much Grace enjoyed talking with you, and I was the envy of every single man in the room."

Before he could reach for the door, a few guys burst through the door, nearly running them over. One laughed at him. "Just kiss her. Hope's too nice to bite."

"That's what you think," she called back, winking at Jay.

He opened the door and waved at her as he walked back toward his car. Near the curb, he turned and looked back. Hope stood just inside the glass doors, smiling at him. She gave a quick little wave before skipping upstairs.

"You know, Lord. You did an exceptionally fine job with her..."

CHAPTER 24

As he flipped through his reports, Hope protested his assertion that he had too much to do. "You have to come! We're making dozens of cookies. I even went home and got all of our cookie cutters and stuff."

Jay still hesitated. He really did need to finish his reports, but if he'd ever made Christmas cookies, he couldn't remember it. "Okay," he relented, "but if I get in trouble with Mike, I'm blaming you."

An hour later, he arrived at the church with arms full of flour, sugar, sprinkles, and a sheepish expression on his face. "I don't know what I'm doing, but I'm here to do it."

Kirky rushed to greet him. "I'm so glad you're here. I was so excited when Hope told me about your baptism! Welcome to the family!"

Hope's natural propensity for enjoying every moment to its fullest shone as the cookie assembly line began. She chided friends for sloppy cutting, rearranged sprinkles on cookies, and adjusted icing colors until the group teased her mercilessly. Only her good-natured attitude and self-criticism kept her managerial attempts from being annoying.

They sang Christmas carols and silly holiday songs. Dan Shatternmann came in the room as they were singing "I Saw Mommy Kissing Santa Claus" and teased them about secularizing Christmas. "Besides, we all know that 'Winter Wonderland' is the best secular song out there—Parson Brown and all..."

Before Hope could turn on him with jokes about his name, Jay grabbed his box of cookies and hurried to his car. The cold air felt odd—suspiciously like snow. His *amma* would like that. She had asked about snow every time they spoke since she'd left.

As he returned to help with clean up, he rounded the corner near the kitchen and overheard Kirky question Hope about her friendship with him. "So give me deets, girl! He watches you—like all the time. I thought I noticed it at your birthday, but it's even more obvious now."

He grinned as Hope tried to dodge the question. Kirky refused to give up until Hope said, "Fine! I just don't know. He's my friend. I've never had a friend I was so attracted to *and* who was sort of available."

"Sort of?"

"I don't know what kind of cultural things go on there. Right now, I'm focusing on friendship. I like him—know him better than anyone except maybe you."

Kirky snickered. "Things are going to get interesting as soon as he figures out that you're as interested as he is."

Before Jay could move, the girls stepped out of the pantry and Hope bumped into Jay. Kirky snickered, stepping aside. Hope whirled around in an ineffectual attempt to hide her flaming face, while Jay thanked the Lord for dark skin that usually hid a blush.

"So," he murmured, a trace of amusement in his tone, "is anything *interesting* going on this afternoon, or am I free to finish my reports?"

Hope whirled to face him, riled. "Sorry, you're not free. You're driving me home to give cookies to Dad and Mabel. By the way, she wants her receipt so she can pay for the stuff you bought her. Then we're going caroling with the Shatternmanns and some of the others. And finally, you're going to drive me home after a side trip to that living nativity, and I'm wearing warm clothing so I can stand out there as long as I like."

Jay allowed his shoulders to droop exaggeratedly. He tried to assume a whipped-puppy look before leaning close and whispering, "But what if I get cold?"

198

Hope swatted at his arm as she squeezed past, her faded blush returning once more. "You now have Jesus to warm your heart."

He didn't move. "Where do I find that?"

"Second Hopians chapter three."

Jay grabbed her arm playfully and allowed his hand to slide down and grab hers as he whispered, "I wasn't worried about my heart being cold. It's plenty warm, but my hands..."

Hope jerked away and put her hands on her hips. "You are being very flirty. Shame on you. I might have to tell my daddy."

"Go ahead. He'd be on my side anyway." He frowned. "Wait, did you say second *Hopians*?"

Hope dashed for the kitchen, calling, "I gotcha, I gotcha..."

"That's what you think," he muttered to himself as he joined the group. He avoided Kirky's knowing expression and attempts to catch his attention. Some things were best left alone to unfold naturally.

Pastor Shatternmann introduced a group from The Assembly in Brunswick. Jay tried to remember names, but failed. After several wrong names for both the Marshfield group and the Brunswick group, he gave up and avoided names whenever possible.

However, one name became forever etched in Jay's mind. Chuck Majors. Deceptively normal and innocent sounding, Chuck proved to be the opposite. He took one look at Hope in her powder blue sweater and white corduroy jeans and zeroed in on her like a Kamikaze pilot.

Disgusted at the man's obvious self-absorption and the way he salivated over Hope, Jay grew quiet—reserved. Hope seemed to notice—or she enjoyed flirting with the creeper. "I'm so glad you all joined us, Chuck. Hey, Jay, isn't it wonderful to have more singers?"

"Wonderful," he agreed growling. "I'm sure we're in for an *interesting* evening."

His inflection on the word "interesting" made her choke

199

back laughter. Jay pounded her back helpfully while she led him, Kirky, and the unshakeable Chuck, to Jay's car. "Come on, we can all ride together."

Clueless to the disaster she created, Hope asked, "So, Chuck, what do you do?"

Chuck swelled like the prize-winning hog owner at a country fair—or perhaps it was the hog. "I'm a collection officer for Rockland Motors—largest dealership in the state. Top guy, too. I have the highest success rate in the whole office."

"I don't doubt that," Jay muttered under his breath.

"What was that, *San*jay?" Hope said in a flirtatious tone. He knew she expected to trip him up; it backfired.

"Ahh, my Hope, I said that I do not doubt that Chuck is an excellent collections agent. He seems uniquely suited to that profession." His eyes met Kirky's in the back seat as he added, "Not everyone finds such a perfect calling."

Kirky choked back laughs, resulting in a fit of coughing that sounded suspiciously like laughter. Chuck, in what seemed an uncharacteristic effort at helpfulness, pounded her back, creating more coughs. Kirky protested. "I'm fine, Chuck! Really!"

"How long have you been with The Assembly?" Hope asked, trying to distract Chuck from bruising her friend further. "Do you know the Burkes?"

"Oh, I've known Grace for a long time. I went out with her best friend until my brother met her. I stepped aside for him— always doing that. Gotta stop, or all the good ones will get away."

Hope clapped her hand over her mouth and raised wide, watering eyes at Jay, begging for him to rescue her. "I see."

Jay groaned to himself and gave her a sidelong glance he hoped she'd understand. From the look on her face, she understood his silent, "I'll get you for this."

Hope tossed her hair and tried again. "So your brother is going out with your ex-girlfriend? Grace was your ex-girlfriend. Who else have you let slip through your fingers?"

"Oh, Grace was never a girlfriend. I'm not into the ugly fat ones. I go for the *hot* chicks like *you*."

200

Chuck's emphasis on "hot" had been annoying, his insulting description of a woman Hope admired infuriated Jay, but when he added to it the obvious emphasis on "you," Jay ground his teeth and managed to avoid sideswiping a bicyclist— barely. "So are you looking for a girlfriend, a wife, or a trophy?"

Hope gasped, but Chuck seemed unfazed by the insult. "Well, I want a wife someday, but I have to have a girlfriend first, of course. And what guy doesn't want a cool trophy wife?"

Kirky choked and muttered, "I've heard people in he—"

"Hey, Kirky, do you remember if we're starting at the retirement center or in Marshfield Heights?"

She didn't get a chance to answer before Chuck interrupted. "Isn't that an oxymoron? Marshfield Heights?" He laughed loudly at his own joke, oblivious that only he was amused.

"Retirement home. Turn left at the light. One block on your right." Even Jay could tell by her clipped tones that Kirky was at the edge of her patience.

"So what songs are we singing, Hope?" Chuck asked, once again ignoring everyone else in the car.

"The usual." She turned to Jay, "Do you think you'll need a songbook?"

Jay struggled to keep his tone civil. "I assume so. I only know a few Christmas songs, and I doubt we'll be singing 'Frosty the Snowman.'"

Chuck perked up at those words. "So, Jay, are you Hope or Kirky's little outreach project?"

Before Hope could find the words to respond, Jay pulled to the curb at the retirement home and said, "I'd be Hope's project. She brings Kirky along as a chaperone. Whose project are you?"

Once more, Chuck seemed unaffected by the retort. "I'd love to be Hope's project. Hey, Kirky, don't you want to take on Jay and leave Hope to me?"

Kirky and Jay exited the car exchanging disbelieving glances. Hope seemed to know how to handle the jerk from Brunswick. She hurried to Jay's side of the car and tucked herself under his arm, forcing his to wrap around her shoulders. He saw fury in her eyes as she gazed up at him with a look he assumed

201

was supposed to be "adoring."

"Oh, I could never do that. I'm devoted to Jay's welfare, and well, he's just so *interesting!*"

Hope led Jay to the crowd gathering by the front door of the home. Stunned, he hissed, "How could you leave Kirky back there with that odious oaf—"

"Odious? Oaf? Oh, that is funny. Been watching Austen or something lately?"

Jay started to protest, but it occurred to him that his mother had been on a BBC kick before she left. "As if. Meanwhile, have you no heart? That poor girl—"

"She knows I'll rescue her. She's just giving us a chance to escape."

"Well, that's *interesting…*"

Hope started to make a retort, but Brian Donaldson passed. She grabbed Brian's arm and whispered something. Brian grinned, his eyes searching the street, and then raced for Jay's car. Hope beamed.

"What did you do?"

"Gave Brian the things he loves most—Kirky and a chance to be a hero."

"Kirky, eh?"

"Yeah, he's been in love with her since the first day I brought her to church—honestly," she added at the look of skepticism on Jay's expression. "He's just too much of a goof to know how to show it."

"But that's been a few years, hasn't it?"

"Yeah, but by the time he wanted to do anything about it, she saw him as a pal and didn't pick up on the signals."

"I know how he feels," Jay whispered as Dan Shatternmann called the group together and named the four songs they would sing as they strolled through the retirement home.

By the time the group sang, "We Wish You a Merry Christmas," Chuck had Brian's spot in the Shatternmann's car and Brian rode comfortably next to Kirky on the way to Marshfield Heights. As they rode, Kirky gave them a live replay of Brian's rescue.

Mimicking Brian's voice perfectly, she barely kept a straight face as she said, "Oh, Kirky. How could you leave me like that? I'm so sorry. I didn't mean it, honestly I didn't. Please say you'll forgive me. I'll just go crazy if you don't forgive me."

"I try," Brian admitted with affected modesty.

"Honestly, I almost missed my cue. I had a cutting rebuff all ready to fire when Brian showed up on his white Nike chargers and threw my plans out of whack."

Hope groaned. "Oh, this I've gotta hear. What did Chuck say?"

"He offered me the choice between forgiving my beloved Brian or a life of insipidry with him."

"Is insipidry a word?" Hope gasped between fits of giggles.

"It is now. I worked hard on that word and I'm not about to relinquish it just because Mr. Webster was too dense to recognize the necessity of a word like insipidry."

Brian laughed. "It is a brilliant word," he agreed. "It also fits." He nudged Kirky, smirking at her and said, "You know, I'm going to have to keep playing the besotted and repentant boyfriend all afternoon or Chuck will return to claim you as his bride before he drags you off to his cave."

Hope snickered. "Cave at the collections department! Aaak!"

Kirky grabbed Brian's arm in mock horror. "Vapors! You dasn't leave me! Whatevah will ah do!"

As Jay watched the theatrics in his rearview mirror, he saw something Hope had missed. Kirky seemed just as oblivious to Brian's interest as he was to hers. Oh, yes. Kirky was definitely *not* immune to Brian Donaldson. How had she kept such an interesting tidbit of information from Hope?

As they reassembled with the rest of the group, Jay held Hope back for a second. "Watch Kirky. Closely. I think you'll discover that there are revelations inside and outside of the Bible."

She gave Jay an odd look and started to move away, but the sight of Chuck drew Hope nearer to him. Jay saw their new "friend" nearing and as casually as possible, draped an arm across her shoulders. The disappointed look in Chuck's eyes told him his efforts hadn't been wasted.

"Man, Jay. You'll have to help me find another good one like Hope. I don't think even I can tempt her. Must be that exotic thing going for you."

Before Jay or Hope could manufacture a response, a man and an incredibly beautiful blond arrived, pulling Chuck away. The blonde hung back for a second and winced apologetically. "Hi. I'm Paige. Sorry I didn't get here fast enough. Your faces tell me I didn't make it in time."

"He—"

Paige shook her head. "No, really. He's just like that. Harmlessly, obnoxiously, offensive. He'd never deliberately hurt anyone, but he does—every single time he opens his mouth."

Before they had to reply, Paige gave them an embarrassed little smile and returned to where Chuck and the other man stood next to others from The Assembly. Hope whistled low. "Wow. That was weird."

"But nice." Jay gave her a knowing smile and opened the songbook.

Hope stared at him, confused. "What?"

"Well, it was nice for me anyway."

"I missed something," Hope said, eyeing him as if he'd lost his mind, "It was nice to be called someone's project? It was nice for me to be indirectly labeled a 'hot chick?'"

"Well, if the description fits…"

"Jay!"

He grinned down at her as another song began. He bent low and murmured, "Ah, Hope. You're so fun to tease. I *am* sorry that I allowed him to insult you. Forgive me?"

She didn't answer. Jay's eyes followed hers, trying to figure out what captured her attention, but it could have been anyone in the group—or something else altogether. "Hope?"

"Shhh. Later."

By the time Hope and Jay left Marshfield, Hope looked ready to burst. The moment Jay pulled away from the curb, Hope pounced. "You meant earlier that Kirky cares about Brian, didn't you? You know, when you talked about revelations?"

Jay nodded.

"I was so confused when you said that, but I saw — or I think I saw — a window into her heart that I've never seen open before."

"Yeah," Jay agreed. "I saw it in the car. She let her guard down for just a second, and I managed to catch it. She really enjoyed the repartee with him."

Hope sat, lost in thought. "She's always sparred with Brian more than anyone else," she said at last. "We all joked that only he could take as good as she gave, but now..."

"If he opened up, do you think she'd respond?"

"I don't know." Hope's voice sounded a little down. "I mean, I'd probably swoon right there. I've always been more of a romantic about things like that, but Kirky?"

"I don't get it. Why not her?"

"I just don't think she'd trust him. She had a hard life before she became a Christian — ugly. I think she's resigned herself to being single." Hope whispered, "I don't think she'll trust a man."

"But at your party — she had a boyfriend there."

Hope nodded. "Oh, she has boyfriends, but they all know it's just some laughs. She won't get serious. Actually, I think that's what some of them like about her; no worries about commitment."

For several miles, neither of them spoke. Remembering something Mike had once said, Jay finally risked a question. "Can you tell me if she was promiscuous — I mean, do you think she'd mind if you told me. I might be able to help."

Hope nodded. "Totally. She's not private about it. The first time I really talked to her was in P.E. She didn't want to dress out and I asked if I could help. She just lost it. I mean, totally lost it. Ranting, crying, screaming. It was terrible."

"What —"

"When I couldn't understand what she was saying, she tore off her shirt." Hope's voice choked. Jay reached for her hand. "Jay, the bruises..." She wiped her eyes. "Sorry. I thought it was her dad, but it wasn't. It was her boyfriend. *Her boyfriend!*"

"Oh, man."

"That part of the story is public record — everyone knows

205

about Kirky Laas. There's more, though, and it's bad. Really bad. I had no idea how ugly the world could be until I met Kirky. She's lived it."

He swallowed hard, squeezing her hand. "I know someone who might be able to help—I mean who has lived it. Traci Finch."

"Really? She—"

"Yep. She talks to people and helps them. I thought maybe Kirky—"

"You're a good man, Jay," she whispered.

"Good," he said thoughtfully. "Is that anywhere close to *interesting?*"

"Just what were you doing listening in on our conversation?"

Jay grinned. "Just trying to discover if you'd say anything *interesting.*

CHAPTER 25

The lights of Rockland rushed to meet them as they whizzed onto the Rockland Loop. Hope's stomach growled. Jay smiled. "Hungry?"

"Not at all."

"Liar." He began naming off restaurants. "What sounds good? We can see the nativity after we eat."

As she named different restaurants, Jay mentally debated the merits and defects of every restaurant he could remember. He wanted some place—nice, but they weren't dressed for his favorites. A new idea hit him and he whizzed across all lanes, barely catching an off ramp. "There's a great bistro on Chestnut, off Ninety-First Street. Let's go there."

"Are we dressed for it?" Hope flicked imaginary lint from her pants before Jay, once again, caught her hand.

"A new excuse. This is getting fun. Your pants are fine, Hope. They're spot free."

"I think we're both dressed too casually for this end of town."

"Trust me," he said as he pulled into the parking lot.

Jay parked the car, opened Hope's door, and led her into the restaurant. Once seated and their orders taken, Hope leaned forward, hands in her lap, and smiled at him. "What's going on?"

Jay understood the question but feigned ignorance. "I'd say 'we're eating,' but somehow I don't think that's the answer you're looking for."

"You're right. It's not. So what's the answer?"

He knew it would frustrate her, but he didn't directly answer the question again. "What is the question?"

Hope chewed her lip and rearranged her words to form a more specific question. "You're a little different lately. Why?"

"Different how?"

"I'm supposed to be asking the questions," she growled. When he responded only with a questioning gaze, she sighed. "You flirted with me."

He smiled. He took a drink of water and smiled again, enjoying seeing her flustered. "I enjoy it too." He winked. "You're blushing again."

"Why do it, though. What's the point?"

"Ah, Hope. I thought you knew that. I thought all girls knew that."

She took a deep breath. He knew what was coming and prayed she'd understand. "Why now?"

"Because I can. I probably would have flirted with you that first day if I hadn't discovered that you are a Christian."

"My being a Christian was that big of a turn off?"

Jay shook his head emphatically. "Of course not. I just knew enough about Christians to know it would put you in an awkward position. I liked you. I wanted your friendship, so that's all I allowed myself to consider." He shrugged. "What can I say; having a Christian boss can be a perk."

"So when —"

"I realized on the way to Mike's party that now I could tell you how beautiful you are without it being inappropriate. I could hold your hand and it wasn't — I mean —"

"I know. I was so surprised. I've never —"

Jay misunderstood her to mean she wasn't interested. "I understand. I won't push it, Hope."

"I don't think you do understand." She toyed with her fork. "I learned as a little girl how to control my emotions — how to deal with disappointment."

"I didn't realize I am a disappointment," he said before he could stop himself.

"No, no. See, when I got old enough for boyfriends, I knew they had to be Christians. So, when I met guys who weren't, they got put in the 'just friends' category and learned not to let my heart go there."

"And I was not a Christian," Jay said, feeling a little more hopeful.

"Yep. It was hard at first. I mean, come on. Teenaged girls want to be liked. They want a guy to find them attractive, and it's exciting when they realize someone does." She dropped her eyes to her hands. "I just had the distinct honor of attracting only unsaved guys. None of the guys at church liked me."

"Fools."

She laughed. "Thanks. I learned that lesson well, Jay. Too well. I never knew how to react when a former 'off limits' was suddenly ok. I still don't."

She had no idea of the hope that her words gave him. While she finished her meal, he allowed himself the privilege of realizing that not only did he have a chance, but that Kirky was right. He was more important to her than a good friend she would hate to lose. He was special to her. How was that even possible?

Hope grew restless. Jay realized that she felt as vulnerable as he had when her father asked about his love for her. "Hope?"

She glanced up at him, her eyes struggling to meet his. "Hmm?"

"Do you know why I didn't call you or write you to have a big discussion about this?"

Frozen, she shook her head, watching him with confused eyes. Jay found himself struggling words. At emotional times, he sometimes found his English weak and easily broken. "I did not want to be making a big deal out of something before I knew — I wanted to test the waters — to go slowly. And if something did not be going right, then our friendship would not be destroyed."

"Practically speaking, what does that mean?"

Now Jay was confused. "I don't think I understand the question."

"You used phrases that I don't understand in the context of me — us. 'Go slowly' and 'test the waters.' Where are we going

209

and what are we testing?"

Jay understood. Sometimes, he felt as if he had a direct link to Hope's mind, and when he didn't understand something, it was because he didn't trust the pictures he saw. This time, he trusted. "It means you are Hope. Not Hope the 'just a friend' or Hope the 'girlfriend.' You're just Hope. If that means you don't want to discuss something, you don't. If it means you tease me, you do. If it means that you hang on my every word and adore me..."

"I get the picture. Thank you." Hope's sarcasm left him breathless as he realized she meant it to be overt flirtation.

They paid the bill and left, Jay feeling a little unnerved at how easily they flip-flopped from friendship to something less platonic within the space of a meal. A delightfully awkward silence hung between them as they drove to the living nativity. Jay wanted to say or do something to break the silence, but it was too emotionally exhilarating to change.

They stood, leaning against the warm car hood and watched as the nativity filed out of the stable to reenact the scenes of Luke chapter two. Hope shivered. Jay saw it and pulled her close, wrapping his arm around her and trying to block the night wind. "Are you cold?"

"No, but thank you. I needed that."

Torn between the desire to know what she meant and not wanting to push things, Jay hesitated. Curiosity won. "What did you need and why?"

"Oh hush. Stop being a man and just hold me. It's been a very traumatic day."

"Traumatic?"

She leaned her head against his chest and nodded. "Mmm hmm. I've bossed people, made hundreds of cookies, been eavesdropped on, teased, accosted by a creeper, and discovered that my best friend isn't really my best friend anymore." She glanced up at him. "Someone else took her place." Burying her head in his chest again she added, "I just need to be held for a while, and if you don't do it, I'll go home and sit on my daddy's lap."

With his arms around her, Jay chuckled at the delightful

combination of bossy woman and little girl he held. They stood, watching as the scene unfolded before them. The innkeeper led Mary and Joseph to the stable and handed them a blanket. Hope's eyes widened as a very large-looking Mary clutched at her middle, in mock pain. "They wouldn't!" she gasped.

Jay pointed to the animals that the shepherds drew close to block the view. "I think they're going to give Mary some privacy that way."

A star lit up on the church steeple as more shepherds pulled sheep with them from around the corner of the church. It slid down a wire from the steeple and shone over the manger, the steeple now dark. Hope gasped and a little girl next to them said, "Oh Daddy! It's Him! He's here!"

Hope tilted her head and gazed into Jay's face. His attention was fixed on the little girl's face. His eyes slid to hers. He leaned close and murmured, "Jesus said that we have to become like children, didn't He?"

They left at the arrival of the wise men. The ride back to the dorms remained as silent as their ride to the nativity, but this time they only felt comfortable. Hands laced together, they pulled up to the dorm and walked to the common room. Jay glanced at the doorway as he opened the door for Hope. "No one has fixed that. Oh well, next time," he murmured.

He gave her hand a squeeze and shooed her inside. Hope watched again as he walked away, as he paused again near the curb, and drove away. She climbed the stairs slowly. Each step punctuated one of the day's memories. As she closed the door to her dorm room, she leaned against it, deep in thought. What was wrong with the door to the commons? She didn't remember it needing to be fixed.

Half an hour later, as she climbed into bed, she grinned, realizing what was wrong with the door. Mistletoe. "Oh, Jay. I'll get you for that."

CHAPTER 26

Jay's cellphone rang, the new ringtone he'd added just that morning bringing a smile to his face: "Only Hope."

"Hey there."

Hope's voice warmed his heart. "I'm home and it's so empty. I've put up the tree, put up the lights, and even did shopping for Christmas dinner."

"Busy."

"I'm going crazy. Maybe I should do my gift shopping. Everything is just so empty."

Jay glanced at his calendar. He could take half a day off the next day and go visit for the weekend, but that meant no work on his house until after Christmas. The work would wait. "How about I come get you tomorrow and we go shopping. We can do a marathon trip—I could even bring you back here and show you all of *Amma's* favorite shops."

"That's silly. Why don't I just meet you there? You can follow me home and help me wrap."

He smiled at the interest he heard in her voice. It had been the right decision. "I'll go one better. We can wrap at my house. You can see my new house and then go from there to your dad's school. We'll arrive like Santa Claus with armloads of packages for Ron."

"Tomorrow?"

He smiled at the eagerness in her tone. "Twelve-thirty."

"I'll be there." Silence hung between them until she added,

"Thanks, Jay."

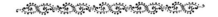

The next afternoon, they browsed through a shop in Little India, Hope entranced by traditional and modern Indian jewelry. "Oh, look at these bangles! They're so pretty." She leaned over a display of Indian mirror work and lacquer bangles and barrettes.

Jay leaned close, pointing to an azure set. "That'd look great on Kirky with her dark hair."

Feeling mischievous, Hope nudged him. "What looks good on boring blonde?"

His tone dropped to an almost inaudible whisper. "Nothing, but I think that purple would look wonderful on a beautiful blonde I know."

Turning to the sales woman, Jay pointed out which bracelets they wanted. Hope watched as the woman glanced coyly at them as she wrapped the bangles. When she spoke to Jay in some Indian dialect and Jay responded, Hope walked around the shop, examining everything from breathtaking saris to hand-carved tables.

Just as Jay paid for his purchases, Hope saw the most beautiful cloth she'd ever seen. Large enough for a king-sized bed, the silk batik was liberally sprinkled with hand-sewn sequins. She hurried to Jay's side and sent him from the store. "Go find me a bunch of spices for Kirky's mom. Mrs. Laas will love that."

Once Jay was out of sight, Hope led the saleswoman to the spread. "I want this, but I can't see a price. If it's less than a car payment, I have to have it."

She choked a bit when the woman told her it was two hundred dollars. Desire won out over sense. "Oh, man. I have to have it. I just have to."

"He seems like a very nice man. You are a fortunate woman."

Hope smiled but kept silent as the woman wrapped the spread in several layers of tissue paper and slipped them into a plastic bag. As she signed her receipt, she smiled up at the girl. "I'll be back. I have a feeling you'll be my go-to place for gifts for years."

Jay stood leaning against the wall that separated the windows of two shops, waiting for her. Hope shook her bag, delighted with her purchase. "I have a housewarming gift for you. You're going to love it, but I get to wrap it first. Now, where to?"

"Well, I got your spices, but there's another gift shop around the corner that has everything—furniture, fabric, jewelry, vases, saris, food items. It's like the Wal-Mart of Little India."

"And do they have pretty Indian girls fetchingly perched behind the counter to tempt unsuspecting men?"

Jay's chuckle rumbled in her ear. "I do believe you are a bit jealous, Hope Senior... and she was *not* flirting. That is something called courteous customer service. Some American stores could learn from her."

"Courtesy? Since when is it courteous to speak in a language that everyone present doesn't understand?"

"You walked away; she felt free."

Hope shook her head. "Nuh uh. I waked away when she started speaking Indian."

"Tamil," he corrected. "She's from the same province we are. *Amma* shops there often. And," he added with that crazy, endearing chuckle that melted her heart a little more every time she heard it, "She said that my girlfriend is beautiful."

Hope cocked an eyebrow. "Uh huh."

"She also said that it's hard to find nice girls these days and that her brother needs a nice girl. She sounded like *Amma*. 'Jay, you must find a nice girl. You should not be alone. It is not good. You need a good wife.'"

"Your mom knows Scripture and doesn't even know it," she teased. At his questioning look, she quoted, 'It is not good that man should be alone. I'll make a helper suitable for him.' Genesis chapter three."

"I remember that one. I liked it."

"So," Hope said, changing the subject, "do you think I'd

215

look good with a nice diamond chip in my nose like she had? I thought it was quite fetching."

Jay whirled to face her, looking deep into her eyes. She kept her expression curious, forcing herself not to smile at the look of panic on his face. "You wouldn't."

"Don't you think it'd be pretty? Your mother's is gorgeous."

He groaned, leading them away from the store she had hoped to enter. Hope pulled away and frowned at him. They sparred for a moment until Jay relented. "I'll make you a deal. You forget the stud, and we go into the store." Before she could argue, he added, "You know I'm stronger than you."

"No deal. Up the ante, and I might agree."

He glared at her in mock disgust. "I promise not to tell your father that you even mentioned it."

Hope's eyes grew wide. "You play dirty. Deal. And I'll get you for that."

The next store made the last one look like a shabby flea market stall in comparison. Silks and scarves draped over rich, ornate furniture. The jewelry caused her to gasp as she skipped from vases to candles and back to the silks. She almost bypassed the saris, but the sight of a purple one wrapped on a mannequin caught her attention. "Oh, look at that. Isn't it beautiful?"

Jay fingered the cloth. "It reminds me of one of *Amma's*."

Hope saw him smile and made up her mind. Leaving him behind, Hope found an elderly Indian woman to help her try it on. They sequestered themselves in a changing room, giggling over Hope's pathetic attempts to wrap the sari. A few minutes later, the woman came out, hands over her mouth in delight. "She is exquisite — beautiful! Wait and see!"

Hope heard the woman's words and glanced again at her reflection in the mirror. It was true. The color — perfect with her skin tones. She looked more graceful and feminine than she'd ever looked or felt in anything. Taking a deep breath, she prayed that Jay would like it and stepped from the dressing room.

Jay turned at the touch of her hand. She watched as he swallowed hard and listened as he cleared his throat. He smiled and motioned for her to wait. He took a few steps backward and

216

shook his head as if in a daze. "Stay there. Don't change. Not yet."

Confused, she watched as he dashed from the store. She glanced at the older woman, an unspoken question in her eyes. The woman smiled, reassuring her. "He was speechless. He has gone to buy you a flower or some other trinket to go with the sari. I am sure of it."

"Thanks—"

"I am Chaya. Please call me Chaya."

She waited, growing more nervous every second. "Chaya?" she whispered.

"Yes?"

"You don't think he was offended…"

"No. He will come back with a flower. You will see."

Chaya was wrong, however. Jay returned several minutes later with his camera. "I want a quality picture—not something from my phone. I thought your father would like to see it. If we take it over there by the hanging silks, it will be a good present for him for Christmas."

"Chaya, can you suggest a frame?" she asked as she moved to where he indicated. She posed, trying several things until Jay found what he wanted. As she changed, she wondered at his reaction. A picture was good, wasn't it? No offense if he wanted the memory of it…

Jay paid for his frame as she stepped from the room, the sari balled in her arms. "I tried. I can't seem to get this folded right."

Chaya clucked, smiling as she showed Hope how to fold the sari into a flat bundle of fabric. The petticoat and blouse were much easier. "Thanks. I appreciate you letting me try it on." She started to say something else, but a deep aqua sari on a rack tucked away in the corner caught her eye. "Oh, Jay. Look at this one!"

"I can't, Hope. A guy can only take so much. We'll have to come back sometime."

Disappointed, and just a little hurt, Hope turned to follow him to the door. Chaya's hand stopped her. She turned at the woman's quiet voice, "He is not angry. He is overwhelmed. Give him time. He did not know it would move him. It will be well. I promise."

Hope gave Chaya a grateful look and hurried after him. She debated between being understanding or jovial and opted for both. "Um, did I offend you? I'm sorry if I did."

Jay pulled her into a sideways hug and pointed out his favorite authentic restaurant. As they neared his car, he took a deep breath and tried to explain. "I didn't expect to—It's just that—" He sighed. "Oh, Hope, I don't know how to explain it."

"But was it offensive for me to put on something so cultural maybe? Did it look silly—out of place on a blonde perhaps?"

He tugged her hair playfully. "Not at all, Hope. Quite the opposite I assure you."

Taking that for a compliment, she winked. "So maybe we should rethink that diamond chip. I might look good in it!"

"That's it. I'm telling your father."

"Bully."

He winked back at her. "And don't you forget it."

Jay followed her through his house, laughing at her delight. "I love this house! It's really nice." She jogged up the stairs, looked over the landing, and waved at him. "Somehow it's modern without looking sterile like so many of them do."

"That's why I liked it. I didn't want to look at it, but my realtor kept suggesting, so I decided I could spend an hour to appease her."

"Looks like she knows her business," Hope called, peeking in rooms along the upper floor.

"She worked hard for this sale, but the minute I walked through it, I knew I was home."

He watched as she roamed in and out of rooms, calling out comments of little details she liked. As she began to descend the stairs, she called out, "Don't let me fall!" and jumped on the bannister.

Jay had just enough time to reach the newel before she would have dropped to the floor. He swept her off her feet and spun her around the room until she begged him to stop. "I'm so dizzy!"

"That was the idea." Hope waited for him to continue. Jay waggled his eyebrows, and carried her to the kitchen, setting her on the island. "I figured if you were going to act like a dizzy blonde..."

"Oooh. I am so gonna get yooouuu..."

Changing the subject, Jay swept his arm around the room. "We can wrap the gifts here and use the counters and the island, or —"

"No way! You have to do it on the floor and make a huge bow mess. It's tradition. Come on, I'll show you."

Jay followed and watched as Hope piled rolls of wrapping paper in the middle of his sparse living room. She sprinkled tape dispensers and bows liberally around the pile and lobbed a few rolls of ribbon into the mix. After a few trips to her car, a pile of empty boxes stood nearby, waiting to be put into service. "Well, get your stuff. It's time to wrap."

She reached Jay's present and grabbed it and a few boxes. She dug through a couple of other bags and dragged them and a few rolls of wrapping paper upstairs. "Be right back."

Jay hadn't managed to get one of his gifts wrapped before she returned back downstairs with three perfectly wrapped packages. She thrust one into his hands and said, "Here. Open it. It's a housewarming present. I can't wait for you to see it."

Jay tore into the package, looking quite pleased, and had the box opened before he saw the shocked expression on her face. As he pulled the spread from its package, he asked, "Did you give me the wrong one?"

She snickered. A chortle followed by a chuckle and laugh eventually morphed into a guffaw. It truly wasn't that funny, but she couldn't stop laughing. "Look at the wrappings," she gasped.

Jay examined the shredded paper and found two different wrappings. "Why did you wrap it twice?"

"I was going to torture you," she snickered, still laughing at herself. "I wrapped it in the plain blue paper for your house warming gift. That way, when you opened the first layer, you would see the Christmas paper and I could say, 'Merry Christmas. I guess you have to wait until then.' But you got me. You got me good and you didn't even mean to."

Jay shook his head, smiling at her silliness. As he unfolded the spread, his eyes grew wide. "This is too much. It's beautiful but so expen—"

"No buts. If you hate it, that's one thing. Just wrap it up and regift it—to me preferably. I'll have dad get me a bigger bed. If you like it but it's not what you want in your room, use it for a guest bed. Otherwise, use it and remember a fun day of sari shopping."

She snatched the spread from him and attempted to tuck and fold the fabric around her in the appropriate sari fashion. Jay reached for her, pulling it off again. "Hope, it won't work. There isn't enough length, thank goodness. Have mercy on a guy, will you?"

"Why do you have such a problem with saris? Your mom told me she wore them every day until she became a citizen. Doesn't she still wear them when she dresses up?"

"Why are you so obsessed with them?"

"Because! They're beautiful. I felt so graceful and feminine, and forgive the conceit, beautiful in it. I really wish I would have tried on the aqua."

"That's it. You described my so-called problem perfectly."

As they continued to wrap, she directing him what paper to use for what boxes, Hope thought about what he'd said. After a few minutes, she thought she knew what he wasn't saying. "Jay?"

"Hmm?" He fought an awkward corner with a too-large piece of wrapping paper.

"Do you think Paige—you know, the girl who rescued us from 'What's up Chuck?' Isn't she gorgeous?"

"Definitely." Jay ripped the corner of the paper and sighed.

"I think she's one of the most beautiful women I've ever seen."

"Huh?" Jay looked up at her. "Oh, Paige. Yes, I'd say so."

"Can't you see her in that emerald sari in the window of the first shop?"

"It'd look great on her. She should try one." Jay cut a new length of paper and tried again.

"But you're not really attracted to Paige, are you?" Hope tried to keep her voice nonchalant.

"Not particularly." Once more, Jay fumbled with the corners, nearly tearing the package again.

Hope took pity on him and showed him how to fold and tape corners for a perfectly mitered envelope seal. "I guess if you were attracted to Paige, you'd rethink the idea of her looking good in a sari, though."

Jay nodded absently as he worked on the other end of the package. "Not really rethink, but if it looked anywhere near as good on her as that purple one did on —" He jerked his head up and glared at her. "That was not fair."

She grinned. "Consider it payback for being a bully about the diamond chip. And besides, it's a very *interesting* idea."

"Hope, you have no mercy." He taped the box and displayed it with a flourish. "There are a lot of things that I find interesting — starting with you."

Hope reached for another package, a little smile playing about her lips. She'd have to go back for the sari. Maybe some night she could make him dinner in it. Now *that* idea was interesting. Yes, it was.

CHAPTER 27

Saturday afternoon, Hope and Jay drove to Rockland to skate on the outdoor rink. As she tied her skates tightly around her ankles, Hope told Jay about Grace and Nolan's engagement. "Right here. Just last year. He stopped on the way to Mike's house and proposed with half the pond watching. She said it was incredibly romantic, and I'm sure it was…"

"Just a little public."

"Exactly. I doubt Nolan meant it to be," she hastened to add, "but regardless, it was. Still though, big ol' snowflakes and winter nights are awfully romantic."

Jay smiled as she as she eased onto the ice, her ankles looking much too sturdy for someone who claimed not to have been skating in a while. He tied his own laces slowly, dragging out the inevitable humiliation. As he worked, he said, "I imagine any story is romantic when it's yours."

"That's a good point! He could have proposed with both feet in a cow pie, and she would have loved it. How wise you are!"

"That's laying it on a bit thick—or as *Appa* says, 'napping it on a bit thick.'"

"Napping. Funny. Come on, I want to skate!"

Jay stood on wobbly legs. He slid one leg forward and then the next. Every second that passed, he saw as delaying the inevitable; he would fall. "Go ahead. I need to get my sea legs under me."

"I can just hear your dad saying, 'I need to see my legs under me.' Besides, shouldn't it be ice legs?"

"No, that'll be what happens when you land on your bum in that dress as previously discussed."

Hope chuckled. "Or me in that sari. I'd freeze. How did your mother stand wearing such flimsy things?"

"She adapted. There are these things called coats. You should check them out sometime. She wore things under her pants and a lot of shawls."

He saw her smile at the idea of his *amma* in her saris. It brought a lump to his throat. She wobbled but caught herself before she fell. His concern must have shown, because she said, "Don't worry, I won't fall. And if I do, I know how to fall without hurting myself – usually."

Jay slowly managed a semi-wobbleless glide around the outside of the rink, watching Hope whenever he felt confident in taking his eyes off the ice. Couples skated close together, while small children careened at breakneck speeds, trying to avoid everyone else. Hope, along with a few dedicated figure skaters, spent most of her time in the center of the rink, making light jumps and spins. She made it look effortless, and she had not exaggerated. Hope was good.

She eventually rejoined him, teasing him about his weak corners. "You need to pick up your right foot..." She described her so-called "smooth transition," but it sounded terrifying to him. When he hesitated, she came in on his left and pulled her arm through his. As they reach the next curve, she pulled on him a little as she said, "Pick up your foot now!"

Jay tried to copy her movements, but his feet slid out from under him, taking both of them down, and sliding just out of the path of oncoming skaters. "I'm sorry. I knew I shouldn't have tried it."

"Oh, I knew you'd fall the first time. Everyone does. Let's try it again."

"You knew I'd fall, and you didn't bother to tell me? Your confidence and encouragement are overwhelming," he grumbled.

Despite his protests, Jay found himself skating and then

sliding across the ice in regular intervals. In a last-ditch effort to keep him out of the ditch, Hope moved to his right side, and their next corner went smoothly. "You did it. I think me being on that side just made you nervous about stepping on me or something."

After a few laps, Jay gaining confidence with each one, Hope took his hand and pushed herself backwards in front of him. The evening grew cooler, the rink emptied until only a few die-hards remained, and Jay begged off. "Go do your spins and stuff. I need to sit."

As he removed his skates and warmed his hands, he watched her do sit spins and toe loops, ending with a scratch spin. At times, she was a blur on the ice. After several minutes of strenuous workout, she stopped, panting and grasping her knees.

She skated to where Jay waited and threw her arms around him. "That was so fun. I forgot how much I love this. I have to come more often."

"I agree—very fun," Jay said, nodding. "I especially liked the part where I sat and watched you." He smiled at her indignant expression. "And yes, we should come back much more often."

Hope pulled her knit hat from her head and whacked Jay with it. He grabbed it and took off into the park. "If you want your hat back, you have to come and get it," he called.

"I have skates on! You want me to chase you with skates on?"

He stopped. "I'll give you a sixty second skate change, and then I'm running. One...two...three..."

Hope's first skate was off before Jay said, "one." She pulled her boot on and tore off the second skate. She tore off after him, leaving both skates on the bench before Jay got to forty-five.

He saw her coming and took off. Hope squealed. "Hey! You said sixty seconds before you started running! You're a cheat, and I will make you pay!"

As he ran up the bridge, Hope took an alternate route. Jay glanced over his shoulder, but didn't see her anywhere. Just as he came around the other side of the bridge, she tackled him

225

around the ankles, sending them both tumbling into the snow.

"Gotcha."

"Aah! I couldn't figure out where you went. I'm too tall for that tunnel — no speed hunched over."

"That's why I went under. I knew I'd catch you when you got around the other side of the bridge."

Once her arms and legs were free of snow, Hope held her hand out for the cap. Jay waved it over her head, taunting her. She crossed her arms in mock fury, eyes flashing at his delay in returning her hat. "My ears are getting cold, Jay…"

Jay smiled down at her, brushing a snowflake from her bangs. He brushed aside another, and then another before he realized it was snowing. They looked up, amazed at the size of snowflakes falling around them like swirls in a snow globe. He brushed a few more flakes from her head before he tugged her hat back in place.

"It's beautiful," Hope whispered as she absorbed the snowflakes falling in the light of the park lamps.

"You were right." Jay's eyes never left her face. "Snowflakes at nighttime are incredibly romantic."

Hope smiled up at him as she slipped her hand in his. They strolled back to the bench where they'd left their skates before continuing on to Jay's car. "We have to get you back home now, or we'll be stuck here," he said as the snow fell faster.

"Mmm?"

Jay glanced at Hope as she watched the snow swirl around them. "Mmm hmmm."

Jay awoke to the sounds of the Senior house coming to life and groaned. Forgetting where he slept, Jay rolled off the couch, smashing his knee on the coffee table as he fell. "Guess that means I should get up," he groused to himself.

He grabbed his clothes from the back of Ron's recliner and shuffled into the downstairs bath. A blast of cold water hit him before it grew warm. "Aaak!" He sighed. "So much for not waking the neighborhood," he muttered.

226

As he dressed, Jay tried to work the kinks out of his neck and shoulders—a present from the couch. As much as he had planned not to do it, he changed his mind. If they offered Concord's bed over Christmas, he'd take it. His neck insisted.

He finally dragged himself into the kitchen, freshly shaved and feeling only a little bit more human. Ron raised his coffee as if a silent "Good morning," while Hope jumped up from the kitchen table and pulled a hot plate of eggs and sausage from the oven. She smiled at him. "You really aren't a morning person, are you?"

"How can you be so chipper at this time of morning? It's unnatural."

She pointed to his chair. "Eat."

Jay ate. With deliberate and soothing slowness, he ate, fully aware that it drove her half-insane. As he neared his last bite, she couldn't wait any longer. She stood, pointed to the clock on the stove, and said, "We leave in forty minutes. Be ready, or I'll make a scene as we enter Bible class."

He watched her disappear from the room and shook his head as Ron chuckled. "She's never late, but she does get grumpy if her routine gets upset. Just saying... turnabout is fair play, or so they say."

He debated for exactly three and a half seconds before deciding to take Ron up on his very transparent challenge. He heard her bedroom door shut and dashed up the stairs, taking them two at a time. He entered the bathroom looking for something—anything. Her curling iron sat on the countertop—warming. He shut it off and hurried back downstairs to dress for church.

The two men fought the temptation to look at one another, as Hope's indignant, "Arrgh!" echoed through the house when she discovered her curling iron. Score one for Jay.

The bathroom door shut with a bang, and Jay sprang into action again. He bounded upstairs, keeping as quiet as possible, and grabbed the shoes at the foot of her bed. He barely made it to the bottom of the stairs when Hope opened the bathroom door and called for her father to find her Bible. "I can't find it and don't know where I left it."

227

Jay dumped the shoes at the foot of the stairs and went searching for her Bible. He found it on the end table where they'd used it less than twelve hours earlier. Jay snickered and snuck out the car, setting her Bible on the front seat. Minutes later, Ron called upstairs, "Hope, I can't find it. Maybe it's in your room."

The bathroom door flung open, and Jay saw a pair of stocking feet run across the hall to her room. Moments later, they heard the sound of light thuds, rapidly increasing in frequency. Jay glanced questioningly at Ron, who said, "Shoes. She's looking for her shoes."

"Hope, we have ten minutes!" Never had he enjoyed giving someone a time deadline more.

"Coming! I just can't find my shoes!"

Ron winked at Jay. "Your black ones with the heels?"

"Have you seen them?"

"They're down here at the bottom of the stairs." Ron gestured wildly for Jay to grab Hope's coat and take it upstairs when the coast was clear.

Hope dashed down the stairs and strapped on her shoes. "I can't find anything today. Oh, the communion juice—I almost forgot."

Jay called from the recliner where he sat hiding her coat beneath him, "You probably just need more sleep."

"Very funny, Jay."

Ron gestured for him to go, and Jay made a third trip upstairs, laying Hope's coat on the end of her bed. He barely managed to jump into the recliner before she rounded the corner. "Ok, I'm ready. Did you find my Bible, Dad?"

"Not down here. Did you check your desk?"

Hope nodded. "Wasn't on it."

Jay waited until Ron made another suggestion before offering his. He didn't want to seem too eager to send her on any kind of search. "Is it on the table next to the coat closet?"

Hope looked as she reached for her coat, but the missing outerwear distracted her. "Where's my coat?"

Jay asked, almost before she finished her question, "Hey, Hope. Is your Bible with your skates? Did you have it with you last night?"

Hope looked confused. She seemed to have forgotten her coat as she dashed upstairs to check her skate bag. She returned moments later, obviously confused. Before she could comment on how her coat had ended up on the end of her bed, Ron urged Jay to get his. "We should have left by now. Let's go. You'll have to use a pew Bible or share Jay's."

As Hope climbed into the passenger seat, she spied her Bible. Her eyes flew to her father and then to Jay. "Jay! I can't believe you did that! Dad!"

Ron and Jay laughed as she upbraided them for their serious lack of chivalry and decorum. This earned her further laughter. "Come on, Hope. You have to admit. You asked for it—practically challenged him to do it," Ron insisted.

"And I bet the idea began in that diabolical head of yours."

"Maaayyybeee."

Despite her accusations, by the time Hope entered the church, Jay was as solicitous of her comfort as any girl could desire. He brought her a bulletin when hers was missing an insert. He held the songbook and communion tray. He offered pen and paper and even fetched tissues when she choked down laughter that brought tears to her eyes. After the benediction, Jay held Hope's coat, purse, and Bible as she greeted her friends and talked with loved ones.

Then Jay caught sight of a familiar face in the back of the room. He moved closer to Hope, murmuring in her ear. "Mabel's here. She's waiting to talk to you."

Hope quickly excused herself from the conversation she'd begun and hurried to greet Mabel. Jay followed. Mabel seemed excited to see them again. After a few minutes, Hope had managed to introduce her to people the woman might enjoy, had her signed up for the senior Christmas luncheon, promised her a visit from the carolers, and cajoled several people to offer to give her rides until her ankle healed.

Jay helped her to the curb where her grandson waited. While Hope hugged Mabel and got her settled in the car, Jay smiled at the young man. "Thanks for bringing her. We'd love to have you come back as well, but if bringing her is a time conflict, several people offered to give her a ride. Don't hesitate to call. They were all happy to get to know her."

The boy nodded and thanked them, half-promising to come at least once. As they pulled away from the curb, Hope smiled up at Jay. "You cannot be this charming."

Eyes twinkling, he cocked his head. "Charming?"

"I'm supposed to be mad at you!"

"We'll have to duel it out then. I consider myself challenged without the need for slapping, by the way. Knives, guns, or swords?"

"None of the above. Laser tag. You're doomed. One on one. Three shots and you're dead. At the park. After lunch. Be there."

"In the snow?"

Hope turned and shook her head. "Wimp."

Jay strategized as he watched Hope move toward him. She dodged from tree to trash can to snowman. He tried to calculate the difference between the warmth generated by movement and the warmth he had found tucked away in a corner of the handball court. Each had one shot on the other. Hope had barely missed him just ten minutes earlier. He had also discovered a serious flaw in their game plan. The game could not possibly end before they froze. With just the two of them, they could dodge one another until one or both became permanent ice sculpture on display until the spring thaw.

Risking an irate Hope, he removed his vest, attached it to the tip of his gun, and waved it as he moved toward her. "Hope, we have a problem! Five minute truce!"

Hope jogged toward him, looking too smug for him to ignore. "Cold?"

"Yes, but that's not the problem. We'll be out here until we're numb. We can dodge each other indefinitely. Once either of us gets another shot at the other, that's what we'll be doing. We need another objective."

Hope had to concede his point. She thought for a moment and nodded. "I've got it. We each take off for three minutes

230

further away from home. We get three shots again. First one back to my house alive wins. If one of us gets killed before that, the game is over and we'll either continue home or come back for your car — whichever is closer."

He nodded. "Deal. On your mark, get set, run!"

They dashed through the park and onto nearby streets. At the three minute mark, they began doubling back, running as fast as they could in the cold air. Jay realized as he ran, that within a few blocks, the real game would begin. The only way back to Hope's house was along the frontage road to the highway.

Jay decided to hide and wait once he reached the frontage road. He'd get a shot in there, and then know which side of the road she would travel. He'd try for another shot when she crossed the highway to her development, and then the final one near her street. With careful planning and even more careful aim, he could have her out before she made it to the door.

He jumped into a culvert and saw his vest light up with a direct hit. Hope smirked at him from behind a spindly scrub tree. "One."

Jay scrambled back out and hid behind a bank of security mailboxes before she could get in a second shot. For the first time, he was thankful for the ten-second space rule. "Game's not over!"

Back and forth, from street to cars to trees, Jay raced toward the highway. Before long, he knew he was ahead of her. He crouched behind a concrete support for a drainage pipe and took aim. Any second now, she would be forced to come out of the culvert. It was a dead end. She'd either come out facing him on his side or he'd get her in the back on the other. Either way, unless his aim was horrendous, he had her.

There she was. Her vest lit up. "Gotcha! We're tied!" Jay raced across the highway and dove into a shallow ditch. Snow slid down his collar, and he shivered. "This is so not worth it."

When he saw no sign of Hope, and she didn't acknowledge the hit, Jay became concerned. He waited. Minutes ticked past. "Hope? I don't see or hear you."

No response. He called again. Finally, Jay made his way

231

back across the highway, looking on all sides to see that she hadn't fallen. It seemed as if she'd vanished. He ignored the game and raced around the concrete support. Direct hit.

"Two to one, my favor!" Hope scrambled for the other side of the culvert, but Jay jumped across it and tackled her, sending both of them sliding down into the snow. He pushed her gun away from her and pinned her arms above her head. "Didn't you hear me call?"

"Yep."

"Why didn't you answer? I was getting worried."

"Because you wouldn't have come back, and I couldn't have shot you again."

Jay groaned, pulling her to her feat. "You'd let me worry to win a game?"

"You have to ask that question?" Hope was completely unrepentant.

Jay shook his head, rolled his eyes, and sighed. "You are— oh what's that word from the musical with all the kids— incorrigible."

"Thank you. I like you too. I think you're *interesting*!" Hope pushed the hair from her eyes with her gloved hand.

Jay reached for her hand and caught it. Pulling the glove from his other hand with his teeth, he combed the hair from her face with his fingers. It was just as silky as on Thanksgiving. "Your hair…"

A lump welled in his throat as she copied him, her fingers playing with his too-long curls. "I thought your hair would be a little coarse, but it's not. It's soft." She waited, quiet, her fingers still intertwined in his hair. "Jay?"

He met her gaze and saw something he'd wanted to see for far longer than he cared to admit. "Yes?"

She sighed, exasperated. "I'm not going to pretend that I don't know you're attracted to me. I mean, I got the sari thing after I got the idea of it being some kind of insult to your culture out of my head. You liked it."

Jay adjusted her bangs, putting the long wisps back on the correct sides of her head. "If you expect me to deny it, you'll be disappointed. What's your point?"

"I've seen it in your eyes. I'm quite certain that I'm not wrong."

"About what?"

Hope tugged at curl near his temple, making Jay's eyes smart. She smiled. "Okay, fine. You want blunt. I can be blunt. Why haven't you kissed me?"

He pulled her to her feet, and pulled her close, one arm around her shoulder. "It's going to sound silly."

"I can handle silly. I can't handle seeing one thing and knowing I do but feeling like it's not really there."

"I just like that we didn't rush our friendship. It became important to me very quickly, but we took our time with it."

"Yeah, I remember thinking, 'How can I care so much about someone I hardly know' back when we were dealing with Mom's chemo." Her voice shook, and Jay pulled her even closer, wrapping her in a hug before he began walking again.

"I think that's why our friendship is strong. You could get engaged to Chuck Majors tomorrow, and I think we'd still manage to stay friends."

"Some friend you are."

Jay's eyebrows rose, questioning. "What?"

"Letting me engage myself to that obnoxious pile of half-melted turkey gizzards."

Jay laughed as they turned toward her housing development. "Ahh, Hope."

"Jay, I'm serious. I've seen it. I know it's not my imagination, and well, I also don't think I have to be full of myself to know that I'm not repulsive…"

"Are you saying you're impatient?" Jay teased.

"Well no, I—I mean that—Oh, I'm going to get you. You know what I mean."

His smile spread across his face. "I do. I'm sorry. You're just quite adorable when you're flustered, but you're right. I won't pretend I haven't thought of it. The night of the party at your dorm, for instance…"

"That one I missed until I got to my room." She frowned. "Was it because it was so public?"

"That might have been a factor had I thought of it. It just

233

wasn't the right time."

Hope stopped and stared at him. "What about last night, or even just a few minutes ago when I know you—"

"Let me ask you a question," he said, interrupting. "When did we first hold hands?"

Hope replied instantaneously. "On the way back from the party."

"Exactly. We'll probably never forget it. It wasn't that special of an occasion, but it had its own moment frozen in time. It's the only time we will ever hold hands for the *first* time."

A slow smile spread across her face. "Are you romantic, sentimental, or just a poet? Maybe all three?"

"I wouldn't go that far. It's just that, as far as I'll ever know, this is my first everything. We can never have a second first kiss—a second first real date. A second first anything. I don't want to rush it. I can't imagine that we'd ever regret taking our time and enjoying every second of discovering if you and me make a good 'we.'"

Hope smiled into his eyes. "I can think of another first…"

It was too late. Jay aimed, shot her, and dove behind a parked car. "One more, Hope. You only have one more."

She stood still, absorbing the moment, smiling. For the first time in her life, she didn't really mind being beaten. Jay Brown liked her. Another first. A Christian man was interested in her. "I underestimated you," she murmured under her breath.

She plotted her strategy as she pounded her way toward home. He'd been fooled by her once, but she couldn't do that again. Jay would lose the game before he ignored the possibility of her being hurt. That wasn't a fair way to win, and in games, Hope liked a fair win—within reason.

Jay's vest flashed past. She fired—and missed. "Drat. Now he knows my position," she gasped as she dove for a fence around the corner from his post. Seeing the fence gave her an idea. She ran down the street, counting houses until she recognized the Bjorklunds. Praying they'd be home—meaning their boxers would be indoors—she jumped the fence and ran through the backyard to the side gate. She lifted the latch quietly and shut it silently behind her.

She saw Jay's vest as he dashed down the street once more, giving her an opening. She raced for the Miller house, and waving at Mr. Miller, motioned for permission to run through his back yard. From there she jumped catty-cornered into the Mercer yard, thankful that they were on vacation. Mrs. Mercer would not have been happy. As she shut the gate, Hope saw her footprints and prayed for snow to cover them before the Mercers got back for the New Year's Eve party.

She dashed across the street, through the Wesleys' yard, and into the Calloways'. Mrs. Calloway dropped the garbage when she saw Hope dive over the fence. "Oh! Sorry. We're playing laser tag, and I have to get to my house before Jay, so I was cutting through — let me help."

Able to speak again, Mrs. Calloway waved Hope home. "Just win. I'll clean it up. Hurry!"

Hope dashed through the side yard, banging against the gate. Jay, three houses away from her door, took aim and missed. Hope had a straight shot for the house and took it. Jay came out blazing, but she reached the door first. As he neared, Jay looked positively menacing.

"You went over fences. Clever. Of course, I couldn't do that, not knowing everyone. I'll get you for it, though." He leaned against the door, effectively trapping her. "You win. I accept defeat and humbly beg forgiveness for my antics this morning."

Hope smiled up at him. "You shouldn't. That was brilliant. I had no idea."

She turned to go inside, but Jay caught her hand. "Hope?"

"Hmm?" She didn't trust herself to speak.

"Do you think I'm being ridiculous? I mean, about taking things so slowly?"

"I think you're right. It might drive me crazy sometimes, but who says that's a bad thing?" She winked and added, "Don't answer that."

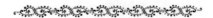

After dinner, Hope drove Jay to his car. They loaded his

235

overnight bags and a few containers of food that Hope insisted he take. "You'll come Wednesday night?"

"It'll probably be nine or later. Are you sure you don't want me to wait for Thursday?"

Her smile was decidedly flirtatious. "I don't want you to leave at all, silly. Of course, I want you on Wednesday." She shook her head, "Oh, and I'll have Concord's room ready for you. You'll have to stay in there. A week is too long for the couch."

"I won't argue unless you think your father —"

She shook her head. "Dad said so too."

Hope shivered. Jay pulled her close into a lazy hug and held her, murmuring into her ear. "I don't want to go either. When we first met, we hardly saw each other — maybe every two or three weeks or even less, and now three days seems much too long."

"I like the way you do that," she whispered.

"Do what?" Jay searched Hope's eyes.

"The way you — talk in my ear. I can't think of the word for some reason — probably because of how you're looking at me with those eyes!"

"You like the way I talk in your ear?"

Hope nodded and pulled his ear close. "It's just so private. It makes me feel like I'm the only one that you care to talk to. Silly, isn't it?" she whispered.

Jay bent his head and murmured one last time before he climbed into his car. "Three days. It'll be torture, Hope."

She stood waving as he drove out of the parking lot. The faint sound of her cellphone ringtone sent her into her car, digging into her purse for it. She pulled out the phone, and a text flashed across the screen. WHERE HAS ALL THE MISTLETOE GONE?

236

CHAPTER 28

The clock taunted him with the lateness of the hour as Jay pulled into the Seniors' driveway. He'd hoped to arrive by nine, but last-minute meetings, a quick report, and a bill-paying marathon kept him from leaving until well after eight-thirty. Thanks to weather and traffic, even pushing the speed limit when possible, it had taken him almost two hours. He sat in the car watching the dark house, hating to have to knock.

With a deep sigh, he climbed from his car and grabbed his overnight bag. A sticky note on the front door told him to come in. *I'll be waiting in the living room. Dad had a hard day. I sent him to bed.*

As he entered, his head brushed a jingle bell. He looked up and found a festive sprig of mistletoe with a bell dangling from the tip. A soft chuckle escaped before Jay could catch himself. He wanted to surprise Hope, if possible.

As he passed the kitchen, he noticed a second sprig, hanging from the entryway. Growing suspicious, his eyes roamed over all the doors and doorways. Mistletoe hung everywhere. From light fixtures to ceiling fans to sprigs on fishing line tacked to the ceiling—there was enough mistletoe overhead to make him feel like a fish swimming in festive seaweed.

The moment she saw him, Hope gave a delighted squeal and rushed to hug Jay, ending her conversation with Kirky abruptly and tossing her phone on the couch. He dropped his bag and spun her in an ark as she flung herself in his arms. "I missed you!"

"I can tell!" Jay glanced around the room. "I see you found the mistletoe. Are you trying to tell me something?"

"Well, you asked where it went. I found it."

Jay gazed down at her, amazed that she chose him — wanted him — and all that mistletoe. "Now, to properly appreciate every single one of the dozens of —"

"That would be four hundred and sixty-three sprigs — before Daddy knocked a few out of place."

Jay nodded. " — To appreciate approximately four hundred and sixty sprigs of mistletoe — individually — could take a great amount of time..."

"But what a way to spend the time!"

"You, my Hope, are shameless."

She smirked at him. "Well, if that's what it takes..."

"So, no taking time to appreciate the firsts of a relationship?"

Hope stood, hands on hips in mock indignation. "There is a first for every single sprig in this house!"

Pulling her close, Jay murmured, "It has been the longest three days of my life. I missed this."

Jay jumped at the sound of banging on his door. "Up and at 'em! We have a busy day."

Groaning, he glanced at the clock. Eight. "It's Christmas Eve! I'm on vacation. Don't I get to sleep?"

Hope peeked her head in the door. "Nope. Not at all. There's a whole day of fun ahead of us. I already let you sleep an extra hour since you got in late. Come on!"

Five minutes later, Jay stumbled from the room and into Ron. "Aak. Sorry. I'm not quite awake."

Ron apologized for accosting him so early. "I had to come get you. You have to stop her. She's trying to do everything that Cheryl did — the dessert baskets, the cards — everything. You have to stop her."

238

"I don't understand."

"She spent all morning making fudge—fudge! She hates making fudge. She threw away more batches than she kept. If she does it all this year, she'll feel like she has to do it forever."

Ron seemed overwrought, but Jay couldn't decide if he was more upset for Hope or for himself. "It's going to hurt her."

"It'll hurt her more if she doesn't release traditions that she enjoyed but weren't her 'projects.'" Ron swallowed hard, blinking back tears. "We're teetering on the edge here. It's hard without Cheryl…"

"I'm so sorry," Jay began, unsure of what to say. "I'll try to scale her back."

Jay dressed and brushed his teeth. He made every move robotically, his mind swirling with plans to convince her to calm down. Hope's third call for him to hurry sent him down without a clue as to what he'd do.

As he passed Ron, he murmured, "I think we need to be alone…"

On a pretext of needing something from his office, Ron drove away, leaving Hope standing at the door looking lost. "I can't believe he did that! He just left!"

Jay laced Hope's fingers in his and tugged her to the couch. He'd prayed for wisdom and now he was curious to see what God would give him as a solution. "I asked him to leave."

Hope snuggled next to him, batting her eyes in comically exaggerated flirtation. "Oh, really."

Jay pushed her away, shaking his head and grinning. "Behave, woman. We have to talk."

As if she knew what he would say, Hope started to rise. He pulled her back down and took a deep breath. "I just want you to tell me about *your* Christmas traditions."

Hope began reciting a list of things to do that made his head spin. From making fudge and divinity to cinnamon popcorn and toffee, the candy making alone would have taken any well-seasoned cook a week in the quantities she mentioned. "Then we make baskets of goodies and take them to everyone at church and to all the neighbors."

"How did your mom do that in the last few years without

you kids home to help her?"

Hope shrugged. "It's almost nine, though, and I haven't even started on the divinity. It's going to take hours. We should really get to work."

Jay held her back once again. "Hope, how much of the baking and candy making did you do?"

She shrugged. "The cookies were my job, usually. I love making cookies. Mom did all the candy and stuff."

"And who made all the baskets?"

Hope frowned. "Well, Mom did, but—"

"Who delivered them?"

"Mom and Dad each took a car and delivered the ones to people at church. I did the neighbors. This year—"

Jay interrupted. "Is your dad up to that this year?"

She looked up at him, her eyes searching his. "What do you mean?"

Jay sighed and ignored the question. "Tell me more. What comes after that?"

"Well," she said hesitantly. "We have Christmas Eve dinner. It's always chili and oyster crackers."

"And who makes that?"

Hope sighed. "Well, Mom usually started it first thing when she woke up—I think. Or maybe she made it during the week. Anyway, I need to go start that too."

Jay pulled her back to the couch once more, trying to smile, but his heart aching for the losses she felt. "What happens after that?"

"We go to church for the candlelight service. After that, we look at Christmas lights. Then we come home and take turns sneaking downstairs to fill stockings."

"Then what?"

Hope glared at him. The first fire he'd seen in her all day lit her eyes. "Then I sob myself to sleep because I had a stinky Christmas Eve because I sat around all day talking about the things I usually do instead of doing them."

Jay sighed, relieved. He had been waiting for a line just like that one since the conversation began. "But Hope, you keep talking about the things your mom did. You didn't do those

240

things. You didn't make chili and the candy and the baskets and deliver them to sixty families at church. You wake up bright-eyed and bushy-tailed, which *Appa* would call 'furry-storied,' and deliver the work your mom has done because she loved doing it."

"But—"

"Do you enjoy—really love—making fudge and divinity? Do you like making cinnamon popcorn and peppermint bark?"

She resisted. He saw in her the truth. None of those things interested her, but she didn't want to admit it. "Well, I love the baskets and giving them to everyone—it's worth the work."

"Is it?" Jay shifted, tilting her chin so he could see her eyes. "Is it really worth the work? Is there something else that you would enjoy doing that you could do next year instead?"

"But it's our tradition! People count on it. The stories I could tell..."

"People do not count on one busy college student and her bereaved father to continue someone else's tradition," he said quietly.

Hope jumped to her feet, eyes blazing. "That *someone* you speak of is my mother. She was loved, respected, and important to a lot of people! Everyone knew my mom, and I'm not going to fail her because our traditions are too much work for you!"

Hope dashed upstairs, the sounds of sniffles in her wake. Jay glanced at the clock. She could never get everything done in one day. Cheryl had to have spent a week—maybe two—doing all the work she had mentioned. Before he tried to comfort her, Jay decided he might want to start a pot of chili.

Upstairs, Hope heard sounds in the kitchen and debated if she should go back downstairs and help or if it would be best not to and just pray that he tossed her crystallized fudge. She wanted to pray. She couldn't. She wanted to cry. Starting would be disastrous. Every moment that she sat alone in her room, she felt more lost and hopeless than she'd ever imagined possible.

The scent of sizzling meat slowly wafted upstairs. Her stomach rumbled. Not eating breakfast—bad idea. Spicy smells followed until Hope almost couldn't stand it. She wanted to go downstairs. She wanted to apologize. She wanted to eat. Pride

241

demanded that Jay come to her.

Pride was appeased. She heard Jay's footsteps outside the door, but didn't roll over to greet him. Still curled in a fetal position, she fought back tears when a plate with sandwiches and chips appeared by her face. She felt Jay sit next to her, his hand on her shoulder.

"Chili is simmering—or will be soon. I have no idea if it will be any good, but it will be chili."

Hope rolled onto her back holding half a sandwich. "That was sooo not fair."

"What wasn't? I'm not—"

"You know I love it when you do that. How can I stay mad at you when my stomach is doing flip-flops?"

With a delighted gleam in his eye, Jay leaned closer. "What, you mean like this?"

Hope bopped him with her pillow and took a bite of her sandwich. "Mmmm… this is good. You remembered salt and pepper. Very nice."

They carried the food downstairs and munched as Hope pulled recipes from her mother's Christmas book. "Mom made scrapbooks for everything—holidays, birthdays, everything. She wrote funny notes, told stories, and just inserted whatever struck her fancy." Before Jay could say anything, she whispered, "Those books of hers are like scrapbooks you can use to live— not just remember."

As she turned to the recipe and instructions for divinity, her shoulders sagged. Jay's voice made her jump. "Hope?"

"Don't say it, Jay."

He sighed. "I have to. You don't have to do this. What about next year? Will you have the time? And the next? What about when you get married?"

Hope eyed him waggling one eyebrow. "Was that—"

He swatted her with an oven mitt. "I'm serious. What if in a few years you're married, pregnant, sick of the baby, and—"

"Sick *of* the baby? If I'm still pregnant, isn't that a bit premature?"

Jay eyed her, clearly not amused. "Hope—"

"But I want to do it. Is it so wrong to want to do it?"

242

Jay sighed. "Do you really want to do *all* of it? What about your father? Is he ready to deal with the memories? How will he feel driving off without your mother? Will he be able to stand a fresh round of condolences at every home?"

"That was low, Jay." Hope's voice now held an edge.

He wiped a few tears from the corners of her eyes. "As low as he'll feel? I don't want to be cruel, *kadhal*, but are you considering your father's feelings at all?"

"What does that mean? Ka—?"

Jay's low chuckle soothed her irritated nerves. "It means 'obnoxious one,' and you're off subject."

"You're cheating—trying to sweet-talk me into seeing things your way."

Jay pulled a barstool to the counter and sat facing her, meeting her eye. "First, I don't have a way. I am perfectly happy to do everything you have always done."

He turned the pages of Cheryl's Christmas book. Hope waited for a moment and then poked him. "And second?"

"Second what?"

"You said, 'first' you were happy to do things with me. What is the second?" She winked at him. "And why do I have a feeling it has something to do with you wanting to avoid telling me what that word means."

"I'm sorry," he said at last. "You're going to be disappointed, but I wasn't trying to sweet-talk you into anything. I didn't realize I said it until you repeated it."

She beamed. "So, why call me obnoxious one?"

"Why does the lavender-haired woman at the grocery store call me hon?"

"But hon is a term of endearment—short for honey. I wonder how you spell that. Maybe there's a Tamil translator on the Internet." At the panicked look on his face, she giggled. "I suddenly do *not* believe you."

Jay groaned. "If I agree that it does not mean obnoxious one, will you agree to leave it alone?"

"You called me something endearing without meaning to!"

He waited, a look of dread on his face. She waited, wondering what his problem was. After several awkward

243

seconds he asked, "Aren't you going to let me have it?"

"Not until I check out one of those translation sites when you aren't looking."

"You're not angry?"

"For calling me something that, based upon your embarrassment alone, is probably charmingly romantic?"

He shook his head. "For doing it without thought or care."

"That's what makes it so romantic. You said it because whatever *it* is, it is a part of how you perceive me. It wasn't just something you said to impress me or manipulate me to do what you want."

"Well, that would be a waste of time; you'll do what you like regardless of what I want."

Hope bit her lip. "Do you really think that?"

Jay muttered something about the air turning cool and moved to the living room. Hope watched him as he piled logs in the fireplace, adjusted the kindling, and nursed it into a roaring flame. It wasn't like him to push her. He usually jumped into her ideas with both feet and seemed to enjoy the ride.

She wondered if Jay saw something in her father... That thought sent her to his side on the floor near the hearth. He sat, staring into the fire, angry. He didn't move to touch her, as he had more recently. She struggled with what to do and then snuggled under his arm until it wrapped around her shoulders.

"Jay, did my father say anything about today?"

Only the crackle of the fire answered her. The grandfather clock ticked in one corner and the faint strains of Christmas music reached them from the radio in the kitchen. Hope marveled at how noisy the silence was as she waited.

"Jay, did my father say anything to you?" Anger welled in her heart.

"And if he did, I am supposed to betray a confidence?"

"So, if my father did not speak to you, did he not say that he does not want to continue our traditions?"

Jay coughed. "I think those are some interesting double negatives, Hope. Your father, if he had chosen to speak to me, probably would have said something about how hard it is for him right now. Seeing you killing yourself while doing things

244

that you don't enjoy—"

"But I do enjoy it!"

"—doing," he continued, "is hurting him. Enjoying the results is very different than the process. Or," he said with pain-filled eyes, "that's what I would think he would say if he said anything that I could repeat of what he did not say that he would have said."

Despite the pain his words caused, she couldn't help but giggle. "I thought he cared about these things as much as Mom and I did—do."

"I think he did, Hope." Jay's fingers played with her hair. "But without your mom, I think some of them are too much for him—especially when you are killing yourself to do in a day what she had to have spent a week or more preparing. Things that she enjoyed doing, and you don't."

"How do you know I don't enjoy it?"

"Well, for one thing, you're sitting here talking about it. If you wanted to be baking cookies, I'd be in there rolling dough and making sure I put them on the sheet in perfect rows. You're procrastinating. But mainly, I think it has to do with how your father didn't tell me how much you didn't like to help your mom with the candy and baskets."

Hope started to speak, but Jay laid his finger gently on her lips. "This tradition of making candy for half of Marshfield was your mother's. Keep your traditions, but don't feel obligated to keep hers. If you do, you'll grow to hate it."

Hope kissed his finger. At his surprised look, she pointed to the ceiling. "I had to. It's tradition!"

"That's one tradition I intend to embrace."

"Oh, really…"

Jay groaned. "Poor choice of words." He glanced at her. "You're not mad at me?"

"Actually, if I'm honest with both of us, I am. I'm hurt, a little scared, and I kind of feel lost. I want to scream. But, I'm also honest enough to admit to both of us that you're right. I was trying to have a good attitude, and now that I think of how much there was to do, I never would've gotten it all done."

"You might want to call your dad. He's probably bored at

245

the school."

Hope called, apologizing to her father, and then turned to Jay. "I made you angry, didn't I?"

"Yes."

"Will you tell me why?" She didn't like the memory of Jay staring stonily into the fire.

"It seemed that you cared more about sticking to your plans than about people — about your father."

"That tradition was more important than the people it was intended to bless."

Jay laced his fingers in hers. "It sounds like something you've heard often."

She stood to go into the kitchen, but Jay didn't release her hand. She tugged; he followed. Ron entered the house just as Hope led Jay through the doorway into the kitchen. Hope flipped to the front of the Christmas book. A handwritten quote stood alone on the page. Jay read it aloud. "'Traditions are not more important than the people they were intended to bless.'"

A voice from the doorway said, "Your mother was a wise woman."

Jay and Hope turned to see Ron standing in the doorway, tears glistening in his eyes. Hope rushed to her father and hugged him. Kissing his cheek, she begged forgiveness. "I'm so sorry, Daddy."

"You should be. All this mistletoe everywhere and that's the first kiss I had. I thought it was going to go to waste."

Hope tripped downstairs in her party dress. Ron watched, amazed. When had his little girl turned into such a beautiful woman? That thought made him smile. There probably wasn't a father alive who didn't or wouldn't think the same thing.

He glanced at Jay and smiled at the way their friend admired his daughter. When the Christian boys had ignored Hope through her high school years, he hadn't minded. She had years ahead of her for boyfriends.

She hadn't met anyone at college during her first two

semesters either. Though not sorry, he had wondered what was wrong with men. The world admired Hope—sought her at every turn. The church, however, as much as they loved and respected her, seemed blind to her. Watching her with Jay as they pulled on their coats and gathered their Bibles, Ron supposed that God must have put blinders on those around her in order to save her for Jay. *You chose well, Lord,* he thought to himself.

Just before Jay climbed into the backseat, he shut the door and retreated to the house. Hope and Ron stared at one another and shrugged as their teeth chattered away, waiting for the car to warm. Jay returned with what appeared to be a package and a blanket. He waved Ron on and climbed into his own car.

Ron turned to his daughter, confused. "What is he doing?"

"Your guess is better than mine."

After church, Jay waited patiently as Hope apologized—again—for not delivering the baskets. Everyone showed genuine surprise that she'd even considered making the elaborate baskets that her mother enjoyed giving. That seemed to fluster her even more.

Mrs. Shatternmann hugged her and said, "Hope, it was your mother's gift to us. No one could have enjoyed something you slaved all day to make. You have a good man here—don't give us or the baskets another thought."

As they walked to Jay's car, she nudged him playfully. "Don't say it."

He smiled down at her. "I don't have to. Mrs. Shatternmann said it better than anyone could have."

At the car, Jay pulled out a gift. "Open it."

Hope watched his face as she tore the paper from the box. "Tights?"

He tilted it toward the streetlight. She squealed. "Did you give me these now for the reason I think you did?"

"I thought maybe you would want to try out your new dress and make a new tradition."

"What about Dad?"

Jay motioned for Ron to join them. "Are you ready to look at Christmas lights?"

"You didn't—I mean, sh—" Ron stammered.

Hope looked at her father, shocked. "You don't *want* to go?"

"I don't expect you to understand," he said at last, "but I just can't."

"Okay. Fine. We're going skating. I'll see you in the morning. Don't wait up. We'll probably be late."

Jay tried to send Ron a reassuring look before opening his car door for Hope. He started the car, backed out of the parking lot, and turned toward Rockland. "I know you're hurting, but so is he. He misses his other half. He was torn in half, Hope. He isn't ready to go on as if she isn't gone."

"So his hurt is worse than mine, and I can just suck it up?"

He sighed. Silence seemed the best course. Hope fingered her tights as she rode along, the fury almost burning him. The air, thick with tension, fairly sizzled as Jay spoke. "How long do you plan to punish your father for his grief?"

Hope gasped. "How can you say that? I can't believe you just said that! What about my grief? We *always* look at lights after church."

"Let's go look at lights, then."

"No offense, Jay, but it's not the same. First I lose my brother, then I lose my mom. Now I just found out that I'm losing that special time with my only remaining close relative!"

"But you don't mind putting that relative through his own private torture so long as you get your way."

Jay kept his voice calm—that maddening, loving calm voice that drove his mother crazy. He knew Hope wanted to throttle him; he just wanted to cry. He hated that he hurt her. Even more, he hated that it was necessary.

"You seem determined to hurt me. I feel like today I lost my mom all over again—mostly thanks to you."

"Imagine how your father feels."

"I'm not going to cry—I won't."

He wrapped her hand in his. "Ah, *kadhal*, why not? I think you need the tears."

She sniffed. "I don't want to look awful. I feel pretty in this dress, but there's nothing pretty about a blotchy makeup job and raccoon eyes."

"Call your father. I think he is now hurting more than ever."

As much as he tried to ignore the conversation, he couldn't help but overhear. Hope apologized, and from what he could tell, Ron did as well. As much as she tried to understand, Hope still seemed wounded — lost.

"You did it again."

Hope's voice startled him from his thoughts. "I did what?"

She covered their hands with her other hand, squeezing them. "You called me the doll thing."

"Did I?" He lowered his voice conspiratorially. "If you can keep a secret…"

Hope leaned closer. "Yes…"

"It's true."

"What's true?"

Jay's voice rumbled with laughter. "Ahh, now that would be telling, wouldn't it?"

Jay waited on the bench by the ice rink, shivering. In the car, Hope was supposed to be putting on her new tights. He thought she was just trying to make him pay for all he'd put her through that day. He whipped out his phone and called.

"What do you want?"

"Get out of that warm car and come freeze with me."

She trudged across the snow, and collapsed next to him on the bench. They laced their skates, and in minutes, she circled Jay, still wearing her overcoat. Jay mocked her. "I knew it was too cold to skate in that dress. "By the time it's warm enough, there won't be any ice left."

Hope rolled her eyes. "I'll have you know that I'm almost too warm for the coat. I just wanted it while I warmed up."

True to her word, she tossed the coat on the bench a few minutes later, skating circles around Jay. "Are you going to tell

249

me what it means?" As she wove figure eights around Jay, Hope teased and cajoled.

"I don't think so."

"What if I guess?"

Jay shook his head. "I wouldn't advise it."

"Is it an insult?" He refused to answer, so she guessed again. "Is it an endearment?"

"Depends on your idea of endearment."

Hope smirked. "Okay, that's a yes."

"You're hopeless."

Just as he spoke, Jay tumbled, sliding across the ice. Hope snickered. "That's what you get for trying to get rid of me."

He skated back to her, pulling her toward the bench. Before he sat down, he murmured, "That's the last thing I want to do."

Hope, fully warmed up and ready for some serious skating, made a few slow sweeps and jumps. As Jay watched, he knew what she meant about her skirt. It flowed and flared beautifully. The skirt was long enough to be modest even in spins, but not so long as to limit movement.

He watched enthralled. Could she have made the Olympic team or gone professional? He suspected she could have. His *amma* needed to see this; she would be delighted.

Hope skated until her ungloved fingers felt numb with cold. Jay helped her with her shoes and then to the car. As he started the engine, Hope smiled at him and said, "I think we've just made a new Christmas tradition — ice skating on Christmas Eve."

"I like it," Jay whispered.

"This is another must-have tradition!"

Jay stared at his bowl, frowning. "I thought it already was a tradition to have chili on Christmas Eve."

Hope smiled wickedly. "It is. The new one is that you make it — and we eat leftovers after we come back from ice skating. This is the best chili I've ever had!"

"So what happens next?" Jay leaned forward expectantly.

"Do you have any idea how fun this is for me?"

Hope gazed into Jay's eyes, searching for something. "You mean that, don't you?"

"Of course! Why wouldn't I?"

She jabbed him playfully as she pulled him into the living room to admire the tree. "You've avoided every hint of any tradition all day."

"Never, Hope. Never. I challenged you to consider if the things you attempted to do were your traditions or if you were trying to keep the traditions of others because they were connected with yours."

The fire left her eyes. The smoke he had expected to billow forth from her ears and nostrils never materialized. Her hands dropped from her hips and her head shook. "Why couldn't you have said that earlier? I understand now. You are so right. That's exactly what I was doing."

He brushed her cheek. "I did say it earlier. You just needed to hear it a few times, get the angst out of your system, and come to grips with the change."

"I didn't have to take it out on you."

With that, she wrapped her arms around Jay's waist, hugging him. Jay had never heard of a more special request for forgiveness. He held her under dozens of mistletoe and smiled at the irony of hugs rather than kisses.

The sound of Ron's throat clearing startled. Jay started to step back, but Hope held fast. "Sorry, Dad. I'm not moving."

"Can you step to the left, then? I need to hang some stockings."

That worked. Hope jumped and clapped her hands, squealing. Her eyes misted as she saw her father hang Concord's and her mother's stockings in their usual places. "Oh!"

Jay found himself left "Hope-less" as she flung herself at her father. "I was afraid—"

Ron smiled at her. "I knew you would be. I waited as long as I could, but I'm an old man. I need my sleep. Pumpkin time in three minutes. Go make this man some hot chocolate or something while I fill your stocking."

She skipped to the kitchen, a trail of delight scattered

251

behind her. Jay and Ron joked as Ron filled the stockings. Once he was done, Jay hurried to retrieve the little gifts he'd purchased just for this purpose, excited to join the one part of Christmas that had fascinated him since his childhood. By the time Hope returned with a tray of piping hot chocolate, the stockings hung from the mantel, bulging with the little surprises that make Christmas morning so enchanting.

"Oh, look! Isn't it beautiful!" She passed them each cups and said, "You guys drink your cocoa. I'm going to get mine. Stockings should never be empty!"

Hope raced up the stairs. It seemed as though she couldn't have even reached the top before she came thundering down again. Jay's eyes widened as he watched her screw a plant hook into the mantel next to her stocking. The most exquisite stocking he'd ever seen swung from its hook minutes later. Ron drained the rest of his hot cocoa, choking a bit. "It burns!"

"It's hot, of course it burns." Hope rolled her eyes at Jay. "If you were in a kettle—"

"Yeah, yeah." Ron retrieved a small box from next to the log basket.

Father and daughter teased and joked as they filled Jay's stocking, emptying it a few times, trying to make everything fit. One package, that looked suspiciously like a book, refused to stay in, no matter how hard Ron tried to make it work. "I give up. It'll have to stay on the mantel."

"It's not Christmas unless a few things fill the mantel."

Ron kissed his daughter's nose, hugged Jay, and wished them a good night. Before he went upstairs for the night, he wrote something on sticky notes from the kitchen organizer and slipped them in Cheryl and Concord's stockings. "Night guys, catch Santa."

Hope watched, her heart in her eyes, as her father climbed the stairs alone. "Oh, Jay, I've never seen him go upstairs on Christmas without him holding Mom's hand ahead of him."

"Can you do anything to comfort him?" Jay asked.

She shook her head. "I think I learned something today. I grieve and am comforted by being with people—by keeping things the same. Dad is the opposite." She pulled him to the couch. "Now that I think of it, Mom was like me. They had trouble like this when Concord died."

"Really?"

"Yeah... there was this one really nasty argument. I was in my room, hands over my head like a five year old, and Mom screamed, 'You act like we never had a son!'"

"I can see why she would feel that way." Anxious to change the subject, he asked, "Where did you find that stocking? I couldn't believe it when you screwed that hook into the mantel. You didn't have to do that. It would have been just fine on the shelf or something."

"The hole was already there. We've put stockings there before for guests on Christmas."

The line of stockings entranced him. "They're all so different. Different shapes, fabrics, styles—all unique."

"Mom found Dad's in a little gift shop on their honeymoon. If you look really closely, it's needlepointed with snippets of Christmas books, poems, or songs."

"And your mom's?" Cheryl's stocking was a strange hodgepodge of fabrics sewn together with sloppy stitches.

"I made that from a box of fabric we got when Grandma White died."

"Grandma White?"

Hope smiled. "Ironic, isn't it? Mom's mom. She saved fabric from every one of Mom's Christmas and Easter dresses. I made that from the Christmas fabrics for Mom's present one year."

"Concord's. Dancing on a record of sequins—and ice skates for you."

"I had one of those red discount store stockings forever. That's what we all had until she found 'the one.' I was fourteen before I got mine." She grinned as he pointed to his. "I found that at the store where I tried on the sari."

"But you didn't buy anything there."

Mischief gleamed in her eyes. "I went back. I didn't want you to see it."

"Ah, *kadhal*..."

"When are you going to tell me what that means?"

253

Jay gave her a small smile and shook his head. Hope stuck out her tongue at him but to no avail. Frustrated, she sputtered and spoke a few nonsensical sounds. "Fine — my — *azhagghee*."

She stared at him with impudent eyes. They widened in shock when he said, "Oh, that is flattering, but I would say that it fits you better than me."

"That means something?" Suspicion clouded her eyes. "I don't believe you. You're 'dragging my leg' or something like that."

"Oh no, Hope. You were very flattering. Let me show you." Jay pulled his laptop from beside the couch and typed 'azhagghee' into Google. "There."

Hope read a message board post, asking for translation help with a song. "I just called you 'my beauty?'"

"I told you it applied better to you."

"I always imagined the Indian language to be exotic and melodic — beautiful. That sounds like someone sneezed."

Before he could stop her, Hope snatched the laptop and typed in 'kadal.' Google suggested an alternate spelling — *kadhal*. Jay smiled at her gasp. "You are surprised? I thought you knew."

"I wondered… I mean, you made it seem like something special and beautiful, but —"

"I once called you my very own *edhirparppu*, but I don't speak Tamil often enough for it to roll comfortably from my tongue in the middle of an English sentence."

"Oh, that doesn't sound nearly as wonderful as *kadhal*. It sounds like the deer poo pooed. What does it mean?"

Jay stroked her cheek. "*Amma* is going to love your interest and appreciation for our language and our culture. *Edhirparppu* means hope."

"Do me a favor, Jay. Call me *your* Hope any time you like. Just do it in English, ok?"

Jay took a deep breath and prayed that his next question was the right one. "Ok, my Hope, tell me about your mother's and brother's stockings. What did you put inside them?"

"That was an unexpected change of subject."

He smiled. "A safe one, I think. What is in those?"

"We did it the first Christmas after Con died. Mom decorated. Dad raged. When he saw her sobbing over Con's stocking, he realized that as much as he wanted to run from the past, she needed the familiar —"

"Sounds familiar…"

She leaned her head on his shoulder. "Yeah. Like I said, we're a lot alike there. Anyway, she needed the stability of the known, you know? Anyway, she hung the stocking. Neither of us knew it, but Dad started leaving notes in it for Con — kind of like his way of saying goodbye."

"Beautiful."

"It was. We discovered it on Christmas Day." She took a deep breath. "Mom and I read his notes and wrote some of our own. His stocking stayed on the mantel until New Year's Eve." A suspicious sniff told him she was crying. "I guess Mom's will too this year."

He passed her the Kleenex. "Do you read them aloud or —"

Hope shook her head. "No, just read them when we feel like it — a few at a time. That's what Dad put in there before he went to bed. We have a box of every year's notes. We add to it each year. This year, I guess we'll start one for Mom."

The grandfather clock struck two. "I guess we didn't catch Santa," Hope said, her attempt at lightheartedness failing. "Dad will be disappointed."

"You should sleep. Do you want me to turn off the tree lights?"

She shook her head and held out her hand. "This is the night we leave them on all night."

With her hand trailing behind her as she preceded him, holding his, they climbed the stairs. They said goodnight, closed their doors, and crawled between the sheets of their beds. Hope lay thinking of the man on the other side of the wall. *He called me his love, Lord. I think he means it.* She sighed. *All those years that I struggled over some boy at church… why didn't I trust that You had something better. Dad loves him. Mom loved him. I think I love him too.*

Her eyes grew heavy. "Happy birthday, Jesus," she murmured.

255

Jay heard Hope mumble something in the other room and smiled to himself. Such a wonderful yet difficult day. He had almost told her he loved her—called her his *kadhal*—his love—and now she knew what that meant. He had no doubt that she knew his heart. He lay praying, his heart overflowing with how much he had been given. *God, you are so good to me. I need her to spend more time with my parents. I need to be sure—be sure that she is sure about us.*

He rolled on his side and pulled the blankets tighter around him. "Do people say happy birthday, Jesus?" he mumbled as his eyes closed.

CHAPTER 29

Tantalizing scents invaded Jay's senses—hinting that breakfast time neared. His stomach rumbled—the traitor. He glanced at the clock, surprised to see it was almost seven thirty. Every instinct protested as he climbed from the warm, comfortable bed. He reached for his clothes and found a thick, velvety robe. The note attached read, *Jay—or is that kadhal? I forgot to tell you that we don't get dressed on Christmas until time for dinner, so here's a robe to keep you warm.*

He wrapped himself in the robe, thankful for its warmth. A look at his feet made him sigh. He'd freeze. He grabbed socks, covered his cooling toes, and hurried downstairs. Although he didn't see Ron anywhere, Jay heard Hope singing in the kitchen. He sneaked in behind her and covered her eyes with his hands. "*Kaalai vanakkam, kadhal.* Merry Christmas," he murmured in her ear.

"Oh! What does the *kali* thing mean?"

"Nothing too interesting. It's equivalent to 'good morning.'" He wrapped his arms around her and asked, "What are you making? It smells marvelous."

"Breakfast casserole. Dad took cinnamon rolls next door, but there are a few on the counter over there if you want one."

Jay glanced up at the ceiling, devoid of sprigs, frowning. "It's mighty bare up there."

"It wouldn't matter if it wasn't," she pouted. "Some people have no sense of honor and respect for age-old traditions."

"Some people have no patience."

Jay watched the mounds of paper grow as Ron tore at his package. Bows and discarded wrappings littered the floor. Hope sat adding music to her new smart phone while Ron bent over and pulled on a new pair of slippers emblazoned with Rockland University's mascot. The sight of the slippers caused Jay to tuck his cool toes under him.

"Here. Open this one." Hope's eyes twinkled as she passed him the package.

He ripped slippers from the package before it was fully unwrapped and shoved his feet in them. Thanks to offensive earth-destroying plastic ties, he could not have walked if he had tried. With one firm jerk, he broke the offensive piece of future landfill refuse and sighed contentedly as his toes began to warm, his twelve seconds of environmentally conscious angst behind him.

Ron glanced at him, amused. "Feet cold?"

"Freezing." His feet swirled in the sea of crumpled wrapping paper and connected with a box. "Oh, I almost forgot this one." He passed the last box to Hope.

As she pulled back the tissue, Hope squealed. "Oh! Jay!"

Hope and a streak of purple flew upstairs. Ron raised his eyebrows at Jay. "Care to elaborate?"

Jay swallowed the lump filling his throat at the anticipation of her return and said, "Prepare yourself. The last time she put that thing on, I couldn't stop staring. I had to get it but—"

"I take it that whatever that was looks too good on her?"

"Something like that."

The clock ticked its rhythmic taunt, each minute feeling like a dozen. The men fiddled with presents, kicked at wrapping paper, and grew impatient. They grumbled, sighed, and almost cheered as Hope's door opened upstairs.

Silver and black silk embroidery on purple fabric danced on her toes as she stepped down the stairs. She looked regal. The graceful drape of the sari made every step she took seem more elegant than the last. "How does it look? Isn't it the prettiest thing you've ever seen?" She twirled. "I could live in this. Thank you, Jay!"

Ron grabbed two stockings and moved toward the stairs, tugging her ponytail as he passed. Hope's face clouded. "Where are you going?"

What Ron said, Jay couldn't hear, but he saw a look of understanding pass between father and daughter—one that warmed his heart. Though he knew it was foolish, he had begun to feel like a wedge between them. With each change and every memory, Jay saw one or the other wounded, and he felt like the attacker.

Hope spun again as her father disappeared up the stairs. "It's just so beautiful. How did your mother ever give up wearing these every day?"

"I seem to remember you asking me how she ever wore them in the cold. Now you can't see her choosing anything else."

She waltzed around the room, trying to convince Jay to dance with her. "Come on, I'll show you!"

Humming the "Merry Christmas Waltz" as they danced, she beamed as Jay caught onto the simple steps. "With you in your robe, me in my sari—we even look the part of Indian royalty—well, we would if I had a nice fetching little chip in my nose and dyed my hair."

"And got a good tan," Jay interjected. "Indian men do not dress in robes as a general rule, but you do look amazing."

She gazed up at him. "Say something in Tamil."

He bent close and murmured, "Like what?"

The sound of his voice near her ear brought a bemused smile to her lips. "Anything. Just don't tell me if it's insulting. As long as it sounds wonderful, I'll assume it is."

"*Naan eppavume unnai kadhalippen,*" he murmured, deliberately keeping his voice low.

Hope's breath caught.

Jay's eyes questioned hers. "What?"

"I caught a word. The last one. It sounded like the root word was *kadhal.*"

"It is," Jay smiled. "I said, 'I love a good meal.'"

259

She shook her head. "I can read your eyes better now. They're telling me you mistranslated." Before he could reply, she said, "Oh, and what did you say to Dad? He acted like I was going to break your heart or something."

Jay didn't know what to say. "I don't know. He asked about the sari—he didn't see what it was before you vanished upstairs."

"Well, what did you tell him?"

Jay smiled and pulled her closer. "I said to be prepared—that the sari looks too good on you."

Her pleased blush faded to doubt in the space of seconds. "Is it—it's not indecent, is it?"

Jay glanced at the ceiling above. Her eyes followed. Dozens of mistletoe sprigs hung gaily over their heads, taunting them. His hand reached for the tie that held her hair back and sighed as it spilled over her shoulders. "Your hair is so beautiful—silky like the sari," he whispered.

A tiny part of Jay resisted as he lowered his lips to hers. He had waited so long—wanted to savor every second—was it too soon? The answer no longer mattered. It was too late now, and he was not sorry—not sorry at all.

He didn't quite know when the kiss began, but by the time it ended, he knew everything had changed. "Oh, Hope... As *Amma* would say, 'My heart is chasing tigers.'"

"Mine is running from them," she said, giggling. "Will you rescue it?"

Feeling as silly as she seemed to, he nodded. "Always."

Time became nebulous—an indeterminate moment frozen in history—as they stood beneath a sea of mistletoe, lost in their own world. Jay finally took a deep breath and said, "I didn't answer an important question."

Hope seemed bemused as she whispered, "You didn't?"

"I didn't. You are beautiful in that sari. It affects me deeply but not improperly. I do not know how to explain it—not logically—but seeing you in that sari feels as I would imagine a groom feels when he first sees his bride. It is very special to me." His fingers traced her jaw. "Never think it improper."

Hope kissed him. Jay's eyes lowered and he pressed his

forehead to hers. "And you thought I was silly for treasuring those firsts. Already you have given me a second."

"Actually," she corrected, "you kissed me the first time. This is actually the first time I kissed you…"

"Ah, *kad* — "

She covered his mouth with her hand. "Don't say it again — not until you tell me what the other thing you said means."

"*Naan eppavume unnai kadhalippen*," he said clearly before leaning to murmur in her ear. "I will love you always."

Hope and Jay sat together on the couch, reading the messages in the stockings. To their surprise, Concord's was full of loving notes from a mother preparing to see her son again. Tears flowed as Hope read several of the messages, and Jay prayed that the pain would not spoil the day for her — not this time.

"Oh, Jay. Look at this one from Dad."

Jay read it, his throat swelling with emotion. *Cheryl, How I wish you could see Hope and Jay. He is here, and the care and attention he lavishes on her is an answer to all of our prayers. You were right about him. I look forward to meeting his parents.*

"I can't believe he wrote about me. That is amazing."

Hope snuggled a bit closer as she found a note from Jay to her brother. Tears filled her eyes as she read it, glancing up at him between sentences. As she finished, she sighed. "Con always wanted a brother. He would have liked you." She peeked in her mother's stocking. "Where is the one you wrote Mom?"

Jay pulled several pieces of paper from the stocking until he found his. Hope's hand shook as she tried to unfold it. She handed it to him and asked him to read it to her. He pulled her closer, his arms wrapped around her and his lips close to her ear.

He read of his respect for her, how much he found himself missing her. He poured out his amazement and gratitude for her daughter. And, he read of his love for Hope. By the time he finished, his own tears flowed. He wiped at them frequently, but they soaked his tissues faster than he replaced them.

Just as Hope gathered control of herself, she sat up abruptly. "Jay! What will your mother say! What would she think if she knew you were in this house where every available horizontal surface over six feet tall is plastered with mistletoe — which, I might add, has been properly initiated."

"Don't you remember how my mother enjoyed your visit? She will be thrilled."

"You think?"

"She chides me every time she sees me, admonishing me to find a girl. 'You need to find a good girl. Marry. Give me grandbabies. I am not young and I won't be again.' Or she will say, 'When will you bring me home a daughter. I was not given a daughter of my own, so you must bring one home for me.' She's very eager for me to find someone who makes me happy." He winked at Hope's disbelieving expression. "I think she really just wants me to find someone I can tolerate so she will be happy."

Hope's eyes grew wide. "Is it possible that she would be looking for someone in India — to — well, I don't know. Someone for you to get to know?"

Jay demurred but stopped himself. The more he considered the idea, the more he realized it was not as farfetched as he first thought. His parents were not so traditional as to expect to arrange a marriage, but if they could find someone he might be interested in, he knew they would find a way to introduce him. Finding someone in India sounded like his mother's idea of a dream vacation. "I — oh. Hmm... I think I should Skype my uncle."

CHAPTER 30

She felt like a teenager again, flopped sideways on her bed, her elbows propping up her phone as she chatted with her best girlfriend. " —didn't know what to say. I mean, you know how I am. I don't do the whole coy thing. It just felt awkward asking, 'So, is that a hint you have plans for us someday?'"

When Kirky didn't respond, Hope grew impatient. "Spill it, girl. What aren't you saying?" Hope shifted the phone and rubbed her sore ear. They'd been talking for an hour.

"You're going to get married. How did it never really sink in that you would get married?" Kirky sighed.

"Because you pictured me as a dried up old spinster librarian."

"Funny. What am I going to do without my goof buddy?" The hint of a wail in Kirky's voice brought a lump to Hope's throat.

"I could always light a fire under Brian —"

Kirky cut her off midsentence. Hope recognized the tight voice, the slow, measured words, and the formal speech patterns. Kirky wanted her to back off —now. "I think that is quite enough. I do *not* want to discuss it. When do you think Jay will propose?"

"It's kind of soon for that, isn't it?"

"You've known him for almost a year-and-a-half. Not too soon at all."

"Kirky…"

"Hope, not now. Do. Not. Do. This. Now. If you say another word, I will fly to Las Vegas with Chuck Majors and return as his wife."

"You don't have to go to Vegas. You can get married in minutes, right here in Rockland."

"But Chuck deserves only the best that Vegas can offer."

"Got that right," Hope agreed. As much as she joked with her friend, a hint of dread crept into her heart. It almost sounded as if Kirky really would do it—just to spite her.

"So, what about going to the mall and watching a movie?"

"Oh! M & M. The perfect recipe for an imperfect day."

Late that night, she called Jay. "I wish you could have heard her. She closed up so tight you would have thought she was glued shut!"

"That's an interesting metaphor."

Hope smiled as she realized she knew exactly what the expression on his face looked like. "I think I just realized how well I know you."

"And how well is that, *kadhal*?"

It seemed that the more he saw how affected she was by his occasional endearing lapses into Tamil, the more he did it. "You cannot expect me to carry on a reasonably intelligent conversation if you are going to turn my insides into mush. It's almost cruel."

"I'm sorry, *kad*—oops. I won't do it again, *kad*—I mean, Hope. Don't you have a question to answer?"

His teasing sent silly butterfly flutters through her. Though she laughed at his teasing, that same new uncharacteristic shyness shrouded her at every attempt to share her feelings. Was he disappointed that she had not said how much she loved him too?

An expectant silence from Jay reminded her of his question. "Oh, well, when you mentioned metaphors, I could just see your expression in my mind. It was kind of funny."

"I would have thought you would be tired of my face. I

was there for four days!"

"You were supposed to be here through Sunday!"

"Work is a pesky thing."

"Speaking of which..."

"I know what you are thinking, Hope. Would you like me to talk to Mike?"

She sighed, relieved. "Do you think he'd mind? How would we even get them together? I can't just say, 'Kirky, talk to this stranger about the most private details of your past, and you will be all better.'"

"No, but Traci can invite you to their home, you can ask to bring a friend, explaining to Kirky that you hardly know her and would like to have someone there with you. Traci can try to strike up a friendship..."

"And when it doesn't work, will you comfort me while I sob over the loss of almost my dearest friend?"

His chuckle warmed her heart as he said, "We'll practice when I get there tomorrow—just to be sure I know how to do it right. I would not wish to disappoint you, Hope of my Hope."

Laughing at his silliness, she asked, "Where did that come from?"

"I heard a song sung by a barbershop quartet in Rockland Center last night. You should have heard them sing that song you sang at New Year's last year."

"'Auld Lang Syne?'"

"Yes. That one."

"And this group," she clarified, "sang something about Hope."

"Actually, it was heart—'Heart of My Heart,' but I thought Hope worked well."

She sighed again. "Jay, you are such a sap. I never imagined I would fall—um—fall for a guy who was so romantic. I always liked guys who were practical and logical."

"I'm glad to hear that I do not have the obnoxious fault of being practical or logical. Impracticality and illogicality are much greater virtues to be desired in men. After all, they are the very virtues that drew me to you."

"That's it," she retorted. "I challenge you to a duel. Six

o'clock at the ice rink. Don't be late." Hope let the phone click as she hung up. She smiled. Somehow, some way, tonight she would tell him — something.

Jay stood, his back to a tree, and watched Hope skate. The rink, although dotted with a few straggling skaters, was left for her to enjoy unimpeded. She jumped, spun, and almost floated across the ice. He snapped a few pictures on his phone, but he regretted not bringing his camera.

The moment she saw him, she skated across the ice. He met her at the edge, wrapping his arms around her as she panted to catch her breath. She smiled up at him. "I didn't see you. I'm sorry. Have you waited long?"

"Too long, and not long enough. You know I enjoy watching you skate." Her hat muffled his voice, but her smile assured him that she heard and understood.

"I demand satisfaction."

His eyebrows rose, questioning. "Satisfaction for what?"

"You insinuated that I lack logic and common sense."

"I did no such thing!"

Hope stared at him, daring him to deny it again. "Oh?"

"I insinuated nothing. I spoke truth. Insinuation is rude — something in which I refuse to indulge."

"I will not laugh," she snickered.

"You will if I tickle you."

"Back to the duel at hand," she protested, laughing. "I, as the injured party, *again*, choose snowballs. You have ten minutes to make as many as you can. You can recruit anyone you like to help. A direct hit to the face determines the winner, so be careful not to get rocks in the snowballs. You break my teeth, you buy 'em. Anything else?"

"Just one thing." Jay kissed her before shaking his head and trudging through the snow to his side of the indicated battlefield.

They faced off on opposite sides of the bridge, each amassing an arsenal of frozen missiles. Her propensity to create

266

memories for him, tugged at new and tender heartstrings. Did she do this with everyone or just him? *And why,* he wondered, *do I think the answer is both?*

Snowballs flew with utter disregard for safety. Both of them risked a hit for the pleasure of lobbing another snowball at the "enemy" on the opposing side of the little park bridge. The "duel" morphed into a cross between forty paces and firing and old-fashioned battle tactics. They faced off on opposite sides, half-standing, exposed and ready to fight until the other side fell. The guerilla warfare tactics of the laser tag games gave way as each tried to fool the other into standing and throwing first.

He glanced around him, anxious to recruit someone to build snowballs while he threw them, but few people remained. Hope did the same before turning and sticking out her tongue at him. She ducked, presumably to grab a few balls. He waited, counted to three, and threw his snowball, hoping she'd stand at just the right time. She did, but to his consternation, her head was turned just enough for it to graze her ear rather than hit her in the face.

"Missed!"

"Barely!" he called back as he lobbed another one.

After dusting the snow from her ear, she had stood, glancing his way to note his position. His snowball hit her squarely in the face. "Ugh!"

"Yes!" Jay pumped his fist and hurried around the bridge to crow — and help remove the snow from her eyes and nose.

"You got me this time, but wait until we do it with water balloons. I'm better with those."

Jay shivered. "Can we do that when it's over sixty degrees? I'm cold."

"Come on," she said, lacing her arm through his and leading him to her car.

Within minutes, he regretted not driving them. She wove in and out of traffic like a pro, but that did not assuage the quasi-terrifying nature of the ride. Every move by any other car received a comment, sandwiched between her natural, running conversation with Jay. He sat, a bit tense and a good deal confused, as he listened to her tell about the movie she and

Kirky had seen.

" —this guy jumped—if you're going to go under the speed limit, you're supposed to stay in the lane for that—and we thought he was dead. I heard some of the people around me grumbling, but Kirky said—lookout! Where is your blinker— 'They won't kill off one of the main characters before half the movie is over.' She was—oh, that's my lane, excuse me—right too. I mean, I never saw the trap door or the net. They showed it though, once I realized what happened—do you know if I go right or left here? I can't remember."

Jay indicated left, and Hope promptly flicked on her blinker and eased into the proper lane, barely missing the bumper of the car ahead of them. He refused to ask any question or offer any comment until they arrived at the restaurant— presumably in one piece, although Jay did wonder if part of his stomach was being pulverized by tires on the Loop somewhere.

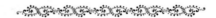

Jay's phone rang. Seeing Hope's name flash on the caller ID, Jay answered it. "Hi."

"Where are you? I thought you left like two hours ago?"

"Got hung up at the last minute, and now I'm on the road waiting for a ticket."

Hope sounded apologetic. "You were speeding? I didn't mean to put *that* kind of pressure on you."

"Not speeding, I don't think. I think the ticket will be for something like reckless driving or some equally disturbing crime."

Hope demanded an explanation and added, "You have to get here alive, you know."

"I was thinking of dark-haired, dark-skinned, blue-eyed daughters and sons that look like Concord, and almost sideswiped a Mercedes. It would have been a crime for sure— great car."

"I'll come up with a crushing reply when I get the picture of a large doe-eyed little Jay out of my mind. Wow. You know how to get my mind spinning."

268

"Sorry, Hope, I see her coming back. I'd better go." Without waiting for a goodbye, Jay slapped the phone back on the holder and put his hands back on the wheel. Visions of drawn guns kept him from giving the officer any doubt as to what he'd been holding. He punched the window button down again and resumed his teeth chattering exercises.

An hour later, he stood leaning against the kitchen island, telling Hope about the ticket, while she made hot chocolate. "What had you thinking of children?"

"I remembered you talking about playhouses and tree houses, and I just got caught up in little Hopes."

She sighed as she passed him a cup of steaming hot chocolate and a candy cane. He held it up questioningly. "You stir the chocolate with it. It's good."

He took her advice, stirring before he took a sip. "Delicious," he agreed, taking another one.

"Now tell me something; what *do* you think of children?"

Jay choked, spewing his cocoa all over her white sweater. "Oh, I'm sorry!"

"For panicking at the thought of children, or for my sweater?" she teased.

"Your sweater. Ugh. I'm actually delighted at the idea of children. I have been, ever since I pictured you sick of one." His wink brought a blush to her cheeks.

While he sipped his cocoa, she changed into a RU sweatshirt and doused her chocolate-stained sweater with pre-wash. Sheepishly, he admitted, "*Amma* would have scolded me for ruining her sweater and then made me do the washing."

"Well, I'll have to take lessons in managing Jay then, won't I?"

269

CHAPTER 31

After a tour of New Cheltenham, Jay and Hope found a corner in a tearoom to defrost. Occasional snowflakes swirled outside as they nibbled their cranberry-mandarin scones and sipped hot tea. Nothing could have felt more Authentically British on the North American continent.

Jay played with Hope's fingers as they talked. "Will you come with me tomorrow?

"Where?"

"To the airport. I pick up my parents at eleven-fifty. I think they would like to see you too."

"Didn't they leave at like nine o'clock today?"

"It's a twenty-seven hour flight. I'll bring them home, they'll sleep until dinner, stay up just a little later than normal, and then they'll try to get up the next morning close to normal time. They'll take a nap all week and be normal by Friday."

"You're rambling."

"I'm trying to keep you from saying no," he admitted.

Hope giggled. "Afraid Mommy will give you the fifth-degree?"

"I don't know what degree she has, but my *amma* could teach the CIA a thing or twenty about interrogation tortures. I do not want to be alone with her."

"Coward."

Jay nodded solemnly. "Guilty."

"I'd love to go. We can make them dinner while they sleep,

271

and you can introduce me to your delightful neighbor."

Jay groaned. "And I thought, just for a second anyway, that you were being merciful."

"Never."

⁓⁕⁘⁘⁘⁘⁘⁘⁘⁕⁓

Hope spied Amala before Jay returned from the restroom. Rushing forward she grinned at the tired-looking woman and said, "Do you remember me? It's Hope."

Jay's father hugged her. "Wish! I am happy to see you, but where is Sanjay?"

Amala's eyes grew concerned. "Is he all right? Has something happened?"

"Jay is fine. He just had to excuse himself for a minute."

Jay arrived seconds later, much to her relief. As much as she had looked forward to seeing them again, she now understood why Jay wanted backup. The look of curiosity in Amala's eyes almost choked her.

Mayhem reigned in the car as they sped toward the Brown home. Raj and Amala talked at once; Jay interrupted with his own comments. Occasionally, the discussion lapsed into Tamil until someone, usually Raj, realized that Hope no longer answered questions or made jokes. Hope loved every second of it.

While the Browns napped, Jay and Hope worked together in the kitchen on the Senior favorite "company dinner." As she put the roast in the oven, her eyes grew wide. "Um, Jay?"

"Yeah."

"Do your parents eat beef? I thought Indians —"

"Hindis in India, Hope. My father loves beef. He says it's the American dream... all the beef he can eat without offending his neighbors."

Relieved, she washed vegetables and tossed a salad. She scrubbed potatoes and carrots and added them to the roast after an hour. Thankful for a double oven, she mixed a cheesecake and baked it, praying it wouldn't crack in an unfamiliar oven.

Raj and Amala awoke to the tantalizing scent of sizzling

272

roast in the oven. They found Jay and Hope snuggled on the couch, Jay reading the Bible aloud to her. Amala sighed. "Raj, he has found a wonderful girl. She appreciates him, look."

Hope blushed and rose to check on the food and set the table. As she worked, she prayed for him—for all of them. He would have to tell them of his baptism soon. According to Jay, baptism to his parents would mean more than saying, "I believe in Jesus." To them, a "ritual" meant commitment.

Aside from slightly undercooked carrots, dinner turned out perfect. The cheesecake came out of the fridge with only a minor crack, and little canned cherry pie filling covered it well. As she sliced the pieces and took inventory of the meal, she called it a success.

Over cheesecake and tea, Jay told his parents of his conversion and invited them to visit the church with him the next week. "I'm not asking you to do anything. I wanted to invite you because this is very important to me, and I thought you might like to see why."

Raj questioned Jay about what he believed and why, but Amala looked at Hope and shrugged. "I don't understand. I cannot think when I am so tired. Would you like to see what I brought home from India? Oh, and I have a gift for you."

They escaped to the guest room where Amala unpacked the extra suitcase she'd brought for her purchases. "I thought I might not make it all fit, but look! It is all here."

Amala showed her hair ornaments, perfumes, shawls, and saris. Hope fingered an aqua one, very similar to the one Jay had practically dragged her from on their trip to Little India. Hope sighed. "This one reminds me of the one Jay wouldn't let me try on when we went shopping."

"He wouldn't let you try it on? What is wrong with my Jay? That color would look wonderful with your eyes and hair!"

Hope suspected that Amala would have continued her rant and gone to scold her son, but Hope stopped her. "Oh, it wasn't like that. Jay treats me like a princess. He's a wonderful man. He just—I don't know how to explain it." She fingered the fabric again. "Would you mind if I tried this on? I'll show you."

"The top will be too large, but I can pin it for you. Let me know when you are ready, and I will wrap it for you."

Hope assured Amala that she knew how to wrap the sari and sent her to find a good place with a view of Jay's face. The men stopped talking the second Hope entered the doorway. This time, Hope had complete confidence in wearing the sari — something she'd never felt. "Look, Jay. It's like that aqua one you dragged me away from." She stepped closer, "Well?"

Jay pulled her onto his lap. "I thought I was an old pro at seeing you in a sari," he whispered. "I danced with you and sat with you, but you kill me."

"Jay, tell her she is pretty! What is wrong with you!" Amala's indignant face brought a burst of laughter from the other three.

"She is beautiful, and I am telling her so, *Amma.* Let me make my Hope blush my way." To Hope, he added, "I hope I never lose the deep emotion that you create in me whenever I see you in one of those." As she turned to follow Amala from the room, he murmured, "Talk my mother into giving you that one. I'll buy her the one at the market."

Like a teenager waiting for the latest gossip, Amala eagerly pulled Hope into the guest room. "My son loves you — really loves you." Her eyes scanned Hope's face. "He has told you, hasn't he?" She leaned close and whispered, "I think he was afraid I would try to find a girl in India, but we knew before we left, his heart was yours or would be soon."

Hope sat on the bed, fingering the beautiful saris, unable to meet Amala's curious eyes. "Yes, he has told me that he loves me. Sometimes I still can't believe it."

"Do you love our Sanjay? May I ask this?"

A tear escaped, and Hope brushed it away as she tried to answer. "I do. I am sure he knows it, but I don't know how to tell him." Her eyes slid sideways to catch Amala's gaze. "That sounds silly, doesn't it?"

"It is refreshing. I have noticed that in America, girls are often aggressive in pursuing men, but at the same time, they can be so cold. You want to express your heart; that is a beautiful thing."

Hope sighed, another tear splashing on her cheek before

she wiped it away again. "He—"

"What is it? What about my Jay is right for Hope Senior?"

"He makes me laugh, think; he challenges my beliefs and makes me feel cherished." She smiled up at Amala. "I think he got that from your husband. I've watched how Raj treats you. Jay emulates that." Hope felt her cheeks grow warm as she added, "He even speaks to me in Tamil when he feels especially tender."

"My Jay is so different than he was—before. He was more like Raj, always joking, always loud. He was a handful as a little boy." Amala shrugged. "We indulged him. After the accident though, that was gone. Sometimes I think it's there—somewhere inside him. I see it. He just had to push it aside so he could cope with all the changes."

Hope hugged Amala. "I think he's wonderful, and I think it is because of how you were there for him after the accident."

Amala brushed her own tears away and asked, "Did you say Jay speaks to you in Tamil? That is very romantic of him. Will you tell me what he says?"

"He called me *'kadhal'* first. I thought it was probably something like 'silly pain in the neck.'"

"Oh, love. That is very romantic—a bit British too."

"Right! I thought that too. I wondered if it was common or what."

Amala nodded. "So what else?"

"Well, he translated my name into Tamil. I thought it sounded like deer poo-poo." Amala giggled as Hope continued. "Then he said something once. He translated it, 'I will love you always.' I didn't know what he was saying, but I knew it was good because I recognized *kadhal* in the last word."

"Oh, you are very clever. You must have an ear for language to catch that. That is very good."

Hope's eyes widened. "Amala, would it be too weird for a guy's mother to teach his girlfriend a few words in Tamil to tell him how she feels about him?"

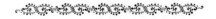

Jay sat on the couch, Hope using his leg as a pillow while they talked. Raj and Amala were asleep, leaving the couple alone to talk about their respective conversations. Jay felt quite optimistic after his discussion with his father. "He said he would read Mark. If Mark has anything that interests him, he will start over in Matthew and read through Acts. Then we will talk."

"Your mother doesn't seem interested or bothered."

"She trusts *Appa*. Once he has done his research and come to a decision, she'll decide if it is worth her time."

For some time, they didn't speak. Exhausted, Jay rested, feeling too tired to get up and dreading the early morning drive to work. Just as he decided to suggest that they go to bed, Hope pulled his head closer, gazing into his eyes. *"Naan unnai kadalikiren*, Jay. *Naan unnai kadalikiren."*

"Remind me to hug my mother in the morning," he whispered, kissing her.

"As long as you don't forget me."

CHAPTER 32

Hope's spin created a blur of blue on the ice. Valentine's Day had turned out to be a slow night for the rink as few braved the icy cold for a chance to skate with their sweethearts. Amala sat with Jay on the bench, wrapped in blankets, watching Hope skate.

"Isn't she a natural, *Amma?* She hasn't skated but a few times this year, and look at her. She did almost as well that first night we came out here." He watched as she jumped. "I think she comes during the week between classes now, though."

"And do you skate more now?"

He nodded, smiling down at his mother. She had teased him in past weeks—always asking about his "*kadhal.*" If he arrived home alone, she asked, "Where is your *kadhal*?" If invited to a meal, she encouraged him to bring, "your *kadhal*" with him. His father, in typical Raj fashion, called her Jay's "true Wish" and refused to correct it to "wish come true." Through their teasing, Jay learned to share his affection for Hope openly with those around him.

As Hope paused in the center of the rink, leaning her hands on her knees to catch her breath, Jay slid out from beneath the blankets and skated toward her. He wrapped his arms around her, giving her something to lean on for support. "Let's skate and cool you down—no more leg cramps for you."

From the bench, Amala watched them skate. Hope adjusted her cadence to Jay's slower pace, as they circled the rink several times. Jay's devotion to his little figure skater warmed her heart, even as her teeth chattered in the cold. She would soon have a daughter — one with blonde hair and blue eyes. Who would have ever thought it possible?

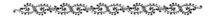

"Your mom should have come with us. How often do you get a reservation at The Palace, much less on Valentine's Day?"

Hope gazed around the room, drinking in each carved balustrade, each marble tile, and each rich, velvet drape. The old theater-turned-restaurant couldn't have been more romantic. Redecorated just for the day, gilt cupids hung from crystal chandeliers, rose petals dusted the tables, surrounded by candles, and each woman received a corsage upon confirmation of their reservation.

"*Amma* wanted to go home and brag of you to *Appa*. She has every second of your 'performance' recorded for him."

"Did you know that the first opera here failed? They printed up the playbills all wrong, and no one showed up." Her eyes became dreamy as she described elegant costumes of vaudeville days. "I can't imagine that life, can you?"

"Nope."

"Did you know that during prohibition, the backstage area was a speakeasy?"

"Is there anything about this place you don't know?"

She nodded. "Yep. When our food will arrive."

After dinner, they pulled on coats, hats, gloves, and scarves and strolled down Boutique Row, window-shopping. At every window, Jay saw a side of Hope he'd never seen. Her opinions regarding fashion had him laughing.

"Ok, look at this one," she said, pointing to a particularly revolting combination. "That is hideous. It's probably a Dominic Original, but it's a pile of wadded fabric with a price tag higher than my car is worth. Why would someone pay that? I'll tell you," she added as he shrugged. "Because that guy's name is on the label. He says it's good, so it must be good. Sickening."

"Well, I agree it's awful, but doesn't the person who pays

that price for it decide that it's good?"

"You'd think," she sighed. "Okay, but look at the one next to it. I bet they're the same price or close. That one is cool. It has artistry to it. Putting it next to that other thing is an insult to it!"

Jay snickered as they strolled down the street. She ranted over purses, shoes, fake furs, and clothing—lots of clothing. The jewelry stores had empty windows, leaving her to speculate whether they had good taste or if their motto in design was simply, "the bigger the rock the better." He couldn't wait to hear what she had to say about the dresses in the bridal shop window at the end of the block.

A few minutes later, Hope stood before the first gown. It took every bit of self-restraint he possessed not to laugh at her disgust at the gown that hung before them. A plunging neckline stopped just above the navel of the strapless gown. It fit, molded to the mannequin's body, until it hit the calves, and then flared into a strange bundle of tulle that fanned behind the gown in the most bizarre train ever conceived by a clothing designer.

"That—that's a travesty—a waste of beautiful fabric. Why would someone want to look like that on their wedding day?"

"How does it stay..." Jay gulped, "up. It seems to defy the laws of whatever it is that holds clothing onto us."

"Decency. And yes, it defies them." She giggled. "It has to be so tight like that to keep it up. And, it probably has that weird fabric-to-skin tape stuff somewhere."

Jay sighed in relief when she stepped to the next window. A gasp of delight told him his plan would work. Plan B, which he still had not formulated, could not possibly be as interesting. All he had to do was wait.

"Oh, look! That is what a bride should look like. See! A gown doesn't have to look like Cinderella to be beautiful. That gown says, 'This is one of the most important days of my life. I respect myself enough to look my best. I have taste, class—"

"That is one talkative dress," he murmured.

"—and thirty years from now, I won't be embarrassed about choosing a silly dress just so I could say that I had something 'different.'" She tossed him a sassy grin. "Don't interrupt me when I'm ranting."

Jay slipped his arm around her shoulder, pulling her close. "That is one dress that could outshine you in a sari."

Hope gazed up at him. "But I can't wear that dress around the house, or to a party, or out to dinner. A sari, I can."

"You could wear that dress to a wedding…"

He watched as Hope reined in her tiger-fleeing heart and gave him a coy smile. "It's not done, Jay. Only the bride wears a dress. Haven't you ever been to an American wedding?"

"Actually, I haven't, but I'd love to if you would go with me."

"But no one is getting married!"

"Ah, *kadhal*, my Hope. You are good to help me with my little charade. Would you go to a wedding with me? Would you go to *our* wedding with me?"

Hope wrapped her arms around his neck and whispered a few words into his ear. The night air nipped at them, but they didn't notice. Jay fumbled with a ring box until Hope took pity and opened it herself. A simple solitaire glimmered against the black velvet of the box, and the streetlight played with the facets. It sparkled as Jay slipped it onto her finger.

Hope sighed. "See, you picked well even before you knew my opinions on jewelry," she whispered.

CHAPTER 33

The week after school was out, Hope stepped into the Brown home, eager to go over last-minute wedding plans. "I brought everything I could think of," she gasped, collapsing on the couch. "I never thought this day would come. One week!"

"Jay is gone. He said to make you wait. He said, 'I haven't had five minutes alone with her in five weeks, and I refuse to wait another day.'"

"Liar. It's only been three. Still too long…"

Amala pulled her into the guest room. On the bed, a richly embroidered and beaded scarlet colored sari lay draped across the bed. "This was my wedding sari," she said, fingering the beadwork. "I want you to have it."

"Oh, no! I—"

"I brought it, even when we didn't have the room, when I came to America. It was silly, but I couldn't part with it. I thought maybe someday—we might have a daughter here, but we never did."

"I—"

"You will be my daughter. I want to give it to you. Wear it as a special thing for Jay sometimes, or save it for your daughters. It is time for me to pass it on. I have a daughter now."

Hope's fingers skittered across the sari. Every stitch of the intricate embroidery was still perfect. "Oh, I can't take this. It's your wedding dress. I—"

"Hope," Amala said, her hands cupping Hope's face, "Take

it, my almost-daughter. It is the only gift that I can give to you that is truly mine."

Jay watched, his heart in his throat, as Hope walked down the aisle. He stole a glance at his mother and swallowed hard when he saw the tears she tried to hide. The scarlet sari seemed a bit out of place amid jeans and athletic shoes, but as the bride, Hope could pull it off, and she did — well.

They stood before the minister who instructed them in the order of service. Jay tried to imagine the row of girls in their saris, carrying jasmine, and his groomsmen in their kurtas. Had he been crazy to insist on a traditional bridal gown and tux for them? Would it look out of place?

"It's going to be so beautiful," Hope sighed.

"What?" Dan Shatternmann stopped his direction of the bridesmaids and stared at Hope.

Jay laughed. "I was imagining it too." As he saw the weariness in Hope's eyes — the emotions that hovered near the surface — Jay suggested that they call it a night. "I think we all know what to do."

The room emptied, the bridal party off for an evening at a local restaurant, but Hope didn't move. Jay tugged at her arm, but she didn't budge. "I don't want to leave yet."

He pulled once more, but Hope smirked at him and sat at his feet. Resigned, Jay dropped to the floor next to her. "What are you thinking?"

"About tomorrow — about how beautiful the contrast between the bridal party's clothes and our formal wear will be. It's going to be the prettiest wedding I've ever seen." She gazed up at him. ""I'm so glad you talked me into buying that dress."

"*Amma's* sari is so beautiful on you, but I wait impatiently for the sight of you in that dress."

"I spent too much on it. I could have bought a good used car for the price of that dress."

Jay tucked a stray hair behind her ear. "It pleased your father to do it. Don't begrudge him that pleasure."

"I couldn't even if I wanted to," she admitted. "I love that dress. It makes me feel like a princess."

Jay gazed around him, taking in all the details of the decorations that had taken up so much of his mother's and Hope's time. "*Amma* is so grateful that you allowed her to help with your plans. Did she tell you?"

"She shouldn't have to be grateful. She's our *amma*!" Her eyes filled with tears. "Tomorrow, I will have a mother arranging my veil for me. I thought I'd lost that."

His fingers played with the hem of her sari. "You wore her sari. Do you know how much that meant to her?" Jay's eyes grew moist at the memory. He wondered, again, how he had found a woman like her. He prayed that he'd see Josh Graham, the paper extortionist, again someday — thank the jerk.

"I wanted to wear it to the ceremony, but I've already bought the other dress, and some people might be shocked to see me married in red."

"In northern India, they would have thought white meant you protested the wedding — white is for funerals."

"Really?"

He shrugged. "Well, I know they wear white in northern India to Hindu funerals anyway." He sighed. "I am glad you are wearing white. It reminds me of Paul describing the church as the bride of Jesus and then says that He will present it without blemish or wrinkle."

"You're reading in the epistles again."

Jay smiled, tracing her cheek with his fingers. How well she knew him. "I am not the only one reading the Bible these days. My father, it seems, has read more than the New Testament through Acts."

"Really? I thought he hadn't brought it up for discussion."

Jay grinned. "He didn't. I thought he wasn't interested. I've been praying so much about it."

"And..."

"And," he said, his voice low, "when I left last night, he stopped me at the door and asked me if I had read Song of Solomon lately."

Hope blushed.

Books by Chautona Havig

The Rockland Chronicles

Noble Pursuits
Discovering Hope
Argosy Junction
Thirty Days Hath...
Advent (Christmas 2012)
31 Kisses (Christmas 2012)

The Aggie Series _(Part of the Rockland Chronicles)_

Ready or Not
For Keeps
Here We Come

Past Forward- A Serial Novel

Volume 1
Volume 2
Volume 3
Volume 4 (coming 2012)

Historical Fiction

Allerednic (A Regency Cinderella story)

The Annals of Wynnewood

Shadows and Secrets
Cloaked in Secrets
Beneath the Cloak

The Not-So-Fairy Tales

Princess Paisley
Everard (Coming 2012)

CPSIA information can be obtained at www.ICGtesting.com
Printed in the USA
LVOW071446231212

312975LV00002B/254/P